The brilliant...
TH

Richard Matheso ... _ble_
Shrinking Man.

Harlan Ellison . . . winner of the Hugo, Nebula, Bram Stoker, and Edgar Awards.

Charles Beaumont . . . best remembered for his classic teleplays for _The Twilight Zone._

William F. Nolan . . . 65 books, 800 articles, 140 stories, and 13 novels including _Logan's Run._

John Tomerlin . . . 10 novels, more than 36 teleplays, and numerous short stories to his credit.

Robert Bloch . . . award-winning author of short stories, screenplays, and the novel _Psycho._

Ray Russell . . . bestselling author of _Mr. Sardonicus_, among other novels and short fiction.

Jerry Sohl . . . novelist and SF TV writer for _The Twilight Zone_, _Outer Limits_, and _Star Trek._

Chad Oliver . . . count _Shadows in the Sun_ and _The Winds of Time_ among his many classic SF novels.

Charles E. Fritch . . . wry SF writer best known for the Group story "Big, Wide, Wonderful World."

George Clayton Johnson . . . many short stories as well as teleplays for _Star Trek_ and _The Twilight Zone._

Ray Bradbury . . . multi-award Nebula Grandmaster of SF and author of _Fahrenheit 451._

CALIFORNIA
SORCERY

edited by
WILLIAM F. NOLAN
and
WILLIAM SCHAFER

ACE BOOKS, NEW YORK

CALIFORNIA SORCERY

An Ace Book / published by arrangement with
William F. Nolan and William Schafer

PRINTING HISTORY
Cemetery Dance hardcover edition / August 1999
Ace mass-market edition / February 2001

The Penguin Putnam Inc. World Wide Web site address is
http://www.penguinputnam.com

ISBN: 0-441-00808-9

ACE®
Ace Books are published by The Berkley Publishing Group,
a division of Penguin Putnam Inc.,
375 Hudson Street, New York, New York 10014.
ACE and the "A" design
are trademarks belonging to Penguin Putnam Inc.

PRINTED IN THE UNITED STATES OF AMERICA

10 9 8 7 6 5 4 3 2 1

Acknowledgments

We owe many fine people for their efforts, advice, and encouragement in bringing this book to print, primary among them:

Christopher Beaumont, Eleanor Bloch, Leslie C. Braunbeck, Chaz Brenchley, Richard Chizmar, Peter Crowther, Stefan R. Dziemianowicz, Susan Ellison, Ed Gorman, Martin H. Greenberg, Tim Holt, George Clayton Johnson, Lola Johnson, Chris Lotts, Bob Morrish, Mark A. Nelson, Norman Partridge, David J. Schow, and finally, especially Harlan Ellison, whose faith and understanding are greatly appreciated.

—W.K.S. & W.F.N.

For
RICHARD CHIZMAR
a fine writer and publisher,
and an even better friend.

CONTENTS

INTRODUCTION

CALIFORNIA SORCERERS
Christopher Conlon

The stories are magical.

. . . A fireman rebels against a society which expects him not to put out fires, but to start them—by burning books.

. . . A traveler stops at a strange, remote monastery one night and must decide whether the man imprisoned there is an innocent victim—or the Devil himself.

. . . A couple desperately struggles to survive in a youth-obsessed world in which people are automatically euthanized when they grow old—21 years old.

They have the power of fables: simple, direct, allegorical, they pull you in and hold you—but they teach you something, too. They're the kind of stories SF master Theodore Sturgeon called "wisdom fiction." And while these particular tales are the work of completely different writers—Ray Bradbury (*Fahrenheit 451*), Charles Beaumont (*The Howling Man*), William F. Nolan and George Clayton Johnson (*Logan's Run*)—they almost seem as if they might all have been hatched from a single brilliant, fantastically inventive imagination.

This is no accident. For these men were, from the early 1950s to the mid-1960s, part of a close-knit brotherhood of writers centered in the Los Angeles area that came to dominate not only printed SF and fantasy, but movies and TV as well—scripting, among them, many of the period's best-known films (including most of the Roger Corman/Edgar Allan Poe movies), along with classic segments of *Thriller*, *Alfred Hitchcock Presents*, *One Step Beyond*, and virtually every episode of *The Twilight Zone*. At its peak this association of creative artists also included, among others, Rod Serling, Richard Matheson, Robert Bloch, Jerry Sohl, Ray Russell, and Harlan Ellison. These outstandingly gifted men were collectively referred to by several names, including "The Southern California School of Writers" and "The Green Hand" (after the Mafia's "Black Hand"). But they were most commonly called, simply, "The Group."

"It's an astonishing story," says Marc Scott Zicree, author of *The Twilight Zone Companion*. "Many of these writers would not have been nearly as creative without each other. It was genuinely a gestalt that made these people deeper, better—made them stretch to places they never would have gotten to without each other." Group member William F. Nolan, whose film credits include *Burnt Offerings* and *Trilogy of Terror*, explains: "We'd talk plot, read stories we'd finished for opinions, talk about markets and what was selling and who was buying, discuss character development and structure, and, yes, we'd argue, but in a constructive way. We all helped each other . . . and interconnected on projects."

"Sometimes, of an evening," Ray Bradbury has written, "Richard Matheson would toss up the merest dustfleck of a notion, which would bounce off William F. Nolan, knock against George Clayton Johnson, glance off me, and land in [Charles Beaumont's] lap. Sometimes we all loved an idea so much we had to assign it to the writer present who showed the widest grin, the brightest cheeks, the most fiery eyes."

Direct collaborations between Group members were common. And no wonder. In those early days, most of them—particularly the "inner circle" of Nolan, Charles Beaumont, George Clayton Johnson, and novelist John Tomerlin—were men in their twenties who were just beginning their careers. They found strength, encouragement, and a sense of solidarity in the company of other struggling young writers. Because of the Group, says Nolan, "We were not alone; we had each other to fire us creatively, to bounce ideas around, to solve plot problems. It was the best kind of writing class that could ever be imagined."

But the closeness of the Group members went beyond the writing. According to Johnson (scriptwriter for *Twilight Zone* and *Star Trek*): "We knew each others' wives, we went to each others' houses, we shared holidays together, we went to movies and other things together . . . [We] would go out on the town and zoom around from place to place, stay out all damned hours. We'd just do anything you can think of. We'd go to strip joints to watch the strippers strip and be embarrassed to be there, but nonetheless whistling and whooping it up and trying to act like college kids . . . We'd go to nice restaurants like Musso and Frank's or we'd end up at Barney's Beanery. Or someplace along the beach. It hardly mattered." The central members were as open to a carnival as they were to an art-house film. More than any particular activity, the joy was in each others' company.

And, most especially, the joy was in the company of one man—a lanky, charismatic young author of screenplays (*The Seven Faces of Dr. Lao*) and teleplays (*Twilight Zone*) as well as essays, short stories, and novels, who is described by Nolan as having been "the hub of the wheel," the Group's "electric center": the vibrant, brilliant, and tragic Charles Beaumont.

I. Gatherings

The genesis of the Group dates back to the summer of
1946, when a 26-year-old professional writer happened to
bump into a hyper-energetic 17-year-old in a Los Angeles
bookstore. As the older man was later to write, the teenager
"began babbling about his *Terry and the Pirates* comic
collection, plus *Tarzan*, plus *Prince Valiant*, plus who-
can-remember-now how many other truly amazing and
life-enhancing subjects. It could only follow, out of such a
passionate encounter, that a friendship developed." It was
a friendship that was to last the rest of the young boy's life,
some twenty more years. The professional writer's name
was Ray Bradbury. The teenager called himself Charles
Beaumont.

Bradbury was by that time already a well-known name in
the field of fantasy and horror. His stories, written at the
feverish clip of one or more per week, had been selling for
the past several years to the pulp magazines of the time—especially *Weird Tales*, to which he was a regular contributor.
Within a year of meeting the young Beaumont, Bradbury
would publish his first book (*Dark Carnival*, 1947) and sell
several of his stories to William Spier, then the producer of
an immensely popular radio series called *Suspense*, whose
adaptations would help catapult Bradbury's name onto the
national stage. Soon thereafter Bradbury would find himself
able to place his bizarre, poetic fictions not just in pulp magazines but also in prestigious national publications such as
The Saturday Evening Post and *Collier's*. Movie work (*It
Came From Outer Space*) and such powerhouse literary
classics as *The Martian Chronicles* and *Fahrenheit 451*
would soon follow. But on that summer day in 1946, Bradbury was still making only thirty or forty dollars a week selling short stories to the pulps.

The name Ray Bradbury was, however, quite well-
known to the teenage Charles Beaumont. An avid reader of

science fiction and fantasy, he had written letters—many of them published—to nearly every magazine in the field, and ran his own fanzine called *Utopia*. He had suffered, in Marc Zicree's words, an "odd, dark beginning"; born Charles Nutt in Chicago in 1929, he had stayed with his parents until he was twelve, in a life he would later describe as "one big Charles Addams cartoon." His mother, in particular, caused the young boy grief—dressing him in girl's clothing and at least once killing one of his pets as a punishment. In part to get him away from this unstable woman, young Charles was sent—in the midst of a bout with spinal meningitis—to live with, as he later said, "five widowed aunts who ran a rooming house near a train depot in the state of Washington." But if the hope was that the boy would enjoy a more normal life with his aunts, the experiment was a failure. "Each night," Beaumont said, "we had the ritual of gathering about the stove and there I'd hear the stories about the strange deaths of their husbands."

By 1946, the young man—who had aspirations to be an actor, an artist, a writer—had changed his name to Charles Beaumont, and had surfaced in Los Angeles. His wandering days were not over—he would soon, for instance, find himself in Mobile, Alabama, working as a railroad clerk (where he would meet his future wife, Helen Broun). But he would return to California to stay shortly thereafter, taking a succession of jobs (disc jockey, usher, mimeograph operator) as he struggled to break into professional writing. Part of the attraction of Southern California to young Beaumont was the presence of the movie industry—he eventually got a job in the music department at Universal Studios—but another major element was surely the presence of the man who grew to be his professional mentor: Ray Bradbury.

"Chuck showed up at my house one night in the early fifties," Bradbury later wrote, "with his first short story. He handed it over, his face flushed with excitement, and cried, 'It's good! Or—I think it is!'" Bradbury had promised Beaumont that if the young man would come to his house every Wednesday evening with a newly written story, Bradbury would read it and comment. But though the established writer might have expected his eager apprentice to have some talent, he could not have suspected just how much. "When I read the first one," he later said in an interview, "I said, 'Yes. Very definitely. You are a writer.' It showed immediately. Chuck's talent was obvious from that very first story." Bradbury showed him how to cut, how to make transitions, how to make his stories move faster, but the raw talent was all Beaumont's. With Bradbury acting as "friendly agent" to help place the stories—Forrest Ackerman would later provide more official representation— Beaumont's tales eventually began appearing in pulp magazines such as *Amazing Stories*, *Orbit*, and *Fantasy and Science Fiction*. The young man had begun a career.

In late 1952, over lunch at Universal, Bradbury introduced Beaumont to another young, yet-to-be-published writer friend of his, a native Missourian named William F. Nolan. At that time Nolan was living in San Francisco, writing stories and trying to find a job. But he "hated the cold and fog," he says, and so, a few months after that initial meeting, he moved to the Los Angeles area and re-contacted Beaumont. "We became instant friends," he remembers, in part because their life circumstances were so similar: "We both wanted to be full-time writers, yet we had to hold down other jobs to pay our bills." Upon arriving in Los Angeles, Nolan—who came to be known among his friends as "The Windmill" because of his tendency to flail his arms wildly in the air when enthused about something (which, according to Bradbury, happened "about two dozen times daily")—secured a position in the credit department of a paper company. But, as with Beaumont, it would be a while before he could sell his writing consistently and easily.

Meanwhile the mercurial Beaumont had been making other friends. During a stint as a tracing clerk for California Motor Express he met John Tomerlin, a future novelist (*Challenge the Wind*), TV scenarist, race car enthusiast, and writing collaborator. Chad Oliver, called "Big Chad" by his friends (he was 6'3" and weighed 200 pounds), was attending UCLA, working toward a degree in Anthropology while also writing science fiction novels for young adults and short stories for the pulp market. And then there was Richard Matheson, shortly to become one of the best-known fantasy writers in the country with such novels as *I Am Legend* and *The Shrinking Man* (filmed as *The Incredible Shrinking Man*, 1957).

Matheson and Beaumont met in 1951. The two men shared a close relationship for many years, acting as spurs to each other's creativity—which is not surprising, considering the similarities in their work as well as their careers. They broke into professional writing at the same time, working the same markets; they also wrote TV and films simultaneously (and sometimes in collaboration, as in the TV series *The D.A.'s Man* and the film *Burn, Witch, Burn*). Predictably, there were feelings of competition; but, Matheson later said, "only of the friendliest sort. We were not jealous of each other but happy for each other's success."

And yet in terms of personality, the men were completely different. Matheson was as quiet, steady, and family-oriented as Beaumont was wild and impulsive. It was a difference that, while not affecting their friendship, would impact upon Matheson's relationship with what was rapidly becoming a recognizable "Group." For by 1954 an "inner core" was beginning to form, consisting of individuals ready to follow Beaumont on whatever new outing he had suddenly decided upon: a seedy nightclub, perhaps, or an all-night talking jag at a coffeehouse. "Then there was the evening," says Nolan, "when Chuck phoned to say 'Be at such-and-such hotel in Chicago at noon tomorrow. We're spending the day with Ian Fleming!' So that night I flew to Illinois. And I recall, a year later, when he told me we were going to Europe next weekend to attend the Grand Prix of Monte Carlo. And we did. Plus another whirlwind trip to Nassau in the Bahamas on 24-hours' notice. All great times!" But Richard Matheson was too much the stable family man for such adventuring. While he remained very cordial with all the Group members, who would frequently arrive *en masse* at his house for talking and laughs (as they would at Bradbury's), he left the restless wanderings to Beaumont and the others.

Thus, with Matheson as an anchoring influence and Bradbury as professional mentor and friend, a Group was born. Charles Beaumont, William F. Nolan, John Tomerlin, and Chad Oliver were set to conquer the world—or at least the worlds of publishing and filmmaking.

II. Flowerings

"It's fascinating," Marc Zicree remarks, "when you think of these guys driving around night after night, talking about stories, talking about the world. They had that enormous enthusiasm of youth and that sense of 'The sky's the limit.'"

Indeed, 1954 to 1958 were years of testing limits and undergoing transitions within the Group. All of the inner core began selling their writing: Nolan, for instance, saw his first publication in 1954 in *If: Worlds of SF*, a pulp of the time, while also working in collaboration with Beaumont for the Whitman comic book company, helping "to guide the destinies," as Beaumont later remembered, "of such influential literary figures as Bugs Bunny, Mickey Mouse, Donald Duck, and Andy Panda." Oliver and Tomerlin were also selling stories. Predictably, however, it was the meteoric

Beaumont who was having the greatest success. His tale about a terminally-ill jazz musician, "Black Country," was published in a then-new magazine out of Chicago called *Playboy*, whose fiction editor, Ray Russell (eventually to collaborate with Beaumont on the 1962 Roger Corman film *The Premature Burial* as well receive screenplay credit on *Mr. Sardonicus* and *X—The Man With the X-Ray Eyes*), was to become a welcome presence at Group get-togethers when he visited Los Angeles. Beaumont's writing so impressed Russell that he placed the writer on a $500 monthly retainer for first refusal rights to all his stories. Beaumont had quit his job at Universal in 1953 to become a full-time writer, but it was only now that he truly had enough money to raise a family.

In 1955 the Group lost Big Chad Oliver, who had always been conflicted between his love of writing and his desire to teach Anthropology at the university level. When a job opened in Texas, Oliver's home state, he and his wife packed their bags. He remained close to the other Group members, however, and saw them on visits to California—managing to keep together his dual life of author and professor for many years.

The inner quartet was now a trio, a situation that would not change until 1958. But the trio was wasting no time. In addition to ever-increasing sales of their writing, all three had become race-car enthusiasts. Nolan remembers, "Tomerlin raced his Porsche and Chuck, who began with an MG-TC, also had bought a Porsche Speedster, while I had a British Austin-Healey. We used to stage illegal races on abandoned roads, but John was actually competing in 'real' race events by then. The sport became a huge passion for [us], and we attended sports car races at various circuits around Southern California." Nolan recalls with particular clarity watching a young movie star named James Dean racing his Porsche a few months before the actor's untimely death in a highway crash.

It was around this time that a new face appeared in the Group, a young man from Wyoming with the sale of a film treatment (*Ocean's 11*, which became a Sinatra cult classic) to his name and little else—he had been writing stories for five years without publication. A few years before, Ray Bradbury had been sought out as a mentor by Charles Beaumont. Now Charles Beaumont would be sought out in his turn by an apprentice writer named George Clayton Johnson.

Johnson had been a design draftsman who worked for companies in the Los Angeles Basin such as U.S. Steel, Lockheed, and Douglas Aircraft. But his real desire was to write. When his grocer informed him that one of his regular customers was a professional writer named Charles Beaumont, Johnson recognized the name from the pulps and obtained his telephone number, carrying it around with him for several days before getting up the nerve to dial. To his surprise, Beaumont suggested a meeting at a local coffee shop, and turned out to be friendly and supportive. Most importantly, says Johnson, "He took me seriously. Which was a compelling reason for me to want to spend as much time with him as he would allow." In due course Johnson also encountered Nolan and Tomerlin, and tried to ingratiate himself with them: "I tried to sort of get in with them, through the help of Chuck Beaumont, who liked me. So when the three of them would get together sometimes I would be there, by invitation or just by happenstance. I'd be sitting with Beaumont in the evening and the other two would show up and then there'd be the four of us."

Johnson was impressed with their personal and professional closeness, which by that point was expressing itself in a number of ways. Beaumont and Tomerlin had collaborated on a novel, *Run From the Hunter*, published under the pseudonym "Keith Grantland." Beaumont and Nolan were co-editing a large book about auto racing entitled *Omnibus of Speed*. But it was not all fun and success,

Johnson discovered—these men also had deep personal ties which allowed for an uncommon frankness in their lives together.

"What I learned from these guys," Johnson says today, "was honest encounter. Let's call it like it really is and not avoid the target by pretending to agree with each other when we really don't. If we have a dispute, let's have the dispute out, and whoever is right is right. Not who is oldest or who is richest or who is best connected or who is the most powerful and the most threatening. None of that stuff . . . We would end up encountering each other over things. Maybe even just a story: 'No, I think it's a piece of crap. Who would believe this, this, and this?' We would tangle with each other over story points."

But there was a personal side to these encounters as well.

"I remember once," Johnson says, "on the way back from a road racing trip, Chuck and Helen Beaumont, John and Wilma Tomerlin, Bill Nolan and myself were talking and we got into an analytical mood where we were discussing somebody's flaws. And Helen stopped us and said that it was like being taken to the beach for the purpose of being drowned. After that we started referring to it as 'being taken to the beach.' You'd be warned: 'We're going out. We've all decided to take you to the beach, George.' And I'd say, 'Yeah, okay, fine.' And you'd spend four or five hours driving up and down the beach or through town or wherever, while three guys told you what was wrong with you. But you have to understand, we weren't setting out with an objective to destroy; we were setting out with an objective to heal."

In an essay published in the late 1980s, Johnson eloquently remembered the very real terror of these encounters.

"For Chuck they were fun," he wrote, "but for me those confrontations were often nightmares as I defended myself against self-satisfied challengers: John, who figured out how he should feel before becoming emotional, with visions of himself as a no-nonsense executive with a taste for the finer things in life; Bill [Nolan], who would kid his way out, the willing focus of Chuck's jokes who never forgot or misplaced anything, happy when the heat wasn't on him; and Chuck Beaumont, keeping things moving with his aggressive manner and willingness to go first, somehow knowing that he was bulletproof, that he was the master of verbal judo who was living a charmed life."

In particular, the Group forced Johnson to look realistically at his writing career, challenging him to stop talking and begin making sales if he expected them to take his opinions seriously. Fortunately, there was a new television series on the horizon that would ultimately allow him to do just that—a series that, in addition to introducing a famous new member to the Group and becoming a national cultural touchstone, would become perhaps the clearest expression of the Southern California Group's peculiar gestalt: Rod Serling's *Twilight Zone*.

Serling had arrived in Hollywood in 1957, as the days of live television (usually broadcast from New York) were waning. He was at that time television's most famous writer, with Emmy Awards for *Patterns*, *Requiem for a Heavyweight*, and *The Comedian*. He was also a controversial figure, constantly battling the sponsors over issues regarding censorship of his often politically-charged teleplays. But as his kind of hard-hitting, passionate drama began to disappear from the airwaves, he decided to head west toward the movies and the world of filmed television. After some failures and false starts, the distinguished Serling announced—seemingly out of the blue—that he would be producing and writing a series of half-hour fantasy stories called *The Twilight Zone* for CBS.

It was an announcement that sent shock waves through the industry; it was as if Ernest Hemingway had declared he would stop writing novels and instead concentrate on comic books. But of course, Serling had ulterior motives for moving into the world of imagination. He reasoned that if producers and sponsors were too timid to present real-life, contemporary issues of television, he might be able to mask the same concerns behind a veil of fantasy: remembering the troubles he had had with a *Studio One* presentation dealing with the U.S. Senate, for instance, he said: "I was not permitted to have my Senators discuss any current or pressing problem . . . To say a single thing germane to the current political scene was absolutely prohibited. In retrospect, I probably [should] have made it science fiction, put it in the year 2057, and people[d] the Senate with robots. This probably would have been more reasonable and no less dramatically incisive." From this kind of reasoning it was an easy step into *The Twilight Zone*.

Serling was contractually obligated to provide 80% of the first season's scripts himself. But, as executive producer, it was up to him to see that the remaining 20% would also be of high quality. To that end (after a disastrous open-call for scripts that yielded nothing useful), he invited a number of professional writers to meet with him, read some of his scripts, and decide if they thought they had what it took to enter *The Twilight Zone*. Among those who attended were Charles Beaumont, Richard Matheson, and Ray Bradbury.

"With great misgivings," Beaumont later wrote, "and after a suitable period of grousing about outsiders and why didn't the networks buy *our* shows, we . . . agreed to discuss the possibility of joining the program. I don't know what we expected Serling to be like, but we were all surprised to find that he was a nice guy who happened to love good science fiction and fantasy and saw no reason that it shouldn't be brought to the screen." But Beaumont still had his doubts: "Nothing galls a science fiction pro more than to see an 'outsider' bumble into the field, rework a whiskered theme which, in his naiveté, he takes to be supremely original, and make either, or both, a fortune and a critical splash."

With these "poisonous thoughts" in his mind, Beaumont took Serling's first nine *Twilight Zone* scripts home with him to read, "determined to hate them." But the quality of Serling's writing won him over. "At midnight," he wrote, "when I'd finished reading the material, I knew that Serling was an 'outsider' only in terms of experience; in terms of instinct, he was a veteran. Bradbury and Matheson read the scripts also, and in very little time we all decided to join the *Twilight Zone* team."

More than any other single program, film, or book of the time, *The Twilight Zone* expresses the heart and soul of the Southern California Group. Beaumont and Matheson became major contributors, penning such classic episodes as "The Howling Man" and "Nightmare at 20,000 Feet." George Clayton Johnson broke through into professional writing on the show, first by providing story ideas to Serling (including "Execution" and "The Four of Us Are Dying"); then, in large part because of Beaumont's encouragement, bulling his way into being allowed to write the teleplay for his story "A Penny for Your Thoughts" himself. He went on to several other scripts for the show, including the now-classic "Kick the Can" and "Nothing in the Dark" (the latter starring Robert Redford).

During this period many writers began to float into the Group orbit. They would not belong to the inner core—those most closely tied to Beaumont—but would nevertheless be greeted warmly when they appeared and might participate in the often vigorous debates about stories (sometimes their own). The casual, amorphous nature of the Group allowed in such disparate figures as Frank M. Robinson and OCee Ritch (best-known as an automotive writer), as well as Bill Idelson, Charles E. Fritch, and Jerry Sohl—all budding freelance authors trying, like the others, to break into the TV, movie, and fiction worlds of the time. Several would ultimately work on *Twilight Zone*.

What Jerry Sohl—who met most of the inner core at a 1958 SF convention and who would go on to write for all three of the seminal SF series of the 1960s (*Zone, Outer Limits*, and *Star Trek*)—found most attractive about the Group was its lack of pretentiousness. "If any one of us was snooty," he says, "and confessed to being the best writer east of the Pacific Ocean, we would have laughed. And if the person persisted in saying he alone knew the answer to everything we'd have let him stew in his own jejune flatulence." This down-to-earth quality translated into down-to-earth success for its members, too. "When I joined the Group I was making maybe one or two thousand dollars' advance for something that took me three months to write"—that is, a book. But through the Group's influence—especially Beaumont's—Sohl quickly broke into television. "The first television thing that came my way I did in one day and took in nearly $900. My thought was, I'd better stick with this Group! Which I did."

Another attraction was the comic repartee of close pals Chuck Beaumont and Bill "The Windmill" Nolan. They were "a great comedy team," remarks Sohl. "They would give each other straight lines. We roared with laughter at their antics. Bill had a mind like Beaumont's in the sense that it was lightning fast." George Clayton Johnson agrees. The two men had, he remembers, "the zaniest sense of humor. They could get really wacky with each other in a verbal kind of a way. It was fun to be around them because they could get really lighthearted and fanciful." Johnson's voice transforms into something like that of a drunken cowboy's as he recalls Nolan saying sardonically to Beaumont, 'Well, here we are, Beaumarg, about to encounter the highlights of Hollywood! Are you prepared for it? Into the cesspools we go!' " Sohl adds, "They were great innovators, very inventive. It made the rest of us look stolid."

Indeed, their wild senses of humor extended even into their writing, as in Nolan's short story "The Lap of the Primitive," an amusing tale featuring a certain crazed anthropologist by the name of "Boliver Chadwick." For his part, Beaumont gleefully gave a murderous robot the name "Nolan" in his story "In His Image."

By this point it was not only writers who were finding themselves attracted to this uniquely creative and witty affiliation. Composer Herman Stein often hung out with the Group, and several actors as well—including a young, little-known TV performer named William Shatner.

"I was allowed in," Shatner told biographer Gordon Sander, "because I had done some Richard Matheson and George Clayton Johnson stuff. But the best of them was Beaumont. He was their mentor, and they met at his house. And he'd say 'Let's do this!' and they'd all charge out into the night to do something or other." Shatner recognized that, while most of them were working in television and in movies, none of them were major players in Hollywood. Only their mentor Bradbury had written a truly A-list film: John Huston's *Moby Dick*. The rest were writing mostly B-movies. Matheson and Beaumont became involved with Roger Corman around this time, ultimately penning most of the low-budget producer's Edgar Allan Poe films; Beaumont also adapted his mainstream novel about racism in the South, *The Intruder*, for Corman, and even played a small role in the film, which starred Shatner (Johnson and Nolan made cameo appearances). Even the Group's TV work was largely on minor, now-forgotten programs. "These guys were on the fringes of success," Shatner said. "If they had been more successful, they wouldn't have been what they were. They were a rat pack on the fringes of the successful writers."

But *The Twilight Zone* was different. It was a "prestige" production, never a ratings blockbuster in its initial run but nonetheless a show the network could be proud of—and

which won for Serling two more Emmys for Outstanding
Writing. The *Zone*'s main man was, however, quite well
aware of the role of his supporting writers, whom he referred to as his "gremlins," in the success of his show.
When the second Emmy came along, in fact, Serling held
up the award during his acceptance speech and, addressing
his "gremlins," said: "Come on over, fellas, and we'll
carve it up like a turkey!"

Twilight Zone was, indeed, virtually unique in the history of American TV in its respect for the written word. In
an industry which routinely revises, rearranges, bowdler-
izes and homogenizes the work of its writers, *Zone*—created and controlled by one of the finest writers in the
history of the medium—stood by itself in honoring the cre-
ators' intentions. Beaumont, for instance, reported his feelings of "amazement" at seeing his first teleplay for the
series, "Perchance to Dream," being filmed exactly as he
had written it—"Nothing was changed. Not one line. Not
one word." In later years Matheson and Johnson have
often expressed anger, even grief, over the industry's cal-
lousness toward their words, but both invariably cite *Twilight Zone* as one of the shining exceptions, considering it
perhaps their happiest experience ever in Hollywood. Serling was smart enough to realize that when one hired mas-
ters in the field, it was best to let them control their own
work—and as a result, with only a handful of exceptions in
the program's 156-episode run, the script accepted for production was exactly the script filmed. It is this "writers
first" policy that allowed such unforgettable episodes as
Beaumont's "Long Live Walter Jameson" and "Shadow
Play" and Matheson's "The Invaders" and "Death Ship" to
be broadcast in precisely the form their authors intended.

Serling himself became part of the casual alliance of
writers who floated around the inner core of the Group, attending Beaumont's parties and occasionally joining in
with workshopping someone's story. But the glamorous

and now world-famous Serling never quite fit in with the rest, despite their affection for him. "He was just a different kind of guy," Marc Scott Zicree says. "Somewhat more vulgar. Serling was always a wonderful, sweet-hearted man, but he was of the Hollywood scene . . . a 'guy's guy,' kind of in the Hemingway mold." Nolan remembers Serling's awkwardness in trying to fit in with the Group: off-balance at not being the center of attention (as he was in virtually any other situation at this point in his life), he often embarrassed himself by telling off-color jokes that landed with a thud. "Rod was making a big effort to be liked," Nolan remembers. "He wanted people to like him and thought they would if he played it funny."

One writer who had decided he didn't much care for Serling's sense of humor, or indeed anything else about the man, was Ray Bradbury. Despite the fact that at the onset of *Twilight Zone* Bradbury was listed as being a major contributor, he had only one teleplay ("I Sing the Body Electric") produced for the series. Other scripts were rejected, and soon Bradbury was criticizing Serling and the series for ostensibly plagiarizing his work as well as that of other science fiction writers. "Bradbury got so angry about this kind of thing," Nolan says, "that he broke off his friendship with Rod." Serling had his defenders, however, who wondered if Bradbury's irritation might not have been fueled at least in part by professional jealousy. But whatever the merit of Bradbury's assertions—and they are debated by fans of both writers to this day—they did not keep *Twilight Zone* from continuing to rack up awards (including two Hugos) on its way to becoming a cherished television classic.

Meanwhile, adding to the confusion, Charles Beaumont had begun using ghostwriters—for *Zone* as well as magazine pieces—when he found himself overwhelmed with writing commitments. Newly successful and seemingly unable to say no to any good offer, Beaumont took to farming out many assignments to his less-established friends in the Group. One such "ghost" was George Clayton Johnson.

"When Beaumont would overwork himself," Johnson says, "and had too much to do, and being faced with being exposed because he's taken money, contracts have been drawn, he's made agreements . . . he would take his problems" to the Group. The other writers would take on Beaumont's overload, splitting the money with him 50-50, so that between his script and article assignments, Johnson says, "You've got people like Bill Idelson writing one, OCee Ritch writing one, Tomerlin writing one, Sohl writing one, me writing one." Jerry Sohl admits that Beaumont paid well for their services, but there turned out to be a catch with the TV work: "We forgot that he would get the residuals and we would get none of the rerun money." During his life Beaumont was always careful to pay his ghosts their agreed-upon share, but tragic events would soon overtake this process and the writers found their residuals drying up. Sohl, who ghostwrote such classic episodes of *Twilight Zone* as "The New Exhibit" and "Living Doll" for Beaumont, estimates that he lost at least $25,000 because of this. And yet it is a testament to the Group members' love for their friend and mentor that no one pursued the matter later. "It would have been taking food out of the Beaumont children's mouths," Sohl comments. "None of us complained. Not a single one of us."

In any event, the *Zone* made its writers highly visible in Hollywood, and most worked on other series at the same time. Beaumont received credit on *Alcoa Goodyear Theater* and *One Step Beyond*, while Matheson, Bradbury, Sohl, and Beaumont all worked for the Alfred Hitchcock show—which also featured the work of a gregarious, humorous writer who had come to Hollywood in the late fifties in the wake of one of his novels being adapted into a film by Hitchcock. The film, released in 1960, was *Psy-*

cho; the novel's author, Robert Bloch, would often host the Group he referred to as the "Matheson Mafia" at his home. He went on to write many of the finest episodes of the Boris Karloff *Thriller* series, for which Beaumont, Matheson, and Tomerlin also penned scripts.

As the Group prospered, a young writer named Harlan Ellison arrived in Hollywood fresh from a stint as co-editor of Chicago's *Rogue* magazine, for which he had purchased the work of Johnson, Tomerlin, and other Group members. He was also friendly with Chad Oliver, whom he visited many times in Texas. But his greatest closeness was with Beaumont, whom he got to know when Beaumont would come to Chicago on business for *Playboy* or to auto race. In fact, Ellison says, "It was Chuck who got me into sports cars. I bought a gun-metal blue Austin-Healey . . . and almost got killed! Chuck always laughed at the way I raced. He called me a leadfoot." Ellison's career as a sports car racer was mercifully brief.

His friendship with Beaumont, however, proved more enduring. Although by the time he arrived in the Los Angeles area—on New Year's Day, 1962—Ellison had already published several books in a variety of genres, he did not yet enjoy the major reputation that would come a few years later with such stories as "I Have No Mouth and I Must Scream" and " 'Repent, Harlequin!' Said the Ticktockman." Indeed, he says, "When I got to Los Angeles all I had was, literally, ten cents in my pocket. That's not hyperbole, that's *exactly* how much I had. And I used that money to call Chuck." The two men met at a local pool hall, and over a game Beaumont imparted two pieces of wisdom to Ellison about writing for Hollywood which the young apprentice was never to forget.

The first was to encourage Ellison to always continue writing books and stories and essays, no matter how much money Hollywood might throw at him. Why? "Because," Beaumont told him, "the industry does not understand where these things come from. They don't understand how books and stories are made. If you do nothing but scripts and teleplays, very soon they will come to think of you as one of their bought whores. But if you keep writing books, they will look on you as a Prince From a Far Land."

The other observation was more caustic. "Attaining success in Hollywood," said Beaumont, "is like climbing a gigantic mountain of cow flop in order to pluck one perfect rose from the summit. And you find after you've made that hideous ascent—you've lost your sense of smell!"

Sadly, by this point in his life the overworked and harried Beaumont had begun to feel that he was losing his own "sense of smell." Robert Bloch remembered the writer at this time as "a tired, driven man who, by his own account, was in the process of fleeing Hollywood for good." He intended, he told Bloch, to go to Rome and finish a novel. But it soon became apparent to everyone that something other than simple exhaustion was affecting their friend and mentor, and that the novel would never be written. In fact, though few suspected it yet, Beaumont's writing career was, even then, all but over.

Something awful was happening to Beaumont that was far beyond his feelings of burn-out in the film industry. Friends had begun to notice that he looked old, exhausted; his speech was sometimes slow or slurred; he seemed confused and forgetful. Indeed, by the latter half of 1963, he was no longer able to write. Though it was unknown to anyone at the time, the brilliant, irreplaceable Charles Beaumont—a mere 34 years old—was beginning to suffer the symptoms of the condition that would ultimately claim his life: Alzheimer's disease.

III. Farewells

"The saving grace to it," John Tomerlin said in 1987, "if there is one to a disease like that, is he was not really aware, after the very beginning, that there was anything wrong with him. When he first began to show strong symptoms of it, he would have kind of momentary flashes of great concern, as though he saw something happening and couldn't understand what it was. But it was a fairly gentle process."

Gentle perhaps, but terrifyingly swift. In Ellison's succinct phrase, "It was as if one of his own horror stories had attacked him"—aging him both physically and mentally with astonishing speed. William F. Nolan shares a particularly sad story: once, in the latter part of 1963, he was with Beaumont and Tomerlin at Musso and Frank's Restaurant in Hollywood, with the intention of all of them taking in a movie later. But abruptly, Beaumont put his head in his hands and began to cry, saying, "I can't go to the movies, guys. I can't think about them. I can't follow them. I love you guys, but I just can't go to any more movies with you . . ."

Soon, however, as Tomerlin indicates, the tears would vanish and he would be entirely unaware of anything being wrong. He once announced to Nolan that he had just seen a film he liked very much, called *King Kong*. It had been one of Beaumont's favorite films since childhood, but he talked of it then as if he had just seen it for the first time. Marc Zicree relates that once Beaumont was sitting at home when, apparently, he somehow set the curtains on fire. He simply sat, staring obliviously at the flames, unaware of the danger, until a family member rescued him. He would occasionally try to write, but it was impossible. Ultimately Beaumont would be confined to a rest home where, according to his son Christopher, he would eventually take on the appearance of a 95-year-old man. Friends would visit, but as time passed he recognized them less and less frequently and became increasingly confused as to his surroundings. "I would go out to sit and talk with him,"

Ellison remembers, "but after a while I just couldn't do it anymore. It was just too goddamn painful."

Meanwhile the Group tried to carry on, but with the hub of the wheel stripped away, the spokes flew off in different directions. Johnson remembers: "With Beaumont gone, it was much more distance between us. We wouldn't see each other as frequently. We didn't have common ground to pass back and forth over." The men of the inner core worked at keeping the friendship together, seeing each other from time to time, making friendly overtures—Johnson remembers Tomerlin loaning him a car, for instance, and Johnson helped Tomerlin choose a new house. But as Bradbury has written, without Beaumont, "Our old group would meet less often, and then fall away. What was central to it, the binding force, the conversational fire, the great runner, jumper, and yeller, was gone. None of us felt up to taking his place. We wouldn't have dared."

Alzheimer's disease is extremely rare in men of Beaumont's age, but few of his close friends were surprised at his early demise. Nolan feels that his friend had, somewhere within him, the knowledge that he would die young. As for Johnson, he says he knew from early in their relationship that this Prince From a Far Land was not long for the world. He describes a fragility, a delicately fey quality that Beaumont possessed, that gave him the sense Beaumont was "more of a fawn than a human being. You got the feeling, 'If he falls down, he'll break.'"

Beaumont "fell" on February 21, 1967, aged thirty-eight. In Bradbury's words, "It was, indeed, never the same after that." The Group was at an end, though over the years its members continued to see each other and even collaborate—in the small world of Los Angeles-based SF writers, it would have been almost impossible not to. Perhaps the greatest fruit of these attempts to stay together was generated when Nolan and Johnson decided to collaborate on a novel called *Logan's Run*, which would be pub-

lished shortly after Beaumont's death and go on to become
a genuine cultural phenomenon of the '60s and '70s. It was
made into a wildly popular MGM film in 1976 (which
eventually spawned a television series), and there were
Logan fan clubs all over the country. In many ways,
Logan's Run marked Nolan's and Johnson's emergence
from the long shadow of their brilliant friend. But there
was a sadness that Beaumont was not alive to share their
success.

In addition, Matheson, Sohl, Johnson, and Theodore
Sturgeon re-formed the Green Hand as an actual corpora-
tion in the mid-1960s, with the express intention of bringing quality SF to the small screen. Sadly, none of their
proposals were actually produced, but all of these writers,
as well as Ellison and Bloch, eventually worked on *Star
Trek* (though some discovered that Gene Roddenberry did
not share Rod Serling's respect for the written word).
Matheson and Bloch both worked on Serling's early '70s
series *Night Gallery*. Nolan adapted Matheson's stories for
the acclaimed *Trilogy of Terror* TV-movie in 1975. Matheson adapted Bradbury's *Martian Chronicles* for a TV
mini-series in the late '70s. Johnson and Matheson shared
screenplay credit on *Twilight Zone: The Movie* in 1983, for
which Bloch provided the novelization. And in 1988 there
appeared a massive fiction collection: *Charles Beaumont:
Selected Stories* (Dark Harvest), which featured affectionate reminiscences from most members of the old Group.
The interconnections have gone on and on, including even
Johnson's and Matheson's helping place Rod Serling's
Star on the Hollywood Walk of Fame. But after Beaumont,
no one pretended that there was a Group.

"We just seemed to go our separate ways after Chuck
died," remarks Jerry Sohl. "I think Bill Nolan and Chuck
are what held the thing together. We still talk to each other
now and then on the phone, but that's about all. Richard
Matheson brought most of us together for a dinner early in

1990. We enjoyed it. But it was not fated to be repeated, I guess."

Today many members of the Group remain active and working, but others, including Serling, Bloch, Oliver, and Russell, have passed on. But while the surviving members of the Group are no longer, in George Clayton Johnson's words, "a bunch of excited kids" leaning on each other for support, their closeness and mutual respect remain—as this book so eloquently testifies. And they are still working together. Matheson, for instance, has written a profile of Nolan for a new Nolan book. Currently Warner Brothers is preparing a high-budget, high-tech remake of *Logan's Run*, and Nolan and Johnson recently shared Guest of Honor status at a Logan-themed convention in Arizona. Bradbury, meanwhile, has collaborated with Ellison on a short story to be included in an expanded edition of Ellison's *Partners in Wonder*. And whether or not another face-to-face reunion is in the offing, the members *have* reunited—right here, in the volume you hold in your hands. *California Sorcery* commemorates the special bond of a group of extraordinary writers, gathering both their new and classic works together in pride and celebration.

REMEMBERING "THE GROUP"

William F. Nolan

In his excellent "Portrait," Chris Conlon presents a comprehensive and accurate history of the writers who formed what has now become known as "The Group." In addition, there's a bio/critical preface to every story in this anthology, telling the reader more about each of us.

There's not a lot left to say, so I'll be brief.

The twelve writers represented in this book have all, at one time or another, belonged to what critic Robert Kirsch has called "The California School," yet only one of us (John Tomerlin) is a native Californian. The rest of us hail from Illinois, Missouri, New York, Texas, Wyoming, Ohio, and New Jersey. The fact that we all gravitated to Los Angeles, and produced most of our best work in the Southern California area, justifies the label we now wear.

Why Southern California? (Beyond the great climate, that is.) Because the area is particularly receptive to creativity. Los Angeles is a totally "open-minded" city at the cutting edge of modern culture. It is also the entertainment capital of the world; if you wish to write for films or television you must live in Los Angeles. Thus, we were able to write and sell to a variety of West Coast markets while still maintaining our contacts with the New York publishing world. In L.A. there are no creative limits.

I have many vivid memories of the Group. Of all-night coffee shop marathons . . . of trips to the beach . . . of hot, exciting race weekends when we'd watch the fast cars duel . . . of prowling Valley bookstores to check sales on our published efforts . . . of weekend SF conventions in

L.A., San Diego, San Francisco . . . of movie-location trips and visits to studio back lots and sound stages to see our works being put on film . . . of wild, out-of-state excursions to New York, Chicago, Nassau, Paris, Sebring, Monte Carlo . . . of reading our stories late at night in one another's homes . . . of rushing off to see the latest SF movie . . . of lengthy dinners in Hollywood, rife with market talk . . . of heated arguments over plot and character . . . of joy and pride at encountering our printed works ("Hey, have you seen the new *Playboy*?") . . . of much laughter and camaraderie . . . of the feeling that we were all part of something special, unique, imaginative—that we were "The Group."

When William Schafer phoned me to ask if I wanted to co-edit this anthology with him I was happily stunned. A book about all of us, with samples, new and old, of our best fiction—and with a Group profile by Chris Conlon?

Yes. Absolutely yes.

And here it is.

The Group lives again in this book, brought together at last and for always in these good pages. I'll treasure the memories evoked here . . . of happy days, happy nights, happy years.

Hey, guys! I'm proud of us!

W.F.N.
West Hills, California
April, 1999

ALWAYS BEFORE YOUR VOICE
Richard Matheson

RICHARD MATHESON was born in New Jersey and raised in Brooklyn. He served as an infantry soldier in the Second World War (resulting in his vivid combat novel, *The Beardless Warriors*), and took his Bachelor of Journalism degree from the University of Missouri in 1949. He moved to California, got married (Rich and Ruth now have four children), and went to work for Douglas Aircraft.

Matheson was a founding member of the Group back in the early 1950s when we were unaware of any such title. I met my future wife at a Matheson screen showing of a Poe film he'd scripted.

Rich has had seven of his seventeen novels filmed, the most notable being *The Incredible Shrinking Man*, an SF classic that can still be viewed on late-night television. Most recently, in 1998, Robin Williams starred in Matheson's *What Dreams May Come*. He's written well over 125 scripts for films and TV (including *Duel*, which launched the career of Steven Spielberg), and more than 100 short stories.

When asked to contribute a new tale for this book, Rich declared: "Sorry, but I don't write short fiction anymore. Not since 1970." Then what about one from his files that had never sold?

Well, yes, he *did* have a story he'd always liked, a character study that had failed to find a market. "I wrote it in 1954 when I was working on *The Shrinking Man* in a rented house on Long Island. [The film sale of this novel brought Matheson and his family back to California.] It will be nice to see the story published at last."

We think so too. Offbeat Matheson. A subtle "mainstream" story about frustration and desire.

Meet Mr. Smalley and Miss Land.

W.F.N.

Mr. Smalley moved to Vera Beach on Wednesday, March seventeenth. The morning of that day Miss Land was distributing the 11:30 delivery when he came in. She heard the doorbell tinkle and the squeak of the floor-boards as he crossed over to the stamp and postal order window. She finished slipping the Brook County Newsletter into the boxes and turned.

Through the tarnished window bars she saw a tall, dark-haired man wearing a brown leather jacket. He looked in his early thirties.

"Hello," he said, smiling, "I just moved here. I'd like to rent a box if I could." His voice was mild and deeply-pitched.

"I'm sorry," Miss Land told him, "I'm afraid all the boxes are taken."

"Oh." The man's smile faded. "And I suppose there's only one house delivery a day."

"We don't deliver to the houses," said Miss Land, "You'll have to have your mail sent in care of general delivery."

"Oh. I see." The man nodded, looking a little perturbed. "And—how many deliveries are there a day?"

Miss Land told him.

"I see. Well . . ."

"If you'd like to put your name on the waiting list for boxes," Miss Land said.

"Yes. I would," he said.

After he'd written down his name and said that yes, he'd given his previous post office a change of address card, the tall man left. Miss Land stood at the stamp window watching him walk across the wind-scoured square to a black Volkswagen. She watched him get in and her right hand fingered unconsciously at the gold locket around her neck.

When the man had driven away, she blinked her eyes and turned away from the window. "Hi ho," she murmured. She walked slowly over to her desk, looking at the name he'd written on the list. *Louis Smalley*.

That's a nice name, Miss Land thought. She wondered if Mr. Smalley had brought his family to Vera Beach with him.

Just before one o'clock, Miss Land's mother phoned and told her to bring some lemons and sugar from the store when she came home for lunch.

⚊

Every morning when she'd finished sorting and distributing the seven o'clock delivery, Miss Land walked across the square to Meldick's Candy Store for a cup of coffee and a cruller. By nine-fifteen she was back at the post office.

The morning after Mr. Smalley had moved to Vera Beach, Miss Land found him waiting at the closed general delivery window when she got back.

"Morning," he said.

She smiled and nodded and let herself in through the back door. She took off her coat and put down her handbag. Her hands moved over her pale, brown hair, they ran smoothingly over her dark dress. Then she let up the window.

"That was Smalley, wasn't it?" she asked.

The tall man nodded. "That's right," he said.

She drew out a small packet of envelopes from the *S* shelf and fingered through them.

"No, nothing today," she said.

Mr. Smalley nodded. "Well, it's a little too soon yet," he said and left.

Miss Land stood at the window watching him walk across the square to his Volkswagen. That's a funny car, she thought. She watched him pull open the door and duck in, then she turned away. *Mr. Smalley*. The name was spoken once in her mind.

Later she found the letters and cards he'd put in the box under the stamp window. She picked them up and looked at them. They were all neatly typed. She held them in her hands a moment, then walked over to the mail sack and dropped them in.

Ten minutes later she drew them out again, thinking that she ought to see if Mr. Smalley had put down the correct return address. She swallowed dryly as she held them in her hands.

There were three letters and a postcard. She saw that the return address was correct on all of them. She looked at the letters. Two of them were going to New York City, the third to Los Angeles. The postcard was addressed to New Jersey.

Miss Land turned the card over.

Dear Harry, it read, *Trying the Island on for size. Address is General Delivery, Vera Beach, N.Y. Any word yet from Heller about MIDNIGHT DRUM? Am working on a few shorts before starting the novel for Cappington. Okay? Best to all. Lou.*

Nervously, Miss Land dropped the letters and the postcard back into the mail sack. I shouldn't have read it, she thought as she went over to her desk. She started checking the previous day's postal money order receipts.

⋏

The next morning Mr. Smalley was waiting again.

"I'm sorry," said Miss Land and she explained to him about the coffee break.

"Oh, that's all right," said Mr. Smalley, "If I'd known I'd have joined you in a cup."

Miss Land took off her coat hastily in back. She felt at her curls automatically and adjusted her dress, then drew

up the general delivery window. There were two letters for
Mr. Smalley forwarded from Manhattan. Mr. Smalley said,
"Oh, good."

"Cold for this time of the year," Miss Land said as he
was looking at the envelopes.

Mr. Smalley looked up with a smile.

"Certainly is," he said, "Especially when you're used to
California weather."

"Oh, is that where you're from?" Miss Land's gaze held
a moment on his face.

He told her he'd decided to move east to see if he'd
like it.

"Well, I hope you'll like it here," said Miss Land.

"I think I'll like it very much," said Mr. Smalley.

Miss Land watched him leave. She shivered briefly as
a cold wind from the opened door laced across her
cheek. She crossed her arms and rubbed at them with her
hands. Cold, she thought as she watched Mr. Smalley
walk quickly across the square to his car.

She stood there until he'd read the letters and driven
away. Then she turned for her desk. Well, I hope you and
your family will like it here, her question re-phrased itself
in her mind. She would have found out about his wife and
children if she'd asked him that.

Miss Land went to her work with great efficiency. What
difference, she thought, did that make to her?

▲

It was the following Monday that she found out about Mr.
Smalley.

She was having her coffee and cruller at Meldick's
when Mr. Cirucci who owned the square grocery store
came in.

They said good morning and Mr. Cirucci sat down on
the stool beside Miss Land.

"See we got us a celebrity," said Mr. Cirucci after the topics of weather, business and mail had been disposed of.

"Oh?" said Miss Land. The coffee had steamed up her rimless glasses and she was rubbing at the lenses with a fresh Kleenex.

"Mr. Smalley," said Mr. Cirucci. "He's a writer."

"Is that so?" said Miss Land, enjoying the mild illicitness of already knowing.

"Yes ma'am," said Mr. Cirucci, "He writes books. History stories."

"Oh. How nice." Miss Land was mentally watching Mr. Smalley walk across the square to his funny little Volkswagen.

Then the question occurred to her and she legitimized her nervous swallow with a sip of coffee. How could she phrase it?

"Yes, ma'am. He lives over on Brookhaven Road. Rents Miz Salinger's place."

"Oh. Yes," said Miss Land, nodding. That was a small house.

"He—has no children then," she heard herself saying.

"He's not even married," said Mr. Cirucci, not noticing the color in Miss Land's cheeks.

He only heard her say, quite faintly, *"Oh."*

⋏

She saw his car turn the corner and her half-full cup clinked down loudly in the stillness of the candy store. Mr. Meldick looked up from his newspaper. He saw Miss Land fumbling in her handbag.

"Somethin' wrong?" he asked.

"No, I just have so much work to do," Miss Land said. "I really shouldn't have snuck out this morning. It's a bad habit, I know, but then—"

She cut herself short and put two dimes on the counter

for the coffee and untouched cruller. She turned away before Mr. Meldick could see the flush across her cheeks.

"Bye now," said Mr. Meldick.

"Good—" Miss Land cleared her throat hastily. "Goodbye Mr. Meldick," she said as she started for the door.

Cold wind whipped the hem of her coat around her thin legs as she hurried across the square. She made the post office just as Mr. Smalley came walking up.

"Tie," said Mr. Smalley.

Miss Land smiled nervously, then nodded as he opened the door for her.

"Certainly is cold," she said.

"North Polish," he answered. She didn't hear exactly what he'd said but she smiled anyway.

When she drew up the general delivery window her windblown hair was back in place.

"Well, now," she said and she drew out the packet of letters from the *S* shelf.

"I don't believe I know your name," said Mr. Smalley.

"Miss Land," she said as she looked through the letters. She was pleased at how casual she sounded.

"Miss Land," he repeated.

Two letters slipped from her fingers and fluttered palely to the floor. "Oh, dear," she murmured, hoping that her face felt warm because of the oil stove's buffeting heat. She bent down quickly and picked up the letters.

"There," she said, putting his mail on the counter.

"Well," he said, "I really hit the jackpot today."

"You certainly did," she said, smiling.

He smiled back at her and turned away. She stood there watching him walk across the square, examining his mail. When he'd driven away she got a Kleenex from her handbag and patted at the dew of sweat across her forehead. The jackpot, she thought with a smile.

He was a writer, all right.

⋀

He corresponded with writers in Los Angeles, New York
City, Milwaukee, Phoenix and his agent in New Jersey. He
subscribed to *The Saturday Review*, *The National Geo-
graphic Magazine*, *The New Yorker* and *The Manchester
Guardian*. He was a member of the Book Find Club. He
typed all his mail and sent most of it in envelopes except
for an occasional postcard. As far as could be judged by
handwriting and return addresses he received no letters
from women.

This Miss Land had discovered in several weeks of observation.

She sat at her desk looking at the wall clock. It was
nine-thirty and Mr. Smalley was late. Miss Land fingered
at the magazine on her desk. It had been forwarded from
Los Angeles. There was three cents due on it. That meant
she would have a few moments talk with Mr. Smalley.

She was stroking the magazine distractedly when the
doorbell tinkled. Her fingers jerked away and she stood up
quickly, smiling.

Mrs. Barbara sent a package to her brother in Naples.

Mr. Smalley didn't come in all that day. Miss Land kept
the office open an extra half hour because she had some
special work to finish up. Then her mother phoned and
Miss Land went home to a restless evening.

"I was wondering what happened to you," she said impulsively when Mr. Smalley came in the next morning.

"Oh." He smiled. "I had to drive into the city," he said.

"Oh." She handed him his mail. "There's three cents
due on this," she said.

"Okay." He fumbled in the right-hand pocket of his
trousers.

"Have you given your change of address to them?"

Miss Land asked, looking at the dark tangle of hair as he picked at the mound of change in his palm.

His eyes met hers. "Yes, I did," he said, "I guess I'd better send them another notice."

"It might be a good idea," said Miss Land.

After Mr. Smalley was gone she sat at her desk staring at the clock. After a few minutes she became conscious of the fact that she was trembling and she pressed her thin lips together and looked angry.

I must be getting a chill, Miss Land said to herself and proceeded to identify herself with her work.

⋏

On Wednesday it poured. Mr. Smalley didn't get in until almost one. Miss Land was deliberating whether she should have her lunch in the candy store instead of getting soaked walking home when Mr. Smalley came in, his hat and raincoat darkly wet.

"You're late," said Miss Land, her hands unconsciously smoothing at the skirt of her dress.

"Couldn't get my darn car started," he said, "No garage where I am."

"Oh," she said. She gave him his mail. "Don't catch cold now," she said. Her heartbeat jumped she was so startled at her own forwardness.

"I won't, Miss Land." He looked up from his letters. "That's a nice dress," he said and left.

Miss Land stood watching his tall form run across the rain-swept square. Once he slipped and almost fell and Miss Land gasped, a sudden constriction binding her chest. Mr. Smalley righted himself and made the car safely.

"You'd better be more careful there, my lad," Miss Land said lightly to herself.

She shuddered a little. *No*, she thought. It was all she allowed herself. She got her coat and umbrella and started out, then went back and phoned her mother and said it was raining too hard, she was going to have lunch at Mr. Meldick's candy store.

Which was empty. Miss Land carried her bowl of tomato soup, her chopped egg on wheat bread sandwich and her cup of coffee to one of the wooden booths.

She sat there eating slowly, listening to the drumming of rain on the roof, the splattering of it outside the door. The soup tasted delicious as it trickled warmly down her throat. The sandwich was also delicious. Miss Land kept looking down at her dress.

When she'd finished eating, she sat running one finger around the smooth warm lip of the empty cup. I love coffee, I love tea, the rhyme appeared. She blinked away the remainder of it and took in a deep breath. She looked around the dimly lit candy store. It was peaceful, she thought, very peaceful here in Vera Beach.

She looked at the jukebox a long time and glanced at Mr. Meldick a long time before she struggled out of the booth and walked toward it.

"Somethin'?" Mr. Meldick asked, looking up.

"Just thought I'd have a little music," she replied.

She stood in front of the jukebox's Technicolor bubbling and looked at the titles. There were a lot of love songs. She put a nickel in and the little green SELECT light went on. A little cheerful music, she thought, something relaxing. Her finger wavered over the buttons, then, abruptly, pushed one in.

Before she'd reached the booth the music started.

"If I loved you," sang the woman, *"Time and again I would try to say."*

Miss Land sat looking at her hands on the table, glancing at Mr. Meldick. When she saw that he wasn't paying attention to anything but his *Herald-Tribune* crossword puzzle she relaxed. She leaned her head back against the booth and closed her eyes. Warm breath trickled out between her lips.

The woman sang, *"Wanting to tell you but afraid and shy."*

⋏

The next day Mr. Smalley didn't speak or smile and when Miss Land dropped one of his letters she heard him tap his fingers impatiently on the window counter. When she handed him his mail he turned immediately and left without a word.

Miss Land stood motionless watching him walk across the square. Even after he'd driven away she stared at the place where his car had been, a look of hurt confusion on her face.

She began to recount the sequence of actions between his entrance and his exit. She went over every step, watching herself as she smiled and said good morning and got his mail and handed it to him. Was it because she'd dropped one of his letters? But he'd looked glum from the moment he'd entered.

At five-thirty when she locked up the office she still didn't understand.

A little after seven she got up from the supper table and went for a walk while her mother did the dishes. She walked for several miles along the dark, windy roads listening to the far-off explosions of the surf. She looked at every street sign when she passed it even though she knew that Brookhaven Road was far away from there.

At nine o'clock her mother went to bed and Miss Land sat watching television. It was a comedy program but Miss Land saw only veiled sorrow in it and she turned it off.

It was after eleven when she sat up in bed and stared around her small, dark room. She should take a sedative, she thought. Maybe she'd had too much coffee that day. She decided it was that.

She turned on the table lamp and sat on the edge of the bed, her feet resting in a pool of light. She turned on the radio very softly and listened to Andre Kostelanetz's orchestra playing *"Lotus Land."* She stared down at her white kneecaps and at the pale curl of her toes on the rug. There were veins like blue cords in her ankles. She thought—In a month and a day I'll be thirty-seven.

She took the book off her bedside table and opened it. It was a Modern Library anthology of poetry she'd bought one day on a trip to the city. Her eyes moved idly down the index of first lines near the back of the book until she came to a particular line. Then she turned to page 875. The poem was written by e.e. cummings.

Always before your voice my soul
half beautiful and wholly droll
is as some smooth and awkward foal

She read the entire poem twice and read aloud the lines:

"But my heart smote in trembling thirds
of anguish quivers to your words
as a—"

"Jessica?"

The book thumped shut loudly. Miss Land looked up and saw her mother standing in the hallway like a bulky ghost, her head alive with curlers.

"Are you sick?" her mother asked.

"No, Mother. Go back to bed."

"You've been drinking too much coffee again," said her mother.

"I'm all right, Mother," said Miss Land.

"You shouldn't drink so much coffee," said her mother. "I always said that."

"Yes, Mother."

Later, lying in the warm center of her bed, Miss Land

stared at the ceiling, her shallow chest almost still. There was a tight pain around her heart. Gas, she thought.

Suddenly, with a grunt, she brushed at something crawling down her cheek. And when she discovered it wasn't an insect she rubbed her wet fingers against the spread until the tips felt warm. This is *nonsense!* she told herself.

The next morning Mr. Smalley smiled at her. Miss Land felt very sleepy around noon and took a refreshing nap during her lunch hour.

⋏

It was May and Mr. Smalley had dropped a postcard into the box under the stamp and postal order window. Miss Land had it in front of her on the desk. Her heartbeat staggered as she read it again.

Dear Sir: I am interested in the possibilities of renting a small house in the area around Port Jervis. Would you let me know what you have available? Louis Smalley.

Once when Miss Land was seven her dog had been crushed by a truck. She felt the same way now. That identical sense of frozen disbelief. That almost angry conviction that there was no place in life for such an occurrence.

Five times that day Miss Land took the postcard out of the sack and read it. At last she dropped it for the last time and watched it flutter down onto the pile of mail.

Tuesday nights she and her mother usually went to the movies in Port Franklin but that night Miss Land told her mother she had a nagging headache and went to bed early. Her mother stayed home and watched television instead. Miss Land could hear the programs from her room as she lay there in the darkness, her pale blue eyes staring at the ceiling.

At ten-seventeen p.m. her lips pressed together. So Vera Beach wasn't good enough for him. Well, that was just too bad. Miss Land turned over and beat her pillow into submission.

Later, in the very still of night, she bit the pillow till her jaws ached and her body shuddered on the bed. I *hate* him! someone screamed.

⋀

When the doorbell tinkled in the morning Miss Land glanced over her shoulder, then went back to sorting.

Mr. Smalley said nothing for a moment. She stood there sliding letters into their proper shelves.

"Anything for Smalley?" he finally asked.

"I'll be finished in a moment," said Miss Land.

She heard him exhale slowly. She picked up another bundle of letters she just hadn't had time to get to that morning.

"Can you tell me if there's anything?" asked Mr. Smalley.

"I really don't know," she said, "I'll be finished in a moment." She felt a cold, drawing sensation in her stomach. Her throat was dry.

Finally she was done.

"Smalley," she said and pulled out the packet of mail on the *S* shelf. She looked through them slowly.

"No, nothing today, Mr. Smalley," she said.

She felt his eyes hold on her an extra moment before he turned and left. She shuddered once as she watched him cross the square. There!—she thought suddenly. *There!* She drew in a quick breath and went over to her desk. She sat there with her eyes shut, hands trembling in her lap.

The next morning she glanced over from her desk and said, "No, nothing."

The next morning she came back late from having coffee and found him waiting at the door. When she handed him the magazine with postage due she said, curtly, "I think you'd better tell them your new address again."

The next morning she handed him his mail without a word and turned away.

On Monday she said lightly, "*Nothing*," and she didn't even turn to look at him.

That night she got severe stomach cramps and had to stay in bed for three days and nights. She phoned the office once each day to remind her replacement to be very sure she collected on all postage due items. Like things that were forwarded from other cities. Like Los Angeles for instance.

▲

When the letter in the blue envelope arrived Miss Land only glanced at it before sliding it onto the *S* shelf.

Later, when she returned from Meldick's she drew the letter out again. Even if there were no return address on it she could have told from the delicate curve of the handwriting. As it was the name printed on the flap was Marjorie Kelton.

Miss Land sat at her desk holding the letter in her hands. She could feel her heart beating in heavy labored pulsings that seemed to strike the wall of her chest. Marjorie Kelton. She read the name over and over, the letters dark blue on blue. She read it until the letters blurred. Marjorie Kelton. Personal stationery. The air seemed close. Miss Land seemed to feel the chair rocking slowly under her. Her head felt numb. Marjorie Kelton's personal stationery. Miniature pearls of sweat hung from Miss Land's brow. Marjorie Kelton.

When the doorbell tinkled and Mr. Smalley appeared at the general delivery window Miss Land said, "Nothing."

Aghast, she twitched on the chair. She began to cry, "Wait!" but only made a faintly hollow sound in her throat.

The doorbell tinkled again. Miss Land raked back her chair and hurried to the window.

"Wait," she said.

She watched him walking brusquely to his car.

"I made a mistake," she said. Mr. Smalley got into his car and drove away without answering.

Miss Land turned from the window with a shudder. I made a mistake, she repeated in her mind. A mistake, you see. I didn't put your letter on the right shelf.

A stage smile drew artificially at her thin features. She laughed as she related to Mr. Smalley the humorous incident. I put it on the *M* shelf, you see. I guess I just wasn't thinking. Wasn't that silly?

The scene dissolved. Miss Land had the phone in her hand. She dropped it back on its cradle. No, not so soon. That would be suspicious. Her eyes fluttered up to the wall clock. In an hour. An hour would be appropriate. Mr. Meldick came in for his mail you see and I ran across your letter. I'd put it on the *M* shelf by mistake. Wasn't that—

She went about her work.

At ten-thirty she looked through the telephone directory and a terrible cold stone lay on her stomach when she saw that Mr. Smalley's name wasn't listed.

"Oh." Miss Land shook her head in self-reproachment. Mr. Smalley had just moved in. How *could* he be listed?

But what if he had no phone? Terror scraped at Miss Land's heart. Hastily, she laughed it away. Oh, for heaven's sake, why wasn't she thinking? Mr. Smalley would be in around noon for his second delivery. She'd give him the letter then. That was all.

Mr. Smalley didn't come in again that day. At two o'clock Miss Land called information and requested the number of his newly installed phone.

She sat there five minutes listening to the buzz-click of his unanswered line. Then, almost soundlessly, she slipped the receiver back in place and stared at the blue letter on her desk. Well, it's not my fault, she thought. Well, what am I worrying about? she thought. Mr. Smalley would get it tomorrow.

Tomorrow.

⋏

"You haven't eaten a *thing*," her mother said, threatening with a spoonful of mashed potato.

"I'm not *hungry*, Mother," said Miss Land.

"You had something in Meldick's this afternoon," said her mother.

"No, Mother. Please. I'm just not hungry."

Her mother grunted. Then there was the sound of her mother's fork clicking from dinner plate to dental plate, the sound of water being swallowed, the wheezing breath that passed her mother's nostrils. Miss Land drew tiny roads through her untouched mound of potato. She stared at the plate and there was a sharp gnawing at her stomach.

"Finish the meat," her mother said.

"I'm—" Miss Land cleared her throat. "I told you I'm not hungry, Mother."

"You've been drinking too much coffee," said her mother, "It stunts the appetite. I always said it."

"Excuse me, Mother," said Miss Land, getting up.

"You haven't eaten a *thing*," her mother said as Miss Land left the room.

Quietly, she locked her door and went over to her bed. She sat there kneading white fingers together, trying to catch her breath. Every time she drew in air it seemed to drain from her instantly.

Five minutes. Abruptly, Miss Land slid her hand under the pillow and drew out the blue envelope.

She turned it over and over as if it had endless sides and she must find the right one. The woman's name flared in her mind and disappeared, it flared and disappeared like an automatic sign. She looked at his name and his address written in Marjorie Kelton's exact feminine hand. She visualized her sitting at her desk and writing down that name: *Mr. Louis Smalley*, surely and casually in the quiet of her room.

Suddenly she tore the envelope open and thought her heart had stopped. The letter fell from her hands and Miss Land sat there trembling, staring down at it, her body rocked with giant heartbeats. She dug her teeth into her lower lip and began to cry softly. It was an accident, her mind fled through the explanation. I thought it was for me, you see, and—

Her eyes pressed shut and she felt two warm tears run down her face. He would never believe that.

"No," she whimpered. "No, no, no."

In a little while she picked the letter up and read it, her face set stiffly, a mask of regal justification.

Lou, Darling! I just heard from Chuck that you were back east! Why in God's name didn't you phone? You know I never meant what I said. Never meant it for a second, damn your luscious bones!

It went on like that. Miss Land sat woodenly, a dull heat licking up through her body as she read. Twice she crumpled up the letter and flung it away and twice retrieved it, pressing out the wrinkles with her fingers. She read it seven times completely and then in sections.

Later in the darkness she lay, holding the crumpled letter in her hand and staring, dry-eyed, at the ceiling, breath a faltering trickle from her lips. She watched Marjorie Kelton and Marjorie Kelton was beautiful and desirable. Miss Land's lips pressed together. Any woman who would write a letter like that . . .

Around midnight Miss Land sat up and slapped around in rabid fury until she'd found the letter and then she tore it up with savage jerkings of her arms and flung the ragged shards into the darkness with a choking sob. *There!*

▲

In the morning she burned the pieces. Mr. Smalley got two letters and a postcard and when Miss Land handed them to him he smiled and said thank you. It doesn't matter, Miss Land decided at lunch. It was only one letter and anything could have happened to it. That was the end of it. She certainly wasn't going to make a fool of herself again.

▲

The following Monday morning the letter from the upstate realtor came for Mr. Smalley and Miss Land put it in her desk drawer. When Mr. Smalley came in she gave him his *Saturday Review* and his notice from the Book Find Club. What amazed her the most was the absence of fright she felt. On the contrary there was a feeling of rich satisfaction in her as she put the letter in her handbag and took it home at lunchtime.

After lunch she retired to her room and, after locking the door, took the letter from her bag. For a long time she lay quietly, touching the envelope, rubbing it experimentally between her fingertips, pressing it against her cheek. Once, suddenly, she kissed it and felt a strange hot pouring sensation in her like a sun-baked river. It made her shiver.

It's really, she thought hastily, a delicious conspiracy against Mr. Smalley. It wasn't doing him any harm. After all it was only a letter from a realtor, nothing important. Miss Land writhed her hips a little on the bed and read the letter. There were rentals available. Miss Land shrugged.

"So what?" she murmured and had to giggle over that.

In a few minutes she tore the letter into pieces and held the scraps high above her and laughed softly and contentedly as they filtered through her spread fingers and fluttered down on her like dry snow.

There, she thought. Her teeth clenched together and anger came again. Oh, *there*.

She fell into a sleep so heavy that her mother had to pound on the door for three minutes straight before she heard it.

▲

She took one of Mr. Smalley's *Saturday Reviews* home and put it under her pillow. Now that's all, she told herself. No more. This much was all right because it was nothing important but that was all. After all there was no point to it really. It was just a silly game.

Two days later she took a postcard from a men's shop in Port Franklin. It wasn't very satisfactory. The next day she took a letter from his agent and tore it up without even reading it.

That's all, Miss Land told herself. After all there's no point in going on with such a silly game.

When he wrote to the realtor again Miss Land tore up the letter with her teeth and hands and threw the pieces all over her room.

▲

On the Wednesday morning of June 22nd Miss Land was sorting mail when she heard the door opened. The beginning of a smile twisted playfully on her lips, then was gone. She kept sliding letters and postcards onto the general delivery shelves.

"Pardon me," said an unfamiliar voice.

Miss Land looked over her shoulder and saw a man wearing a dark blue suit and a panama hat. There were palm trees on his tie.

The man pressed his hat brim between two fingers and Miss Land came forward. "Yes?" she said.

The man drew a billfold from his inside coat pocket and opened it. Miss Land looked down at the card he showed her.

"I'd like to talk to you, Miss Land," he said.

"Oh?" she said. Her fingers were rigid on the bundle of mail. "What about?"

"May I come in back?"

"It's against the rules," said Miss Land.

The man held out his card again.

"I know what's against the rules," he said.

Miss Land swallowed once. It made a dry clicking sound in her throat.

"I'm so busy," she said. "I have so much mail to sort."

The man looked at her without any expression on his face.

"The door, Miss Land," he said.

Miss Land put down the bundle of mail on the table. She pushed in at the edges to even them. Then she walked over to the door. The man's footsteps stopped there. Miss Land stood a moment looking through the frosted glass at the dark outline of the man. Then she unlocked the door.

"Come in," she said, cheerfully. "You won't mind if I continue with my work while we talk."

She turned before the man could answer. From the corners of her eyes she saw him walk in, hat in hand, and heard the click as the door was closed again. A shudder laced down her back.

"Well, what is it?" she asked, picking up the mail, "Somebody complaining about me?" Her laugh was faint and hollow. "You can't please all of the people all of the time. Or is it—?"

"I think it would be better if we shut the windows for a while, don't you?" interrupted the man.

"No, that's impossible," said Miss Land with a fleeting smile. "The office is open, you see. People will be coming in for their mail. After all, that's what I'm here for. I can't just close—*just like that*."

She turned back to her bundle of letters and held one up with a shaking hand.

"Mrs. Brandt," she said and slid the letter onto the *D* shelf.

"Miss Land," started the man.

"*Close* in here, isn't it?" said Miss Land, "I've written the main office about it, oh, dozens of times. I guess I'll just have to get a fan for myself."

The man walked to the stamp and postal order window and pulled it down.

"Now *wait* a minute!" Miss Land said shrilly. "You can't do that. This is a public—"

Her voice broke off as the man looked at her. She stood there frozenly, the bundle of mail held against her chest, as the man went to the other window.

"But you can't do that," said Miss Land. She watched him pull down the general delivery window. A giggle hovered starkly in her throat. "Well," she said, "I guess you did it." She shrugged and held the mail bundle out toward the table.

"*Oh!*" she said as the letters and cards spilled all over the tile floor. She crouched down hastily. "Dear me," she said, "I'm all thumbs to—"

"Let them be, Miss Land," the man said firmly. "We'll pick them up later."

"Oh, that's very nice of—"

Miss Land stopped suddenly, realizing that the "we" he mentioned didn't include her. She straightened up dizzily and knotted her hands together.

"Well," she said, "What is it you want to see me about?"

"I think you already know, Miss Land."

"*No,*" she said, too loudly, "No, I have no idea. I—I haven't been honored with a visit from a p-p—"

Miss Land looked stunned. Her shudder was too visible to hide. She cleared her throat suddenly.

"If it's about—" she started, then broke off again.

"Miss Land, we've been checking on this for almost a month. *Twenty-one* items have been reported undelivered by the party in—"

"Oh, that would be Mr. Smalley," Miss Land blurted, "Oh, he's a strange man. *Strange*, Mr.—"

The man didn't say. Miss Land cleared her throat.

"He's a writer, you know," she said, "You can't—rely on that t-type of man. Why he wasn't here more than two weeks before he started looking for another place to stay because he didn't like—"

"We have the evidence, Miss Land," the man said, "I'd like you to come with me."

"Oh, but—" A terrified smile splashed across her lips. "No, that's impossible. I have people here to serve, you see. You don't understand, you simply don't understand. I have *people* here."

"I have a replacement for you out in my car," said the man.

Miss Land stared at him blankly.

"You—" She ran a shaking hand over her cheek. "But, that's impossible," she said.

"Would you get your things," said the man.

"But a replacement wouldn't know where everything *is*," Miss Land told him cheerfully, "You don't understand. I have my own system here. I call it the—"

She bit her lower lip suddenly and drove back a sob.

"No, no, I'm sorry," she said, "It's impossible. You don't understand. A replacement would never be able to—"

"Miss Land, get your things."

Miss Land was a statue except for the vein that pulsed on her neck.

"But you don't understand," she murmured.

Outside, the doorbell tinkled and Miss Land's head turned. She stared at the general delivery window.

"Miss Land," said the man.

Abruptly, Miss Land stepped over to the general delivery window and jerked it up.

"Well, good *morning*," she said. "Isn't it a lovely morning?"

Mr. Smalley looked at her in blank surprise.

"Well, let's see now," said Miss Land, turning toward the shelves. Her trembling hand drew out the small packet and she put one, two, three, four, five letters on the table. She drew a magazine off the pile, then turned back to the window, smiling and flushed.

"Well," she said. "You certainly hit the jackpot this morning."

She looked right into Mr. Smalley's dark eyes and she held on to the counter edge with bloodless fingers.

When Mr. Smalley had left, she stood watching him for a moment as he walked across the square toward his car. Once he glanced back and she waved to him with a delicate flutter of her fingers.

Then Miss Land drew down the window and turned away from it.

THE FUNCTION OF DREAM SLEEP
Harlan Ellison

HARLAN ELLISON is the most honored living fantasist. In a career spanning nearly 50 years, he has won 8½ Hugo awards, 3 Nebulas, 5 Stokers (including The Lifetime Achievement Award in 1996), 2 Edgars, the Silver Pen for Journalism, and, most recently, an Audie for his reading of Ben Bova's *City of Darkness*.

Born in Cleveland, Ohio, in 1934, Ellison has been a resident of Los Angeles since 1962, where he lives with his wife, Susan.

Among his most famous works are *Deathbird Stories, Angry Candy, Shatterday, Mind Fields* (a fiction/art collaboration with Jacek Yerka), and, most recently, *Slippage*. Harlan Ellison has formed his own imprint, Edgeworks Abbey, to republish his works in uniform editions, with the definitive, expanded texts of two separate books contained in each volume.

W.K.S.

McGrath awoke suddenly, just in time to see a huge mouth filled with small, sharp teeth closing in his side. In an instant it was gone, even as he shook himself awake.

Had he not been staring at the flesh, at the moment his eyes opened from sleep, he would have missed the faintest pink line of closure that remained only another heartbeat, then faded and was gone, leaving no indication the mouth had ever existed; a second—secret—mouth hiding in his skin.

At first he was sure he had wakened from a particularly nasty dream. But the memory of the thing that had escaped from within him, through the mouth, was a real memory—not a wisp of fading nightmare. He had *felt* the chilly passage of something rushing out of him. Like cold air from a leaking balloon. Like a chill down a hallway from a window left open in a distant room. And he had *seen* the mouth. It lay across the ribs vertically, just below his left nipple, running down to the bulge of fat parallel to his navel. Down his left side there had been a lipless mouth filled with teeth; and it had been open to permit a breeze of something to leave his body.

McGrath sat up on the bed. He was shaking. The Tensor lamp was still on, the paperback novel tented open on the sheet beside him, his body naked and perspiring in the August heat. The Tensor had been aimed directly at his side, bathing his flesh with light, when he had unexpectedly opened his eyes; and in that waking moment he had surprised his body in the act of opening its secret mouth.

He couldn't stop the trembling, and when the phone rang he had to steel himself to lift the receiver.

"Hello," he heard himself say, in someone else's voice.

"Lonny," said Victor Kayley's widow, "I'm sorry to disturb you at this hour . . ."

"It's okay," he said. Victor had died the day before yesterday. Sally relied on him for the arrangements, and hours of solace he didn't begrudge. Years before, Sally and he . . . then she drifted toward Victor, who had been McGrath's oldest, closest . . . they were drawn to each other more and more sweetly till . . . and finally, McGrath had taken them both to dinner at the old Steuben Tavern on West 47th, that dear old Steuben Tavern with its dark wood booths and sensational schnitzel, now gone, torn down and gone like so much else that was . . . and he had made them sit side by side in the booth across from him, and he took their hands in his . . . I love you both so much, he had said . . . I see the way you move when you're around each other . . . you're both my dearest friends, you put light in my world . . . and he laid their hands together under his, and he grinned at them for their nervousness . . .

"Are you all right; you sound so, I don't know, so *strained*?" Her voice was wide awake. But concerned.

"I'm, yeah, I'm okay. I just had the weirdest, I was dozing, fell asleep reading, and I had this, this *weird*—" He trailed off. Then went back at it, more sternly: "I'm okay. It was a scary dream."

There was, then, a long measure of silence between them. Only the open line, with the sound of ions decaying.

"Are *you* okay?" he said, thinking of the funeral service day after tomorrow. She had asked him to select the casket. The anodized pink aluminum "unit" they had tried to get him to go for, doing a bait-and-switch, had nauseated him. McGrath had settled on a simple copper casket, shrugging away suggestions by the Bereavement Counselor in the Casket Selection Parlor that "consideration and thoughtfulness for the departed" might better be served by the Monaco, a "Duraseal metal unit with Sea Mist Polished Finish, interior richly lined in 600 Aqua Supreme Cheney velvet, magnificently quilted and shirred, with matching jumbo bolster and coverlet."

"I couldn't sleep," she said. "I was watching television, and they had a thing about the echidna, the Australian anteater, you know . . . ?" He made a sound that indicated he knew. "And Vic never got over the trip we took to the Flinders Range in '82, and he just loved the Australian animals, and I turned in the bed to see him smiling . . ."

She began to cry.

He could feel his throat closing. He knew. The turning to tell your best friend something you'd just seen together, to get the reinforcement, the input, the expression on his face. And there was no face. There was emptiness in that place. He knew. He'd turned to Victor three dozen times in the past two days. Turned, to confront emptiness. Oh, he knew, all right.

"Sally," he murmured. "Sally, I know; I know."

She pulled herself together, snuffled herself unclogged

and cleared her throat. "It's okay. I'm fine. It was just a second there . . ."

"Try to get some sleep. We have to do stuff tomorrow."

"Of course," she said, sounding really quite all right. "I'll go back to bed. I'm sorry." He told her to shut up, if you couldn't call a friend at that hour to talk about the echidna, who the hell *could* you call?

"Jerry Falwell," she said. "If I have to annoy someone at three in the morning, better it should be a shit like him." They laughed quickly and emptily, she said good night and told him he had been much loved by both of them, he said I know that, and they hung up.

Lonny McGrath lay there, the paperback still tented at his side, the Tensor still warming his flesh, the sheets still soggy from the humidity, and he stared at the far wall of the bedroom on whose surface, like the surface of his skin, there lay no evidence whatever of secret mouths filled with teeth.

Λ

"I can't get it out of my mind."

Dr. Jess ran her fingers down his side, looked closer. "Well, it *is* red; but that's more chafing than anything out of Stephen King."

"It's red because I keep rubbing it. I'm getting obsessive about it. And don't make fun, Jess. I can't get it out of my mind."

She sighed and raked a hand back through her thick auburn hair. "Sorry." She got up and walked to the window in the examination room. Then, as an afterthought, she said, "You can get dressed." She stared out the window as McGrath hopped off the physical therapy table, nearly catching his heel on the retractable step. He partially folded the stiff paper gown that had covered his lap, and laid it on the padded seat. As he pulled up his undershorts,

Dr. Jess turned and stared at him. He thought for the hundredth time that his initial fears, years before, at being examined by a female physician, had been foolish. His friend looked at him with concern, but without the *look* that passed between men and women. "How long has it been since Victor died?"

"Three months, almost."

"And Emily?"

"Six months."

"And Steve and Melanie's son?"

"Oh, Christ, Jess!"

She pursed her lips. "Look, Lonny, I'm not a psychotherapist, but even I can see that the death of all these friends is getting to you. Maybe you don't even see it, but you used the right word: obsessive. *No*body can sustain so much pain, over so brief a period, the loss of so many loved ones, without going into a spiral."

"What did the X rays show?"

"I told you."

"But there might've been *some*thing. Some lesion, or inflammation; an irregularity in the dermis . . . *some*thing!"

"Lonny. Come *on*. I've never lied to you. You looked at them with me, did *you* see anything?" He sighed deeply, shook his head. She spread her hands as if to say, well, there you are, I can't make something sick where nothing sick exists. "I can work on your soft prostate, and I can give you a shot of cortisone in the ball joint where that cop worked you over; but I can't treat something out of a penny dreadful novel that doesn't leave any trace."

"You think I need a shrink?"

She turned back to the window. "This is your third visit, Lonny. You're my pal, kiddo, but I think you need to get counseling of a different sort."

McGrath knotted his tie and drew it up, spreading the wings of his shirt collar with his little fingers. She didn't turn around. "I'm worried about you, Lonny. You ought to be married."

"I *was* married. You're not talking wife, anyway. You're talking keeper." She didn't turn. He pulled on his jacket, and waited. Finally, with his hand on the doorknob, he said, "Maybe you're right. I've never been a melancholy sort, but all this . . . so many, in so short a time . . . maybe you're right."

He opened the door. She looked out the window. "We'll talk." He started out, and without turning, she said, "There won't be a charge for this visit."

He smiled thinly, not at all happily. But she didn't see it. There is *always* a charge, of one kind or another.

⏶

He called Tommy and begged off from work. Tommy went into a snit. "I'm up to my ass, Lonny," he said, affecting his Dowager Empress tone. "This is Black goddam Friday! The Eroica! That Fahrenheit woman, Farrenstock, whatever the hell it is . . ."

"Fahnestock," Lonny said, smiling for the first time in days. "I thought we'd seen the last of her when you suggested she look into the possibility of a leper sitting on her face."

Tommy sighed. "The grotesque bitch is simply a glutton. I swear to God she must be into bondage; the worse I treat her, the more often she comes in."

"What'd she bring this time?"

"Another half dozen of those tacky petit-point things. I can barely bring myself to look at them. Bleeding martyrs and scenes of culturally depressed areas in, I suppose, Iowa or Indiana. Illinois, Idaho, I don't know: one of those places that begins with an I, teeming with people who bowl."

Lonny always wound up framing Mrs. Fahnestock's

gaucheries. Tommy always took one look, then went upstairs in back of the framing shop to lie down for a while. McGrath had asked the matron once, what she did with all of them. She replied that she gave them as gifts. Tommy, when he heard, fell to his knees and prayed to a God in which he did not believe that the woman would never hold him in enough esteem to feel he deserved such a gift. But she spent, oh my, how she spent.

"Let me guess," McGrath said. "She wants them blocked so tightly you could bounce a dime off them, with a fabric liner, a basic pearl matte, and the black lacquer frame from Chapin Molding. Right?"

"Yes, of course, right. Which is *another* reason your slacker behavior is particularly distressing. The truck from Chapin just dropped off a hundred feet of the oval top walnut molding. It's got to be unpacked, the footage measured, and put away. You *can't* take the day off."

"Tommy, don't whip the guilt on me. I'm a goy, remember?"

"If it weren't for guilt, the *goyim* would have wiped us out three thousand years ago. It's more effective than a Star Wars defense system." He puffed air through his lips for a moment, measuring how much he would *actually* be inconvenienced by his assistant's absence. "Monday morning? Early?"

McGrath said, "I'll be there no later than eight o'clock. I'll do the petit-points first."

"All right. And by the way, you sound awful. D'you know the worst part about being an Atheist?"

Lonny smiled. Tommy would feel it was a closed bargain if he could pass on one of his horrendous jokes. "No, what's the worst part about being an Atheist?"

"You've got no one to talk to when you're fucking."

Lonny roared, silently. There was no need to give him the satisfaction. But Tommy knew. He couldn't see him, but Lonny knew he was grinning broadly at the other end of the line. "So long, Tommy. See you Monday."

He racked the receiver in the phone booth and looked across Pico Boulevard at the office building. He had lived in Los Angeles for eleven years, since he and Victor and Sally had fled New York, and he still couldn't get used to the golden patina that lay over the days here. Except when it rained, at which times the inclemency seemed so alien he had visions of giant mushrooms sprouting from the sidewalks. The office building was unimpressive, just three storeys high and brick; but a late afternoon shadow lay across its face, and it recalled for him the eighteen frontal views of the Rouen Cathedral that Monet had painted during the winter months of 1892 and 1893: the same façade, following the light from early morning till sunset. He had seen the Monet exhibition at MOMA. Then he remembered with whom he had taken in that exhibition, and he felt again the passage of chill leaving his body through that secret mouth. He stepped out of the booth and just wanted to go somewhere and cry. *Stop it!* he said inside. *Knock it off.* He swiped at the corner of his eye, and crossed the street. He passed through the shadow that cut the sidewalk.

Inside the tiny lobby he consulted the glass-paneled wall register. Mostly, the building housed dentists and philatelists, as best he could tell. But against the ribbed black panel he read the little white plastic letters that had been darted in to include THE REM GROUP 306. He walked up the stairs.

To find 306, he had to make a choice: go left or go right. There were no office location arrows on the wall. He went to the right, and was pleased. As the numbers went down, he began to hear someone speaking rather loudly. "Sleep is of several kinds. Dream sleep, or rapid eye movement sleep—what we call REM sleep, and thus the name of our group—is predominantly found in mammals who bring forth living young, rather than eggs. Some birds and reptiles, as well."

McGrath stood outside the glass-paneled door to 306, and he listened. *Viviparous mammals*, he thought. He could now discern that the speaker was a woman; and her use of "living young, rather than eggs" instead of *viviparous* convinced him she was addressing one or more laypersons. *The echidna*, he thought. *A familiar viviparous mammal.*

"We now believe dreams originate in the brain's neocortex. Dreams have been used to attempt to foretell the future. Freud used dreams to explore the unconscious mind. Jung thought dreams formed a bridge of communication between the conscious and the unconscious." *It wasn't a dream*, McGrath thought. *I was awake. I know the difference.*

The woman was saying, ". . . those who try to make dreams work for them, to create poetry, to solve problems; and it's generally thought that dreams aid in consolidating memories. How many of you believe that if you can only *remember* the dream when you waken, that you will understand something very important, or regain some special memory you've lost?"

How many of you. McGrath now understood that the dream therapy group was in session. Late on a Friday afternoon? It would have to be women in their thirties, forties.

He opened the door, to see if he was correct.

With their hands in the air, indicating they believed the capturing of a dream on awakening would bring back an old memory, all six of the women in the room, not one of them older than forty, turned to stare at McGrath as he entered. He closed the door behind him, and said, "I don't agree. I think we dream to forget. And sometimes it doesn't work."

He was looking at the woman standing in front of the six hand-raised members of the group. She stared back at

him for a long moment, and all six heads turned back to
her. Their hands were frozen in the air. The woman who
had been speaking settled back till she was perched on the
edge of her desk.

"Mr. McGrath?"

"Yes. I'm sorry I'm late. It's been a day."

She smiled quickly, totally in command, putting him at
ease. "I'm Anna Picket. Tricia said you'd probably be
along today. Please grab a chair."

McGrath nodded and took a folding chair from the three
remaining against the wall. He unfolded it and set it at the
far left of the semicircle. The six well-tended, expensively-
coifed heads remained turned toward him as, one by one,
the hands came down.

He wasn't at all sure letting his ex-wife call this Anna
Picket, to get him into the group, had been such a good
idea. They had remained friends after the divorce, and he
trusted her judgment. Though he had never availed himself
of her services after they'd separated and she had gone for
her degree at UCLA, he'd been assured that Tricia was as
good a family counseling therapist as one could find in
Southern California. He had been shocked when she'd
suggested a dream group. But he'd come: he had walked
through the area most of the early part of the day, trying to
decide if he wanted to do this, share what he'd experienced
with total strangers; walked through the area stopping in at
this shop and that boutique, having some gelato and shaking his head at how this neighborhood had been "gentri-
fied," how it had changed so radically, how all the
wonderful little tradesmen who had flourished here had
been driven out by geysering rents; walked through the
area growing more and more despondent at how nothing
lasted, how joy was drained away shop by shop, neighborhood by neighborhood, person by . . .

Until one was left alone.

Standing on an empty plain. The dark wind blowing

from the horizon. Cold, empty dark: with the knowledge that a pit of eternal loneliness lay just over that horizon, and that the frightening wind that blew up out of the pit would never cease. That one would stand there, all alone, on the empty plain, as one after another of the ones you loved were erased in a second.

Had walked through the area, all day, and finally had called Tommy, and finally had allowed Tricia's wisdom to lead him, and here he sat, in a folding straight-back chair, asking a total stranger to repeat what she had just said.

"I asked why you didn't agree with the group, that remembering dreams is a good thing?" She arched an eyebrow, and tilted her head.

McGrath felt uncomfortable for a moment. He blushed. It was something that had always caused him embarrassment. "Well," he said slowly, "I don't want to seem like a smart aleck, one of those people who reads some popularized bit of science and then comes on like an authority . . ."

She smiled at his consternation, the flush of his cheeks. "Please, Mr. McGrath, that's quite all right. Where dreams are concerned, we're *all* journeyists. What did you read?"

"The Crick-Mitchison theory. The paper on 'unlearning.' I don't know, it just seemed, well, *reasonable* to me."

One of the women asked what that was.

Anna Picket said, "Dr. Sir Francis Crick, you'll know of him because he won the Nobel Prize for his work with DNA; and Graeme Mitchison, he's a highly respected brain researcher at Cambridge. Their experiments in the early 1980s. They postulate that we dream to forget, not to remember."

"The best way I understood it," McGrath said, "was using the analogy of cleaning out an office building at night, after all the workers are gone. Outdated reports are trashed, computer dump sheets are shredded, old memos tossed with the refuse. Every night our brains get cleaned during the one to two hours of REM sleep. The dreams pick up after us every day, sweep out the unnecessary, un-true, or just plain silly memories that could keep us from storing the important memories, or might keep us from ra-tional thinking when we're awake. *Remembering* the dreams would be counter-productive, since the brain is try-ing to unlearn all that crap so we function better."

Anna Picket smiled. "You were sent from heaven, Mr. McGrath. I was going precisely to that theory when you came in. You've saved me a great deal of explanation."

One of the six women said, "Then you don't *want* us to write down our dreams and bring them in for discussion? I even put a tape recorder by the bed. For instance, I had a dream just last night in which my bicycle . . ."

He sat through the entire session, listening to things that infuriated him. They were so self-indulgent, making of the most minor inconveniences in their lives, mountains im-possible to conquer. They were so different from the women he knew. They seemed to be antiquated creatures from some primitive time, confused by changing times and the demand on them to be utterly responsible for their ex-istence. They seemed to want succor, to be told that there were greater forces at work in their world; powers and pressures and even conspiracies that existed solely to keep them nervous, uncomfortable, and helpless. Five of the six were divorcées, and only one of the five had a full-time job: selling real estate. The sixth was the daughter of an or-ganized crime figure. McGrath felt no link with them. He didn't need a group therapy session. His life was as full as he wanted it to be . . . except that he was now always scared, and lost, and constantly depressed. Perhaps Dr. Jess was dead on target. Perhaps he *did* need a shrink.

He was certain he did not need Anna Picket and her well-tailored ladies whose greatest *real* anguish was mak-ing sure they got home in time to turn on the sprinklers.

When the session ended, he started toward the door without saying anything to the Picket woman. She was surrounded by the six. But she gently edged them aside and called to him, "Mr. McGrath, would you wait a moment? I'd like to speak to you." He took his hand off the doorknob, and went back to his chair. He bit the soft flesh of his inner cheek, annoyed.

She blew them off like dandelion fluff, far more quickly than McGrath thought possible, and did it without their taking it as rejection. In less than five minutes he was alone in the office with the dream therapist.

She closed the door behind the Mafia Princess and locked it. For a deranged moment he thought . . . but it passed, and the look on her face was concern, not lust. He started to rise. She laid a palm against the air, stopping him. He sank back onto the folding chair.

Then Anna Picket came to him and said, "For McGrath hath murdered sleep." He stared up at her as she put her left hand behind his head, cupping the nape with fingers extending up under his hair along the curve of the skull. "Don't be nervous, this'll be all right," she said, laying her right hand with the palm against his left cheek, the spread thumb and index finger bracketing an eye he tried mightily not to blink. Her thumb lay alongside his nose, the tip curving onto the bridge. The forefinger lay across the bony eyeridge.

She pursed her lips, then sighed deeply. In a moment her body twitched with an involuntary rictus, and she gasped, as if she had had the wind knocked out of her. McGrath couldn't move. He could feel the strength of her hands cradling his head, and the tremors of—he wanted to say—*passion* slamming through her. Not the passion of strong amorous feeling, but passion in the sense of being acted upon by something external, something alien to one's nature.

The trembling in her grew more pronounced, and McGrath had the sense that power was being drained out of him, pouring into her, that it had reached saturation level

and was leaking back along the system into him, but
changed, more dangerous. But why dangerous? She was
spasming now, her eyes closed, her head thrown back and
to the side, her thick mass of hair swaying and bobbing as
she jerked, a human double-circuit high-voltage tower
about to overload.

She moaned softly, in pain, without the slightest trace of
subliminal pleasure, and he could see she was biting her
lower lip so fiercely that blood was beginning to coat her
mouth. When the pain he saw in her face became more
than he could bear, he reached up quickly and took her
hands away with difficulty; breaking the circuit.

Anna Picket's legs went out and she keeled toward him.
He tried to brace himself, but she hit him with full dead
weight, and they went crashing to the floor entangled in
the metal folding chair.

Frightened, thinking insanely *what if someone comes in
and sees us like this, they'd think I was molesting her*, and
in the next instant thinking with relief *she locked the door*,
and in the next instant his fear was transmogrified into
concern for her. He rolled out from under her trembling
body, taking the chair with him, wrapped around one
ankle. He shook off the chair, and got to his knees. Her
eyes were half-closed, the lids flickering so rapidly she
might have been in the line of strobe lights.

He hauled her around, settling her semi-upright with
her head in his lap. He brushed the hair from her face, and
shook her ever so lightly, because he had no water, and had
no moist washcloth. Her breathing slowed, her chest
heaved not quite so spastically, and her hand, flung away
from her body, began to flex the fingers.

"Ms. Picket," he whispered, "can you talk? Are you all
right? Is there some medicine you need . . . in your desk?"

She opened her eyes, then, and looked up at him. She
tasted the blood on her lips and continued breathing

raggedly, as though she had run a great distance. And finally she said, "I could feel it in when you walked in."

He tried to ask what it was she had felt, what it was in him that had so unhinged her, but she reached in with the flexing hand and touched his forearm.

"You'll have to come with me."

"Where?"

"To meet the *real* REM Group."

And she began to cry. He knew immediately that she was weeping for him, and he murmured that he would come with her. She tried to smile reassurance, but there was still too much pain in her. They stayed that way for a time, and then they left the office building together.

A

They were impaired, every one of them in the sprawling ranch-style house in Hidden Hills. One was blind, another had only one hand. A third looked as if she had been in a terrible fire and had lost half her face, and another propelled herself through the house on a small wheeled platform with restraining bars to keep her from falling off.

They had taken the San Diego Freeway to the Ventura, and had driven west on 101 to the Calabasas exit. Climbing, then dropping behind the hills, they had turned up a side road that became a dirt road that became a horse path, Lonny driving Anna Picket's '85 Le Sabre.

The house lay within a bowl, completely concealed, even from the dirt road below. The horse trail passed behind low hills covered with mesquite and coast live oak, and abruptly became a perfectly surfaced blacktop. Like the roads Hearst had had cut in the hills leading up to San Simeon, concealing access to the Castle from the Coast Highway above Cambria, the blacktop had been poured on spiral rising cuts laid on a reverse bias.

Unless sought from the air, the enormous ranch house

and its outbuildings and grounds would be unknown even
to the most adventurous picnicker. "How much of this
acreage do you own?" McGrath asked, circling down the
inside of the bowl.

"All this," she said, waving an arm across the empty
hills, "almost to the edge of Ventura County."

She had recovered completely, but had said very little
during the hour and a half trip, even during the heaviest
weekend traffic on the 101 Freeway crawling like a million-
wheeled worm through the San Fernando Valley out of Los
Angeles. "Not a lot of casual drop-ins I should imagine,"
he replied. She looked at him across the front seat, fully for
the first time since leaving Santa Monica. "I hope you'll
have faith in me, trust me just a while longer," she said.

He paid strict attention to the driving.

He had been cramped within the Buick by a kind of dull
fear that strangely reminded him of how he had always felt
on Christmas Eve, as a child, lying in bed, afraid of, yet
anxious for, the sleep that permitted Santa Claus to come.

In that house below lay something that knew of secret
mouths and ancient winds from within. Had he not trusted
her, he would have slammed the brake pedal and leaped
from the car and not stopped running till he had reached
the freeway.

And once inside the house, seeing all of them, so ruined
and tragic, he was helpless to do anything but allow her to
lead him to a large sitting-room, where a circle of comfortable overstuffed chairs formed a pattern that made the
fear more overwhelming.

They came, then, in twos and threes, the legless woman
on the rolling cart propelling herself into the center of the
ring. He sat there and watched them come, and his heart
seemed to press against his chest. McGrath, as a young
man, had gone to a Judy Garland film festival at the Thalia
in New York. One of the revived movies had been *A Child
Is Waiting*, a nonsinging role for Judy, a film about re-

tarded children. Sally had had to help him out of the theater only halfway through. He could not see through his tears. His capacity for bearing the anguish of the crippled, particularly children, was less than that of most people. He brought himself up short: why had he thought of that afternoon at the Thalia now? These weren't children. They were adults. All of them. Every woman in the house was at least as old as he, surely older. Why had he been thinking of them as children?

Anna Picket took the chair beside him, and looked around the circle. One chair was empty. "Catherine?" she asked.

The blind woman said, "She died on Sunday."

Anna closed her eyes and sank back into the chair. "God be with her, and her pain ended."

They sat quietly for a time, until the woman on the cart looked up at McGrath, smiled a very kind smile, and said, "What is your name, young man?"

"Lonny," McGrath said. He watched as she rolled herself to his feet and put a hand on his knee. He felt warmth flow through him, and his fear melted. But it only lasted for a moment, as she trembled and moaned softly, as Anna Picket had done in the office. Anna quickly rose and drew her away from McGrath. There were tears in the cart-woman's eyes.

A woman with gray hair and involuntary head tremors, indicative of Parkinson's, leaned forward and said, "Lonny, tell us."

He started to say *tell you what?* but she held up a finger and said the same thing again.

So he told them. As best he could. Putting words to feelings that always sounded melodramatic; words that were wholly inadequate for the tidal wave of sorrow that held him down in darkness. "I miss them, oh God how I miss them," he said, twisting his hands. "I've never been like this. My mother died, and I was lost, I was miserable, yes

there was a feeling my heart would break, because I loved
her. But I could *handle* it. I could comfort my father and
my sister, I had it in me to do that. But these last two
years . . . one after another . . . so many who were close to
me . . . pieces of my past, my life . . . friends I'd shared
times with, and now those times are gone, they slip away
as I try to think of them. I, I just don't know *what to do*."

And he spoke of the mouth. The teeth. The closing of
that mouth. The wind that had escaped from inside him.

"Did you ever sleepwalk, as a child?" a woman with a
clubfoot asked. He said: yes, but only once. Tell us, they
said.

"It was nothing. I was a little boy, maybe ten or eleven.
My father found me standing in the hallway outside my
bedroom, at the head of the stairs. I was asleep, and I was
looking at the wall. I said, 'I don't see it here anywhere.'
My father told me I'd said that; the next morning he told
me. He took me back to bed. That was the only time, as
best I know."

The women murmured around the circle to each other.
Then the woman with Parkinson's said, "No, I don't think
that's anything." Then she stood up, and came to him. She
laid a hand on his forehead and said, "Go to sleep, Lonny."

And he blinked once, and suddenly sat bolt upright. But
it wasn't an instant, it had been much longer. He had been
asleep. For a long while. He knew it was so instantly, because it was now dark outside the house, and the women
looked as if they had been savaged by living jungles. The
blind woman was bleeding from her eyes and ears; the
woman on the cart had fallen over, lay unconscious at his
feet; in the chair where the fire victim had sat, there was
now only a charred outline of a human being, still faintly
smoking.

McGrath leaped to his feet. He looked about wildly. He
didn't know what to do to help them. Beside him, Anna

Picket lay slumped across the bolster arm of the chair, her body twisted and blood once again speckling her lips.

Then he realized: the woman who had touched him, the woman with Parkinson's, was gone.

They began to whimper, and several of them moved, their hands idly touching the air. A woman who had no nose tried to rise, slipped and fell. He rushed to her, helped her back into the chair, and he realized she was missing fingers on both hands. Leprosy . . . *no*! Hansen's disease, that's what it's called. She was coming to, and she whispered to him, "There . . . Teresa . . . help her . . ." and he looked where she was pointing, at a woman as pale as crystal, her hair a glowing white, her eyes colorless. "She . . . has . . . lupus . . ." the woman without a nose whispered.

McGrath went to Teresa. She looked up at him with fear and was barely able to say, "Can you . . . please . . . take me to a dark place . . . ?"

He lifted her in his arms. She weighed nothing. He let her direct him up the stairs to the second floor, to the third bedroom off the main corridor. He opened the door and it was musty and unlit. He could barely make out the shape of a bed. He carried her over and placed her gently on the puffy down comforter. She reached up and touched his hand. "Thank you." She spoke haltingly, having trouble breathing. "We, we didn't expect anything . . . like that . . ."

McGrath was frantic. He didn't know what had happened, didn't know what he had done to them. He felt awful, felt responsible, *but he didn't know what he had done!*

"Go back to them," she whispered. "Help them."

"Where is the woman who touched me . . . ?"

He heard her sobbing. "She's gone. Lurene is gone. It wasn't your fault. We didn't expect anything . . . like . . . that."

He rushed back downstairs.

They were helping one another. Anna Picket had brought water, and bottles of medicine, and wet cloths. They were helping one another. The healthier ones limping and crawling to the ones still unconscious or groaning in pain. And he smelled the fried metal scent of ozone in the air. There was a charred patch on the ceiling above the chair where the burned woman had been sitting.

He tried to help Anna Picket, but when she realized it was McGrath, she slapped his hand away. Then she gasped, and her hand flew to her mouth, and she began to cry again, and reached out to apologize. "Oh, my God, I'm so *sorry*! It wasn't your fault. You couldn't know . . . not even Lurene knew." She swabbed at her eyes, and laid a hand on his chest. "Go outside. Please. I'll be there in a moment."

A wide streak of dove-gray now bolted through her tangled hair. It had not been there before the instant of his sleep.

He went outside and stood under the stars. It was night, but it had not been night before Lurene had touched him. He stared up at the cold points of light, and the sense of irreparable loss overwhelmed him. He wanted to sink to his knees, letting his life ebb into the ground, freeing him from this misery that would not let him breathe. He thought of Victor, and the casket being cranked down into the earth, as Sally clung to him, murmuring words he could not understand, and hitting him again and again on the chest; not hard, but without measure, without meaning, with nothing but simple human misery. He thought of Alan, dying in a Hollywood apartment from AIDS, tended by his mother and sister who were, themselves, hysterical and constantly praying, asking Jesus to help them; dying in that apartment with the two roommates who had been sharing the rent keeping to themselves, eating off paper plates for fear of contracting the plague, trying to figure out if they could get a lawyer to force Alan's removal; dying in that miserable apartment because the Kaiser Hospital had found a way around his coverage, and had forced him into "home care." He thought of Emily, lying dead beside her bed, having just dressed for dinner with her daughter, being struck by the grand mal seizure and her heart exploding, lying there for a day, dressed for a dinner she would never eat, with a daughter she would never again see. He thought of Mike, trying to smile from the hospital bed, and forgetting from moment to moment who Lonny was, as the tumor consumed his brain. He thought of Ted seeking shamans and homeopathists, running full tilt till he was cut down. He thought of Roy, all alone now that DeeDee was gone: half a unit, a severed dream, an incomplete conversation. He stood there with his head in his hands, rocking back and forth, trying to ease the pain.

When Anna Picket touched him, he started violently, a small cry of desolation razoring into the darkness.

"What *happened* in there?" he demanded. "Who *are* you people? What did I do to you? Please, oh please I'm asking you, tell me *what's going on!*"

"We absorb."

"I don't know what—"

"We take illness. We've always been with you. As far back as we can know. We have always had that capacity, to assume the illness. There aren't many of us, but we're everywhere. We absorb. We try to help. As Jesus wrapped himself in the leper's garments, as he touched the lame and the blind, and they were healed. I don't know where it comes from, some sort of intense empathy. But . . . we do it . . . we absorb."

"And with me . . . what was that in there . . . ?"

"We didn't know. We thought it was just the heartache. We've encountered it before. That was why Tricia suggested you come to the Group."

"My wife . . . is Tricia one of you? Can she . . . take on the . . . does she absorb? I lived with her, I never—"

Anna was shaking her head. "No, Tricia has no idea what we are. She's never been here. Very few people have been so needing that I've brought them here. But she's a fine therapist, and we've helped a few of her patients. She thought you . . ." She paused. "She still cares for you. She felt your pain, and thought the Group might be able to help. She doesn't even know of the *real* REM Group."

He grabbed her by the shoulders, intense now.

"What happened in there?"

She bit her lip and closed her eyes tightly against the memory. "It was as you said. The mouth. We'd never seen that before. It, it *opened*. And then . . . and then . . ."

He shook her. *"What!?!"*

She wailed against the memory. The sound slammed against him and against the hills and against the cold points of the stars. "Mouths. In each of us! Opened. And the wind, it, it just, it just *hissed* out of us, each of us. And the pain we held, no, that *they* held—I'm just their contact for the world, they can't go anywhere, so I go and shop and bring and do—the pain *they* absorbed, it, it took some of them. Lurene and Margid . . . Teresa won't live . . . I know . . ."

McGrath was raving now. His head was about to burst. He shook her as she cried and moaned, demanding, "What's happening to us, what am I doing, why is this doing to us now, what's going wrong, please, you've got to help me, we've got to *do* something—"

And they hugged each other, clinging tightly to the only thing that promised support: each other. The sky wheeled above them, and the ground seemed to fall away. But they kept their balance, and finally she pushed him to arm's length and looked closely at his face and said, "I don't know. I *do not* know. This isn't like anything we've experienced before. Not even Alvarez or Ariès know about this.

A wind, a terrible wind, something alive, leaving the body."

"Help me!"

"I *can't* help you! No one can help you, I don't think *anyone* can help you. Not even Le Braz . . ."

He clutched at the name. "Le Braz! Who's Le Braz?"

"No, you don't want to see Le Braz. Please, listen to me, try to go off where it's quiet, and lonely, and try to handle it yourself, that's the only way!"

"Tell me who Le Braz is!"

She slapped him. "You're not hearing me. If *we* can't do for you, then no one can. Le Braz is beyond anything we know, he can't be trusted, he does things that are outside, that are awful, I think. I don't really know. I went to him once, years ago, it's not something you want to—"

I don't care, he said. I don't care about any of it now. I have to rid myself of this. It's too terrible to live with. I see their faces. They're calling and I can't answer them. They plead with me to say something to them. I don't know what to say. I can't sleep. And when I sleep I dream of them. I can't live like this, because this isn't living. So tell me how to find Le Braz. I don't care, to Hell with the whole thing, I just don't give a damn, so *tell me!*

She slapped him again. Much harder. And again. And he took it. And finally she told him.

▲

He had been an abortionist. In the days before it was legal, he had been the last hope for hundreds of women. Once, long before, he had been a surgeon. But they had taken that away from him. So he did what he could do. In the days when women went to small rooms with long tables, or to coat hangers, he had helped. He had charged two hundred dollars, just to keep up with supplies. In those days of secret thousands in brown paper bags stored in clothes clos-

ets, two hundred dollars was as if he had done the work for
free. And they had put him in prison. But when he came
out, he went back at it.

Anna Picket told McGrath that there had been other . . .
. . . work. Other experiments. She had said the word *experiments*, with a tone in her voice that made McGrath
shudder. And she had said again, "For McGrath hath murdered sleep," and he asked her if he could take her car, and
she said yes, and he had driven back to the 101 Freeway
and headed north toward Santa Barbara, where Anna
Picket said Le Braz now lived, and had lived for years, in
total seclusion.

It was difficult locating his estate. The only gas station
open in Santa Barbara at that hour did not carry maps. It
had been years since free maps had been a courtesy of gas
stations. Like so many other small courtesies in McGrath's
world that had been spirited away before he could lodge a
complaint. But there was no complaint department, in any
case.

So he went to the Hotel Miramar, and the night clerk
was a woman in her sixties who knew every street in Santa
Barbara and knew very well the location of the Le Braz
"place." She looked at McGrath as if he had asked her the
location of the local abattoir. But she gave him explicit directions, and he thanked her, and she didn't say you're
welcome, and he left. It was just lightening in the east as
dawn approached.

By the time he found the private drive that climbed
through heavy woods to the high-fenced estate, it was fully
light. Sun poured across the channel and made the foliage
seem Rain Forest lush. He looked back over his shoulder
as he stepped out of the Le Sabre, and the Santa Monica
Channel was silver and rippled and utterly oblivious to
shadows left behind from the night.

He walked to the gate, and pressed the button on the in-
tercom system. He waited, and pressed it again. Then a

voice—he could not tell if it was male or female, young or old—cracked, "Who is it?"

"I've come from Anna Picket and the REM Group." He paused a moment, and when the silence persisted, he added, "The *real* REM Group. Women in a house in Hidden Hills."

The voice said, "Who are you? What's your name?"

"It doesn't matter. You don't know me. McGrath, my name is McGrath. I came a long way to see Le Braz."

"About what?"

"Open the gate and you'll know."

"We don't have visitors."

"I saw . . . there was a . . . I woke up suddenly, there was a, a kind of *mouth* in my body . . . a wind passed . . ."

There was a whirring sound, and the iron gate began to withdraw into the brick wall. McGrath rushed back to the car and started the engine. As the gate opened completely, he decked the accelerator and leaped through, even as the gate began without hesitation to close.

He drove up the winding drive through the Rain Forest, and when he came out at the top, the large, fieldstone mansion sat there, hidden from all sides by tall stands of trees and thick foliage. He pulled up on the crushed rock drive, and sat for a moment staring at the leaded windows that looked down emptily. It was cool here, and dusky, even though it was burgeoning day. He got out and went to the carved oak door. He was reaching for the knocker when the door was opened. By a ruined thing.

McGrath couldn't help himself. He gasped and fell back, his hands coming up in front of him as if to ward off any approach by the barely human being that stood in the entranceway.

It was horribly pink where it was not burned. At first McGrath thought it was a woman, that was his quick impression; but then he could not discern its sex, it might have been male. It had certainly been tortured in flames.

The head was without hair, almost without skin that was not charred black. There seemed to be too many bends and joints in the arms. The sense that it was female came from the floor-length wide skirt it wore. He was spared the sight of the lower body, but he could tell there was considerable bulk there, a bulk that seemed to move gelatinously, as if neither human torso nor human legs lay within the circle of fabric.

And the creature stared at him from one milky eye, and one eye so pure and blue that his heart ached with the beauty of it. As features between the eyes and the chin that became part of the chest, without discernible neck, there were only charred knobs and bumps, and a lipless mouth blacker than the surrounding flesh. "Come inside," the doorkeeper said.

McGrath hesitated.

"Or go away," it said.

Lonny McGrath drew a deep breath and passed through. The doorkeeper moved aside only a trifle. They touched: blackened hip, back of a normal hand.

Closed and double-bolted, the passage out was now denied McGrath. He followed the asexual creature through a long, high-ceilinged foyer to a closed, heavily-paneled door to the right of a spiral staircase that led to the floor above. The thing, either man or woman, indicated he should enter. Then it shambled away, toward the rear of the mansion.

McGrath stood a moment, then turned the ornate L-shaped door handle, and entered. The heavy drapes were drawn against the morning light, but in the outlaw beams that latticed the room here and there, he saw an old man sitting in a high-backed chair, a lap robe concealing his legs. He stepped inside the library, for library it had to be: floor to ceiling bookcases, spilling their contents in teetering stacks all around the floor. Music swirled through the room. Classical music; McGrath didn't recognize it.

"Dr. Le Braz?" he said. The old man did not move. His head lay sunk on his chest. His eyes were closed. McGrath moved closer. The music swelled toward a crescendo, something symphonic. Now he was only three steps from the old man, and he called the name Le Braz again.

The eyes opened, and the leonine head rose. He stared at McGrath unblinkingly. The music came to an end. Silence filled the library.

The old man smiled sadly. And all ominousness left the space between them. It was a sweet smile. He inclined his head toward a stool beside the wingback. McGrath tried to give back a small smile, and took the seat offered.

"It is my hope that you are not here to solicit my endorsement for some new pharmacological product," the old man said.

"Are you Dr. Le Braz?"

"It is I who was, once, known by that name, yes."

"You have to help me."

Le Braz looked at him. There had been such a depth of ocean in the words McGrath had spoken, such a descent into stony caverns that all casualness was instantly denied. "Help you?"

"Yes. Please. I can't bear what I'm feeling. I've been through so much, seen so much these last months, I . . ."

"Help you?" the old man said again, whispering the phrase as if it had been rendered in a lost language. "I cannot even help myself . . . how can I possibly help you, young man?"

McGrath told him. Everything.

At some point the blackened creature entered the room, but McGrath was unaware of its presence till he had completed his story. Then, from behind him, he heard it say, "You are a remarkable person. Not one living person in a million has ever seen the Thanatos mouth. Not one in a hundred million has felt the passage of the soul. Not one in the memory of the human race has been so tormented that he thought it was real, and not a dream."

McGrath stared at the creature. It came lumbering across the room and stood just behind the old man's chair, not touching him. The old man sighed, and closed his eyes.

The creature said, "This was Josef Le Braz, who lived and worked and cared for his fellow man, and woman. He saved lives, and he married out of love, and he pledged himself to leave the world slightly better for his passage. And his wife died, and he fell into a well of melancholy such as no man had ever suffered. And one night he woke, feeling a chill, but he did not see the Thanatos mouth. All he knew was that he missed his wife so terribly that he wanted to end his life."

McGrath sat silently. He had no idea what this meant, this history of the desolate figure under the lap robe. But he waited, because if no help lay here in this house, of all houses secret and open in the world, then he knew that the next step for him was to buy a gun and to disperse the gray mist under which he lived.

Le Braz looked up. He drew in a deep breath and turned his eyes to McGrath. "I went to the machine," he said. "I sought the aid of the circuit and the chip. I was cold, and could never stop crying. I missed her so, it was unbearable."

The creature came around the wingback and stood over McGrath. "He brought her back from the Other Side."

McGrath's eyes widened. He understood.

The room was silent, building to a crescendo. He tried to get off the low stool, but he couldn't move. The creature stared down at him with its one gorgeous blue eye and its one unseeing milky marble. "He deprived her of peace. Now she must live on, in this half-life.

"This is Josef Le Braz, and he cannot support his guilt."

The old man was crying now. McGrath thought if one more tear was shed in the world he would say to hell with it and go for the gun. "Do you understand?" the old man said softly.

"Do you take the point?" the creature said.

McGrath's hands came up, open and empty. "The mouth . . . the wind . . ."

"The function of dream sleep," the creature said, "is to permit us to live. To flense the mind of that which dismays us. Otherwise, how could we bear the sorrow? The memories are their legacy, the parts of themselves left with us when they depart. But they are not whole, they are joys crying to be reunited with the one to whom they belong. You have seen the Thanatos mouth, you have felt a loved one departing. It should have freed you."

McGrath shook his head slowly, slowly. No, it didn't free me, it enslaved me, it torments me. No, slowly, no. I cannot bear it.

"Then you do not yet take the point, do you?"

The creature touched the old man's sunken cheek with a charred twig that had been a hand. The old man tried to look up with affection, but his head would not come around. "You must let it go, all of it," Le Braz said. "There is no other answer. Let it go . . . let *them* go. Give them back the parts they need to be whole on the Other Side, and let them in the name of kindness have the peace to which they are entitled."

"Let the mouth open," the creature said. "We cannot abide here. Let the wind of the soul pass through, and take the emptiness as release." And she said, "Let me tell you what it's like on the Other Side. Perhaps it will help."

McGrath laid a hand on his side. It hurt terribly, as of legions battering for release on a locked door.

⋏

He retraced his steps. He went back through previous days as if he were sleepwalking. *I don't see it here anywhere.*

He stayed at the ranch-style house in Hidden Hills, and helped Anna Picket as best he could. She drove him back to the city, and he picked up his car from the street in front of the office building on Pico. He put the three parking tickets in the glove compartment. That was work for the living. He went back to his apartment, and he took off his clothes, and he bathed. He lay naked on the bed where it had all started, and he tried to sleep. There were dreams. Dreams of smiling faces, and dreams of children he had known. Dreams of kindness, and dreams of hands that had held him.

And sometime during the long night a breeze blew.

But he never felt it.

And when he awoke, it was cooler in the world than it had been for a very long time; and when he cried for them, he was, at last, able to say goodbye.

A man is what he does with his attention.
John Ciardi

THE WAGES OF CYNICISM
Charles Beaumont

CHARLES BEAUMONT was born Charles Leroy Nutt on January 2, 1929 in Chicago, Illinois. He kept neither the surname nor the locale, eventually settling in California in 1949 and adopting the name which he would make famous. It was during this peripatetic period (in Mobile, Alabama) where he met his wife, Helen.

As Chris Conlon's "Portrait" makes clear, Beaumont was the driving force behind the Group. In fact, he wrote, edited, or adapted the work of many of its members, including John Tomerlin (with whom he co-authored *Run From the Hunter*), Richard Matheson (many teleplays), William F. Nolan *(Omnibus of Speed, When Engines Roar)*, and Harlan Ellison (who published him); as well as employing the likes of Jerry Sohl, William Idelson and George Clayton Johnson as ghostwriters when commitments and failing health limited his output.

Beaumont's credits include *The Twilight Zone*, countless teleplays, adaptations of Edgar Allan Poe's works, as well as two novels, three anthologies, and four original collections published during his lifetime.

Death has not silenced him. The decades since have seen the release of two retrospective collections, both featuring previously unpublished material, a movie, *Brain Dead*, and a final gathering of thirteen unpublished stories, *A Touch of the Creature*.

We're pleased to include in *California Sorcery* a slight but charming tale which is not included in that collection.

W.K.S.

You say you believe in ghosts," said Jeremy Dodge, snorting. "Do you know what you're actually saying? That you believe in life after death, in the survival—ecto-plasmically speaking—of the so-called human spirit. But a dismal sort of survival, isn't it, gentlemen? Having to spend eternity clanking chains and roaming through churchyards and floating about in drafty old houses." He grinned wolfishly at his two friends. "Why not believe in witches, too, while you're at it? They make as much sense. Or leprechauns. What about it, Wilson? Seen any leprechauns lately?"

"No," said Wilson, staring down glumly into his glass.

Dodge hawked loose a subaqueous laugh and pounded his thigh. "Demons!" he roared. "Poltergeists! Genies! *Fairies!* Eh, Kagan? Fairies?"

"Don't joke," said Kagan, frowning.

"Oh, but I'm not! I'm simply pointing out the absurdity of your notion. Don't you see? Open one door and you've opened them all. Admit the existence of even one ghost and you must chuck everything we've learned in all these thousands of years. Are you prepared to do that, either of you?"

Wilson looked up from his drink. "I don't know about any of that," he said. "I only know that there is a ghost in the Spring Hill cemetery."

"Oh, really, Wilson! *How* do you know? Have you seen it?"

"No. But I have it on good authority—"

" 'Good authority!' " Dodge rolled his eyes. "In other words, you believe in the after-life because a friend of a friend of a friend had an uncle whose gardener claimed to have seen a spook."

"Not at all," said Wilson angrily. "My information comes directly from—"

"But it doesn't matter, my dear fellow. If all the deans of all the universities in the world were to tell me such a story, I should still regard it as nonsense."

Kagan took a sip of his drink. "And if you were to see it with your own two sober, cynical, scientific eyes, what then?"

"Then," said Dodge, calmly, "I should revise my thinking. However, it isn't very likely, now, is it?"

"That depends entirely upon your courage."

"I beg your pardon?"

"As it happens," said Kagan, "I am the good authority Wilson was about to cite. I have seen this ghost. Of course you will say that I was suffering from an hallucination, that I am so fearful of death that my mind manufactures reassurances of immortality."

Dodge shrugged.

"Nevertheless," said Kagan, "I do not believe that you have the strength of your lack of convictions. In the long run, I doubt that you'll do it."

"Do what?" demanded Dodge.

"Spend the night at Spring Hill cemetery, alone."

"Are you serious?"

"You believe in what you can see and feel and touch," said Kagan, reaching into his breast pocket. "Would a check for five hundred dollars be an adequately tangible demonstration of my seriousness?"

Dodge's eyes twinkled. "It's almost like robbery," he said. "However, perhaps it will teach you both a lesson. Tomorrow night would be convenient—or is this particular ghost to be seen on appointment only?"

⟁

. . . Jeremy Dodge chuckled as he made his way across the weed-choked graveyard. The moon was full and so he could see the ancient tumble of headstones clearly, but this was of no more than antiquarian interest. For an hour or so he wandered about, reading the quaint epitaphs; then at ten o'clock, he settled himself on the soft bed of a grave, leaned his head against a mossy stone and lit his briar.

It was, of course, absurd. But if he had not agreed to come, Kagan and Wilson would doubtless have counted him a member of their little group of superstitious fools, all too timid and weak to face reality. Ghosts, indeed, he thought. When will the human race grow up?

He chuckled again and was about to close his eyes when a high-pitched keening sound hurried his senses to attention. A bird. I shall be hearing various noises, he told himself, and very probably things will begin to move out there in the gloom. Birds, patterns of moonlight, animals. Perhaps even Kagan and—No; however foolish they were, they wouldn't stoop to a cheap trick. But they might. Believe anything, however improbable, before you believe the impossible.

He smoked. The silence deepened. Feeling a small shudder, Dodge cast his mind back to a number of pleasant experiences and relived them. When he glanced at his watch, it was five minutes to twelve.

Witching hour, he thought, smiling. Midnight. Damn silly business, anyway, sitting on the cold ground; I'll catch the flu.

He rose from the gravedirt, brushed at his trousers and struck another match on the headstone. The flame was reassuring. Shouldn't be, though. Of what do I need to be reassured? He pulled his collar up and sighed.

Over there, he thought, nodding in a northeasterly direction: that patch of moving light on the tree: that's what Kagan saw. And he a chemist. Shocking!

But, Lord, it was quiet. And what did you expect? Still, it wouldn't hurt to hum a bit. Dodge hummed, but the noise annoyed him, and he listened again to the utter stillness of the cemetery.

There was a shriek.

Feeling a quick jab of pain at his heart and a sinking sensation, Dodge thought, furiously, "Steady, dammit!" He made out the form of a small, scruffy dog. Ye Gods! Well, it proves one thing, he mused. There's a bit of the fool in the best of us. Being frightened of a dog!

"Shoo!"

The animal barked again and vanished.

Dodge smiled, thought of the pleasure it would be to take Kagan's check, turned, and froze.

By a mossy headstone, not twenty feet distant, was a figure. Very plainly that. A thin, white figure, with large, white, pupilless eyes.

Hallucination, thought Dodge blinking. Hallucination.

He advanced, expecting the figure to vanish. It did not vanish. It lay there, hideous, somehow—familiar?

Latent imagination plus ideal circumstance equals HALLUCINATION.

Dodge reached out. His hand passed through the figure's foot. He blinked again. He reached out again. Again his hand passed through the figure's foot.

Dodge screamed. He ran the length of the weed-choked churchyard, out onto the dark path and toward his car.

There he saw Kagan and Wilson. Unhesitatingly he vaulted over to them and cried, "It's true! There is a ghost! I've seen it!"

"I tell you," said Kagan, "I heard a cry."

"I didn't, but perhaps we ought to take a look," said Wilson.

"It's horrible!" cried Dodge. "Thin and pale and—"

"I think it's gone a bit far," said Kagan. "He'll be properly chastened by now."

"Come on," said Wilson. And together they walked through Jeremy Dodge, who suddenly remembered the face of the figure in the moonlight. If he had had hackles, they would have risen on his neck, if he had had a neck.

LONE STAR TRAVELER
William F. Nolan

WILLIAM F. NOLAN was born in Kansas City, Missouri, where he also attended the Kansas City Art Institute and honed his drawing skills at Hallmark Cards. As one who has received many letters adorned with cheerful doodles, I can attest that this isn't a skill which he has lost.

Bill came to California, to San Diego in the late 1940s, before settling in the Los Angeles area in 1953, where he left art behind for writing, going full-time in 1956. To date, he has over 1500 sales to his credit, including 65 books, 800 magazine pieces, over 140 stories, and 13 novels (the most famous of which is *Logan's Run*).

His most recent efforts include a novella published by Cemetery Dance, *The Winchester Horror,* and the "Black Mask Mystery" book series, which features Dashiell Hammett, Raymond Chandler, and Erle Stanley Gardner, solving murders in 1930s Hollywood. The latest of these (out in '98) is *Sharks Never Sleep,* and the next will be written in collaboration with his wife, Cameron.

As you'll see in "Lone Star Traveler," Bill enjoys nothing more than mixing genres: in this case, westerns, and yes, science fiction.

W.K.S.

A vast stretch of Texas prairie, 1910. Late summer, in the Big Bend country near the Rio Grande. Under the sun's diamond-sharp glare, through the distorting waves of rippling heat, there is movement on the plain. A crawling dust cloud caused by . . . *what*? A string of riders? A herd of wild horses? A stagecoach, perhaps, bound for the modest cowtown of Libertyville at the far edge of the plain?

No, none of these.

A head pokes through the dense swirl. Goggled eyes are revealed under a wide black Stetson, dust-whitened at the crown, its brim curled back to reveal a tanned, heavily-

mustached face. Leather-gloved hands grip a massive,
wood-spoked steering wheel. A long, loosely-buttoned
road duster flaps out to either side.

The moving vehicle is a 1909 Hupmobile, resolutely
driven by its new owner, Texas John Thursday. And John
is indeed resolute—grim-faced at his task of herding this
cantankerous metal beast over the washboard terrain. Gul-
lies and potholes and half-buried rocks assault the machine
in its sputtering passage.

Finally, with a gasping wheeze, its engine dies and the
car rolls to a stop. Texas John, plainspoken and tall, a
wide-shouldered man in his forties who still retains the
rugged handsomeness of his youth, sets the brake and
climbs out, swearing under his breath.

He stares at the silent machine. "Quittin' on me, are ya?
Damn stubborn varmint! I shoulda knowed better than to
take ya into town. Serves me right. Tryin' to impress folks
with my fancy new autee-mo-beel." He kicks the side of
the big, dust-yellow machine. "Damn ya to hell! Any
cross-eyed, spavin-legged mule is worth *ten* of ya!"

Then, adjusting the spark, he moves to the front of the
long hood, leans to grip the crank handle, and goes to
work. Cranking the Hupmobile in the intense heat of the
day is a hellish endeavor. Cranking . . . swearing . . .
cranking. Then, a raw gout of exhaust smoke and the
power plant explodes into life, allowing Texas John to re-
sume his seat behind the wheel.

Popping and sputtering, tires biting into the loose
prairie soil, the ponderous vehicle resumes its forward motion.

The Machine Age has arrived in western Texas.

▲

The citizens of Libertyville were not fools. Thus, they
stayed well clear of this new-fangled road monster as it

bumped down their rutted main street. Dogs whined nervously, tails between their legs. Horses reared up with nostrils flared, neighing in alarm as the big Hupmobile sputtered past them. A wagon overturned. A woman shrieked in fear. Only the young were unafraid.

A ragged pack of children ran boldly alongside the car, hooting like banshees. At the hitching rail in front of the Greater Libertyville Bank, Texas John cut the engine, set the hand brake, and climbed down, discarding his gloves, duster, and goggles.

"Never seen me nothin' like this here critter," said a brightly-freckled ten-year-old boy, staring in awe at the now-silent behemoth. "What d'ya *feed* it?"

"Cactus an' snake eggs," said Texas John, slapping a plume of dust from his Stetson. "Got real sharp teeth, it has, so you'd best stay clear. It *bites*!"

The youngster went pale, edging away from the machine. "Gee, thanks for the warnin', mister."

Chuckling, Thursday entered the building.

Rufus Finley, the bank's owner, came forward to shake John's hand. He was bald and red-cheeked, with shaggy eyebrows and an expansive gut. "Good to see you, John," he said, giving the big man a gold-toothed smile. "How's Anna doing? She any better?"

"'Fraid not," said Thursday. "Sis is still doin' poorly. Doc says it's her heart. Keeps gettin' worse. She's weak as a newborn pup."

"Sorry to hear that," said Finley, knitting his shaggy brows. He peered through the front window into the street. "See you brought your new autee-mo-beel into town. Amazing invention, the autee-mo-beel. Back East, I hear tell, these things run along streets smooth as a baby's behind."

Thursday scowled, tugging at his mustache. "Less said about the dang contraptions, the better. Next time I'll be comin' in on a horse like I shoulda done this time.

Horses make sense—an' ya don't have to crank 'em up, neither."

Finley realized it was time to change the subject. "Town election's next month, John. Lotta folks around here think you oughta throw your hat in the ring and run for sheriff."

"Yeah, an' a lotta folks are fulla hogwash," snarled Thursday. "I'm a rancher, not a fighting man."

"I wouldn't say that," argued Finley. "You're boxing champeen of the whole county."

"Well, boxin' is one thing and bein' sheriff is another. I'll stick to cattle. I come here to make my monthly deposit, not run for no office."

He removed a roll of bills from his coat and passed the money to Finley's cashier.

"I've seen you handle a six-gun," persisted Finley. "And I've seen you tame broncos that'd kill an ordinary man. We need a sheriff around here who knows how to ride and shoot."

Thursday shook his head. "Look, Rufus, I'm not gonna run fer sheriff an' that's a fact, flat and final. So quit pesterin' me about it."

"All right," sighed Finley. "Have it your way."

"I always do," grinned the rancher. And, with his deposit book duly stamped, Texas John headed for the street.

Outside, he unfolded a square of paper from his coat, checked the contents, and walked toward Robbins Mercantile: Stock Feed, Dry Goods, Fine Comestibles.

▲

Shan was saddle-sore. His buttocks ached and his leg muscles were stiff. He was not accustomed to riding a horse, but felt that he should make his initial appearance in Libertyville on the back of such an animal. To blend in with the populace. To attract less attention. He had not come here to attract attention.

Obtaining the animal had been absurdly easy. Shan simply beamed his Disc at a bowlegged cowpuncher who'd stopped at a waterhole a few miles from town to fill his canteen. The beam struck him in the back and he dropped like a stone. The horse, a deep-chested, silk-black stallion with a white mane, was really no problem. The animal didn't seem to care who was in the saddle.

Scanning the main street of Libertyville, Shan decided that the logical place to find out what he needed to know was the saloon. Cowtown bartenders could usually be counted upon as a rich source of local knowledge. Yes, the saloon would do nicely. He cantered the horse in that direction.

Dismounting gingerly in front of O'Rourke's Drinking Emporium, Shan groaned at the sudden ripple of pain that shot through both of his legs. Adding to the misery, his store-tight range boots had already raised blisters on both feet.

He hesitated at the top of the wooden porch steps and glanced back at the stallion's hanging reins. Unaccustomed to horses, he'd forgotten to tether his mount. Looking around to make sure he was alone and unobserved, he slipped the silver Disc from a leather pouch at his belt and beamed it.

Activated, the reins looped themselves securely around the hitching post.

Adjusting the angle of his new ten-gallon hat, he pushed through the batwings into O'Rourke's saloon. At this time of day the place was largely deserted. A half-dozen patrons, talking quietly among themselves, were huddled over drinks at the bar. The gaming tables were empty and a large roulette wheel in one corner stood unattended.

The saloon's most distinctive feature was hung behind

the bar: a long, cut-glass mirror which had been set into an ornate, beautifully hand-carved frame. Shan stared at his reflection in the glass: staring back at him was a clean-featured, thin-shanked man of twenty-one with a thatch of red hair under his hat and guileless blue eyes that hinted of virgin innocence.

"What'll you have, stranger?" asked the bartender, a sweating barrel-shaped fellow in a patched apron.

"Milk," said Shan softly. "With a soda cracker."

The barman grunted. "No milk. No sodee crackers. What we got is beer and bar whiskey, so what'll it be?"

"Beer," nodded Shan. As it was being drawn from the keg he said: "I'm looking for a man named John Thursday. He has a ranch near the river."

"Then you're in luck," declared the barman, trimming a spill of foam off Shan's glass. "Texas John just come inta town in that fancied-up horseless carriage of his. Likely he's over to the feed store. Where do you hail from, stranger?"

Shan sipped his beer, ignoring the question. He pushed a coin across the bar. "I'd best go find John Thursday."

A sudden thunder of hoofbeats from the street. Then an angry shout: "There's my hoss!" Two burly cowpunchers, riding double on a chestnut mare, had pulled to a dusty halt outside the saloon. Through the window, Shan recognized one of them as the bowlegged man from the waterhole. Now the fellow burst in, waving a naked Colt in his right hand. His partner, a massive character with ham-sized fists, was directly behind him.

"By Jasper, here he is!" shouted Bowlegs, pointing the gun at Shan. "Here's the lowdown, piss-ass hoss thief what stole Blackie."

Shan smiled. "I'm truly sorry I had to borrow your animal," he said, "but circumstances called for it."

Bowlegs appealed to the startled bar patrons: "Ya see, gents, this here piss-ass thief *admits* to grabbin' my black."

"Which means we hang him here an' now," declared the second puncher.

And they hustled Shan out to the street.

⋏

Inside the grocery and feed store old Pete Robbins glanced outside, then paused as he filled a barrel with oats. "Happenin' again," he muttered darkly. "Smack dab outside. Bold as brass."

Texas John turned to face the old man. Around him was a week's provision of flour, sugar, coffee, and hardtack. "Somethin' bothering ya, Pete?"

"We got us another hangin'. Right on Main Street, in fronta all the kids an' wommin folk. A disgrace, if you ask me. When are people around here gonna start actin' civilized?"

"Yer right," agreed John. "Just hold onta my order. I'll be comin' back." And he headed for a group of townfolk gathered around Libertyville's "hanging tree," a tall, black oak that towered above the livery stable.

When he arrived on the scene the two determined cowpunchers were in the act of tying a noose around Shan's neck.

"What's goin' on?" demanded Thursday.

"Any pie-eyed, half-wit kin see what's goin' on," growled the bowlegged man. "We're gonna hang a stinkin' hoss thief is what's goin' on."

"Yeah," said his surly companion. "Just you stay outa this, John Thursday. No damn concern a'yours."

"I say different," John told him. "This here kinda thing concerns us all, an' it's gotta stop." He glared at the bowlegged man. "Just how much is yer hoss worth—the one that got stole?"

Bowlegs narrowed his eyes. "Why . . . a *hundred* dollars wouldn't buy ole Blackie."

Thursday took out his wallet and extracted a sheaf of bills. "Here's *two* hundred, an' ya kin keep the hoss. This is just to let the boy go."

Bowlegs ran a slow tongue over his lower lip. "Two hundred is a sizable lotta jack."

"We got a deal?" asked the rancher.

"Yeah," said Bowlegs, stretching out a grimy hand for the money.

Thursday paid him, then removed the noose from Shan's neck.

Excitement over, the crowd broke up and drifted away, followed by the two cowpunchers, now gleefully slapping one another on the back over their newfound riches.

Texas John turned to the young man. "What's your moniker, son?"

"Shan is the name, first and last. And you must be John Thursday."

"That I am."

"I'm glad you arrived when you did. Otherwise, I would have been forced to deal with them."

John snorted. "*Deal* with 'em! Hell, boy, you're not even packin' a gun. You'da dealt with them right enough— by kickin' yer legs in the air while that rope choked the life outa ya."

"It was most kind of you to intervene," said Shan. "How may I reimburse you? I carry very little cash on my person."

"You kin work off the two hundred at my place. Pay's a dollar a day, sunup to sundown, with a bunk fer yerself, an' all the grub ya kin eat throwed in. Sound fair enough?"

"Yes, sir." Shan nodded. "That sounds fair enough."

"An' don't call me 'sir.' I'm just plain John to every-body this side'a Hell. And when I get down there, they can call me any damn thing they've a mind to."

"One fact you should be made aware of," Shan said. "I'm from the city, so I know nothing about ranching."

John squinted at him. "Well, then . . . I guess you'll just hafta *learn*."

Which was how, in the summer of 1910 in the Big Bend country of western Texas, a red-haired young man known as Shan became a working hand at John Thursday's Triple-Z Ranch.

⋏

Shan was impressed with the Triple-Z. Its acreage, blanketed with a multitude of grazing cattle, seemed to go on forever—while its rambling main house, two barns, corral area, and snug, newly painted bunkhouse exemplified the ideal of ranch life. Indeed, John Thursday had carved his own special empire from the prairie wilderness and could take justifiable pride in his accomplishment.

At the house, first thing, Shan was introduced to Texas John's sister, Anna Thursday—a pale, bedridden woman with bright, birdlike eyes and a strong voice that belied her frailty. At her request, the rancher left Shan alone with Anna so she could "get to know the boy."

Shan sat down on a chair next to the bed.

Her first comment was typically direct: "John tells me you're a horse thief."

Shan smiled. "I meant no harm. I simply needed proper transport."

"Mighty odd way to put it," she said. "How is it that you're a cowboy without a horse?"

"I'm not a cowboy, ma'am. I'm a city boy."

Her bright eyes searched his face. "What city?"

"I've lived in a great number of them. No one in particular." He shifted in the chair. "But, if you don't mind, I'd rather not talk about my past."

"All right, although you'll find I'm a very curious woman." She hesitated. "Do you like sagebrush tea?"

"I've never had any."

Thursday poked his head into the room. "Anna makes the best herb tea in Texas!"

Shan grinned.

He was off to a good start.

∧

"This is home fer the next seven months—'till ya work off yer debt," said Texas John.

They were inside the Triple-Z bunkhouse and Shan was trying out an empty bunk.

"Soft enough," he said. "And clean. I'll rest well here."

"Yeah," nodded John, "so long as ya don't mind all the heavy snorin'. I bunk twenty men in here at night, an' most of 'em snore loud as a saw through timber."

"It's doubtful they'll disturb me," said Shan. "I'm a sound sleeper."

A rough-hewn cowboy entered the bunkhouse. Hooded eyes. Bearded. In dusty range gear. And strong enough to wrestle a gorilla.

"This here's my foreman, Jake Slater," said Texas John.

"I'm Shan," said the stranger, shaking hands.

"You'll need a hoss," said Slater, with a sly wink at Thursday. "An' we got jes the proper one picked out, right John?"

"Sure do," nodded Thursday, suppressing a grin. "We call him 'Hellfire' 'counta his red coat, but he's gentle as a lamb."

"As a wee woolly lamb," agreed Slater.

"I'm not much of a rider," Shan admitted.

"Oh, you'll get along fine on Hellfire," said Texas John.

"That you will," nodded Slater. "He's *just* the hoss fer a tenderfoot."

∧

At first sight, Hellfire *did* seem docile as a lamb—head down, eyes glazed with afternoon boredom, his tail casually switching at flies. The copper-hued horse slowly raised its head to regard the foreman as he carried a saddle from the barn and slung it over the stallion's back. Hellfire obediently opened his mouth for the bit as Slater arranged the bridle, then tightened the cinches.

"Ya see," said John Thursday to Shan, "ain't he jes like we said?" He unlatched the corral gate for the young man. "Care to give him a try?"

"All right," said Shan, "but don't expect much."

"Oh," muttered Thursday under his breath, "I'm expecting a *lot*."

Hellfire waited, head down, as Shan approached. Fumbling the reins, the stranger—his foot slipping twice from the stirrup—awkwardly mounted. Throughout, the big horse remained motionless . . . but the instant Shan's full weight descended on his back, Hellfire seemed to go mad.

Throwing himself skyward, he landed with a stiff-legged jolt that snapped Shan's head back, causing his new hat to go sailing into the dirt. Now the young man hung on desperately as Hellfire twisted like a dervish and rotated in frenzied circles.

At the fence, John Thursday and Jake Slater whooped in delight, tears of laughter running down their cheeks. "Stay with him, son!" they shouted. "Ride 'em, cowboy!"

Suddenly, horse and rider vanished behind the barn. As soon as they were safely out of sight, Shan activated the silver Disc in his belt pouch.

Hellfire found himself abruptly airborne, levitated to a height ten feet above the corral floor. The stallion's eyes rolled wildly as—stationary in space—he snorted in fear. A quiver of raw terror rippled the big animal's flanks.

Shan's voice was icy calm: "*Now* will you behave?"

At the corral gate, Thursday and Slater watched as Hellfire emerged from the shadowed edge of the barn, trotting gently, with Shan sitting easy in the saddle.

"You were right," the young man said to them as he neared the gate, the reins loose in his hands. "He's exactly like you said—a wee woolly lamb."

The two older men, staring in shock, did not reply.

▲

The next day, after chores were done, Shan and Texas John stood in deep prairie grass on a flat clearing between low hills. Twelve tin cans had been lined up on a series of rocks some fifty feet away. Thursday had unholstered his heavy Colt .45 and now held it, barrel-down, by his right side.

"An' yer positive ya never fired a weapon at no kinda targets before, livin' or dead?" John asked.

"No, never," declared Shan. "In the city, I had no need of guns."

"Well, out here ya just might have a *big* need for 'em," said Thursday. "Man's gotta know how to defend hisself. This here is wild country, an' a gent without a gun is like a cat without claws."

"I'll take your word for it," Shan said.

"Ya hear a lotta talk about quick draws," said Thursday, "but it ain't how quick ya draw that counts. It's what you kin *hit* once ya clear leather."

Texas John swept the Colt up to arm's length and began firing. Six rapid shots.

Shan blinked. Half of the rocks were bare; six of the tin cans were gone.

"An' *that's* how ya do it," said Thursday, reloading the Colt. "Now try fer the other six while I go fetch us more bullets."

Thursday walked toward their horses, tethered behind a stand of tall boulders at the edge of the clearing.

With the rancher out of sight, Shan removed the Disc

from his belt and beamed it at the remaining targets while, simultaneously, he fired the Colt into the air six times.

When Thursday returned with fresh ammunition, he scanned the rocks. Bare. No tin cans. Six for six.

"Kid," he said to Shan, "you sure as hell are one *fast* learner!"

And the stranger smiled modestly.

⚓

That night Texas John took his new cowhand into town, to O'Rourke's saloon, to meet its owner, Bernadette Mariana Rebecca O'Rourke.

"He don't have no last name," Thursday told her, "or at least none he'll 'fess up to."

"Shan is name enough," she said, shaking the young man's hand with a firm grip.

"Happy to meet you, ma'am," said Shan.

"I'm no 'ma'am' around here," she told him. "Everybody in town calls me 'Becky,' and that'll do fine from you."

She was in her late thirties and dressed in a tight-waisted, red velvet dance-hall gown that displayed an ample bosom. Her smile dazzled, and her eyes were a deep lake-blue. A too-firm jawline kept her from outright beauty, but Becky O'Rourke was attractive enough to capture any man's fancy.

"How is it you don't stock milk at your bar?" Shan asked her. "I had to settle for beer."

"I take it you're not a drinking man," Becky said.

"Liquor addles the brain and destroys the body," Shan declared.

Becky laughed. "I'm mighty glad my customers don't share your view, or I'd be out of business." She clucked her tongue thoughtfully. "Tell you what . . . I just got me three cases of sarsaparilla. Parson MacDougall ordered it for the church ladies' social next week. Maybe you'd like some a' that."

"Sure would," nodded Shan.

"He likely built up a thirst breakin' Hellfire," said Texas John. "That critter near killed three of my best riders, but Shan here stuck to him like a burr on a saddle blanket."

"Well . . . I am truly impressed," said Becky. "You must be *some* bronc buster."

"No, I'm not," protested Shan. "The horse and I simply reached a mutual understanding." He hesitated. "About that sarsaparilla . . ."

"Go ask Joe, my barkeep," she told him. "Tell him I said it's on the house." She took Thursday's hand. "Me an' John here, we got some talking to do."

As Shan headed for the bar, Becky led John Thursday upstairs. Once in her sitting room, she fixed him a drink ("from my private stock"), then settled down next to him on the overstuffed rose-colored sofa.

"What's on yer mind, Becky?"

"You know damn well what's on my mind," she snapped. "Just when in tarnation are you gonna ask me to marry you?"

Texas John sighed heavily. "Ya know I rightly can't. Not with Anna the way she is. She *needs* me."

"So do I, John." Her blue eyes were moist. "We've been sparkin' for two years now. At this rate, I'll be a white-haired old lady before you get around to popping the question."

He looked pained. "I can't, darlin'. We gotta wait. Anna's likely to pass on soon, God help her, an' then it'll be different."

"There's another thing," Becky said. "You keep avoiding my questions about what your life was like before you started the Triple-Z."

"I can't get inta that," he said. "Over an' over I keep tellin' ya I can't."

"And over and over I keep on asking." Her voice was intense. "John . . . if I'm gonna be your wife, I've a *right* to know."

"In due course, Becky," said Thursday. He put down his drink and took her into his arms.

"You think you can just kiss me and that'll shut me up," she scolded.

"That's right," he said, pulling her closer. "That's what I think."

And they kissed.

⚔

Downstairs, at the bar, Shan was finishing his second bottle of sarsaparilla when a calloused, thick-fingered hand gripped his shirt collar and spun him around. He faced an unshaven giant of a cowpuncher whose mouth was twisted with scorn. His breath reeked of stale beer and whiskey.

"Well . . . if it ain't the skinny little runt of a hoss thief what I shoulda hung by now," growled the big man.

Shan regarded him placidly. "Even for this untutored region of the West, your grammar is remarkably poor. Given your atrocious vocabulary, you are particularly fortunate that your raw physical bulk allows you to eke out a crude living and maintain your basic lifestyle, however unsavory."

"Luke," said a fellow cowpuncher standing next to the giant. "I ain't for certain sure, but I'd say yer bein' insulted."

"Yeah? Waal, I don't hafta put up with no yella runt of a hoss thief smart-talkin' back ta me," snarled the giant, as he lifted Shan into the air with one hand. With the other, he jammed a long-barrel Colt against the boy's neck. "I figger he'll shut his yap quick enough once I've blowed his head off."

"Stow the iron, Luke!" Texas John was at the upper stair landing, his own Colt in hand. His eyes burned with anger. "That there boy works for me. Put a bullet in him, an' yer a dead man."

Luke dropped Shan and holstered the Colt. Looking up, he raised a balled fist, round as a cannonball. "C'mon down here, Thursday . . . you an' me, we'll settle this man-to-man."

At this, Texas John jumped over the bannister and landed on top of his challenger, igniting an all-out brawl that bloodied more than two dozen customers and saw most of the room's furniture destroyed.

Including Becky's prize mirror, which had been shattered by a tossed spittoon.

At this point, a shotgun blast rocked the saloon, freezing the combatants. Becky O'Rourke stood atop the bar, brandishing a sawed-off, her eyes points of enraged blue fire. "Get out of my place now—all of you—or by God I'll scatter your guts from here to Christmas!"

When the saloon was empty, Texas John told Shan to wait outside in the buckboard while he talked to Becky.

Flushed with anger, she stood in the middle of the room and surveyed the splintered tables and chairs, the smashed chandelier, the broken bottles. The roulette wheel lay on its side in one corner. Shards of glass crackled under her shoes.

"How *dare* you wreck my place!" she snapped, glaring at Thursday. She turned to regard the shattered mirror behind the bar and sadness filled her eyes. Her voice became muted. "That mirror was freighted in by wagon all the way from New Orleans," she said. "A genuine French antique. Priceless. And now look at it!"

John had his Stetson in his hand and twisted it as he spoke. "First, I didn't wreck yer place. The other boys done that. I jes jumped Luke Henry a'fore he kilt the youngster. I never meant for any a'this to happen, Becky."

She sighed. "No . . . I guess you just did what you had to. God knows that scurvy polecat would have shot poor Shan if you hadn't stopped him."

"Look, I got me more money than I need," said John Thursday. He thrust a roll of bills into her hand. "Lemme pay yer damages, especial fer yer mirror. When I saw ole Seth Johnson heave that brass spittoon, I knew yer mirror was a goner."

"No, John. But I appreciate the offer." She pushed his hand away. "This isn't the first time my saloon's been wrecked, and it won't be the last. Cost of doing business." She sighed again. "As for the mirror . . . it's one of a kind. Money isn't going to bring it back."

John shrugged in resignation. "As ya say, Becky. But if ya ever need cash, ya know where to find it."

He gave her a hug, kissed her cheek, and headed out the batwing doors for Shan and the waiting buckboard.

⋏

Three a.m. in the Triple-Z bunkhouse. The air quivered in a cacophony of snoring from the slack mouths of twenty sleeping punchers.

Shan sat up, slipped out of his blankets, and swiftly dressed. Quietly, he left the building. Walking quickly out to the barn, he saddled Hellfire, mounted the big stallion, and then began galloping into the darkness.

In Libertyville, at Becky O'Rourke's saloon, he tethered Hellfire and climbed the wooden porch steps, making certain the warped boards didn't creak. Main Street was totally deserted; only the questing howl of a distant prairie wolf disturbed the silence.

A new, rough-lettered sign had been nailed to the padlocked front door:

CLOSED FOR REPAIRS

YOU'LL HAVE TO GET DRUNK
SOMEWHERE ELSE

Walking quietly, Shan circled the porch, searching until he found a boarded-over side window. He pried one of the boards loose, then slipped into the building.

Inside, a yellow shaft of moonlight striped the floor, revealing the night's chaos. An abandoned battleground.

Shan moved to the bar, removed the silver Disc from his belt pouch, then beamed it at the shattered French mirror. Instantly, in a glittering, soundless movement, the broken pieces began smoothly refitting themselves, like pieces in a jigsaw puzzle. Once the original pattern had been re-formed, the pieces began seamlessly melding together. Frame and glass were now intact. Perfectly restored.

The flawless, gleaming surface reflected Shan's satisfied smile.

△

Early morning at the Triple-Z.

A sound of hoofbeats.

Becky O'Rourke rode into the yard fronting the main house, calling out: "John! John Thursday!"

The rancher appeared at the doorway, a straight razor in his hand, a white froth of lather covering his lower jaw. He looked stunned to see her.

"Becky, girl. What brings ya out here this time'a mornin'?"

"I'm meeting Hank Sutter over at the Lazy-M," she said from the saddle of her roan. "He wants to buy that acreage I own in the east county. But I had to stop off to say God bless you, John, for what you did."

"I don't understand," John stammered. "I ain't done nothin' that rates no blessin'."

"You call finding me a new mirror—from God knows where—and sneaking in last night to put it up behind my bar . . . you call that *nothing*? I think it's just about the grandest thing a man could do for the woman he loves, and I'd jump off my horse this second and give you a smacking big kiss, except for all that shaving cream under your mustache."

Thursday shook his head. "But I don't fer the life a' me know what yer—"

"I have to go," she declared. "Hank Sutter's waiting. See you later, darlin'!"

She turned the roan and galloped off, leaving Texas John Thursday standing on the porch, looking totally confused.

⋏

Several years earlier Thursday had set up a full-sized boxing ring in his central barn. Although the sport had always been dear to his heart, his workouts at the ranch were generally considered, in the beginning, as evidence of his eccentricity. No one in Libertyville had taken him seriously as a boxer until, despite his age, he'd won the title of Amateur Champion of Western Texas. After that, he was well-respected both for his fistic abilities and for his farsighted wisdom in setting up the boxing ring.

So each day, after the morning chores were done and before the big noon meal, Thursday made it a practice to spend two hours in his converted barn, working the light and heavy bags, skipping rope, and boxing with the other ranch hands. His most frequent sparring partner was a husky, long-armed cowman named Sid Benson.

Shan and Thursday had been repairing sections of north pasture fence since sunup when John called a break and in-

vited the young man to come to the barn and watch him
box Sid Benson.

When the first session had ended, John yelled down
from the ring: "Wanta put on the gloves and have a go?"

Shan shook his head. "I'm no boxer."

Texas John grinned at Benson. "He said he was no rider,
either, an' look what he done with Hellfire. An' he tole me
he couldn't shoot, then knocked off six cans outa six, neat
as ya please." He leaned down toward Shan. "C'mon, take
Sid's gloves and step inta the ring with me."

Reluctantly, the young man removed his shirt and then
climbed over the ropes. He looked frail and vulnerable
next to Thursday's trained, muscled body. Benson helped
Shan with the padded boxing gloves, lacing them tight.
The young man looked nervous and uncertain.

"I don't know about this," said Shan. "I could get hurt."

"Naw!" scoffed Texas John. "I'll be pullin' my
punches . . . jes be playin' with ya."

"All right—but only *two* rounds. Agreed?"

"Agreed," nodded Thursday. He grinned at Benson.
"Sid'll keep time for us."

Shan readied himself for the bell.

The first round proved him hopelessly outmatched.
Light-footed, gliding across the ring, Texas John fast-
jabbed the younger man—pop-pop-pop. Shan reeled back,
his gloves up in an attempt to fend off the barrage.

"C'mon kid, *hit* me!" urged Thursday. "Let's see some
action!"

At the bell, Shan stumbled to his corner and dropped
onto the wooden stool, gasping for breath. His lips were
puffed and swollen, a small cut on his lip was bleeding,
and he told Sid Benson that his right glove needed to be
taken off and retied.

"Gotta watch that left jab a'his," Benson warned as he
removed the glove. "John's killin' ya with his left."

"I thought he was going to pull his punches," groaned Shan.

Benson chuckled. "Oh, he *is*. Otherwise, you'd be out cold by now."

As Sid went to get him a fresh cup of water, Shan eased the Disc from his belt pouch, made a quick adjustment to the shimmering silver object, then slipped it into his right glove before Benson returned.

Round 2. Thursday, in total command of the ring, pressed Shan toward the ropes with a lightning flurry of body blows.

"Hit me!" the rancher taunted. "Let's see ya throw a real punch."

Shan ducked away from another left jab, saw his opening, and delivered a long, looping right uppercut that landed square on the point of Thursday's chin.

The champ was knocked across the length of the ring, through the ropes, and slammed to the barn floor.

Dazed, John sat up, rubbing his chin. "Now *that*," he said, "is what I call a real punch."

And he stared at Shan in genuine awe.

⋏

Later that afternoon Shan took the buckboard into Libertyville to purchase several gallons of maple syrup at the mercantile. "Punchers go through maple syrup faster'n I can buy it," Texas John had complained. "Bring back whatever Pete has."

When Shan entered the store, Pete Robbins was in the back room checking out a new shipment of dry goods, his daughter was filling in behind the counter.

Molly Robbins, an engaging, slim-bodied young woman with merry brown eyes and an inviting smile, walked over to help the new customer.

"I'm Shan," he said. "From the Triple-Z."

"I'm Molly Robbins," she declared, forthrightly giving him her hand. "You're new at the Z."

"That's right," nodded Shan. "John Thursday took me on after he saved me from a hanging."

"He's a good man," she told him. Discreetly, she didn't ask about the hanging; everyone in town knew what had happened. Instead, she asked him what he needed by way of supplies.

"Maple syrup," he said. "John forgot it on his last trip into town. How much do you have in stock?"

"I think we have three gallons left," she said.

"Then I'll take all three." As he was paying her, Shan noticed that she couldn't seem to take her eyes off him. "I notice that you're obviously attracted to me," he told her, "and while I find you to be a very pretty young lady, I am obligated to tell you that there is no possibility of a romance between us."

Molly Robbins stared at him in shock. "What makes you think that I'd ever—" Flustered, she couldn't finish the sentence. "You must be insane to say such a thing to me!"

"I'm sorry if I have offended you," declared Shan. "I am simply trying to be honest."

"*Honest*!" She trembled with anger. "You're outrageous!"

Another young man—dark-haired, with sharp eyes and a wolfish cast to his features—had entered the store during their exchange. Shan noted that the newcomer wore his holstered Colt slung low along his leg in the manner of a veteran shootist.

His suspicion was verified when the youth paused at a rack of weapons, unpegged a new, pearl-handled six-gun, and spun it rapidly in his hand, testing its weight and balance.

"How much for this?" he asked Molly, who had turned her back on Shan. He flashed her a wide smile as he looked her over. "Well, now. This must be my lucky day. Ain't you somethin'."

She smiled back and named a price for the Colt. The newcomer was paying her for the weapon as Shan, carrying the gallon tins of maple syrup, left the store.

Perhaps he *had* been too direct with Molly Robbins, he reflected as he put the syrup into the buckboard. He did, in fact, find her very appealing, but a relationship with her was impossible. Scientifically impossible.

Or so he kept telling himself.

▲

Late afternoon in the south pasture, with a depleted sun riding the tip of the hills, Shan and Texas John had been rounding up strays and now the rancher suggested a break.

Even this late in the day the summer heat was still intense, and they stretched out in the shade of a large boulder. John's back was against the rock as he fired up his pipe.

I been meanin' ta have us a talk," he said.

"About what?" asked Shan. He was sitting cross-legged, whittling at a stick.

"'Bout some stuff I jes don't savvy," said Texas John. "Becky's mirror fer instance. She thinks I went an' got her a new one, an' that's tommyrot. But *somebody* sure did."

The young man shrugged. "No way to figure who," he said.

Thursday looked steadily at him. "I got me a notion you had somethin' to do with it."

Shan said nothing as he continued to whittle.

"Then there's Hellfire—the way he was raisin' high hell one second, an' meek as ya please the next."

"We get along," said Shan.

"An' the way you plastered them tin cans first time

out . . . an' that punch ya hit me with in the barn. John L. Sullivan hisself woulda been proud'a that one."

"I got lucky both times," said Shan. "You're the boxer, not me. And you can shoot better than I could ever hope to do. I was just lucky."

"Uh-huh," nodded John, as he puffed out a thin blue cloud of pipe smoke. "Maybe you'd like to say jes exactly where it is ya hail from."

"It's a place you wouldn't know about," declared Shan. "You'll have to take my word on that." He put the stick aside. "What about you, John? You've never mentioned the death of your wife."

Thursday leaned forward and drew his brows together. "How d'ya know about Elly?"

"There's talk. I just know."

"She died givin' birth to our first child," said Texas John in a quiet voice. "I was right there in the room when . . . when I lost 'em both, her an' the baby." He hesitated, his tone soft, regretful; pain alive in his eyes. "Never had me no sons nor daughters. Guess now I never will."

"There's Becky," said Shan. "She loves you. She could bear children."

"I know . . . an' Becky's a fine woman." He sighed. "But with Anna so sick an' all . . ."

Thursday stood up, knocking the ashes from his pipe against the side of the rock. "Sun's almost down. Let's get back ta work."

And their talk ended.

▲

The pearl-handled Colt flashed against the sun, spinning in a bright arc into the waiting hand of its new owner.

"So that's the fancy piece ya bought in town?" asked Buck Haines. He was as massive as an oak, with untrimmed hair flowing under his black hat and a thick tangle of gray-ing beard. His nose had been broken in two places, and three of his front teeth were missing. His dark eyes were cold and humorless, sunk into a face that seemed skinned in saddle leather.

His son, Bobby Haines, ran a slow finger along the glossy pearl handle of the new Colt. "Bought it in Liberty-ville from a right pretty little store gal. Her name's Molly, an' she's a sweet flower, jes ripe for the pickin'."

"See that ya stay outa her rose garden," warned his father. "Small town like that . . . we don't wanta create us no attention." He scowled at his son. "Didn't tell her yer name did'ja?"

"Naw," said young Haines. "I ain't no fool."

"Gun like that . . . people remember it, an' they remember the man that packs it. When we hit the stage, you keep that pearl job outa sight."

"Sure, Pop. You can count on it."

Buck turned to the others in his gang: five desperate looking characters whose hard faces and low-slung Colts revealed their trade. They sat around the ashes of the previous night's campfire which had been built in a clearing, within the shelter of scattered boulders.

"You boys ready?" Buck asked.

They nodded. Colts had been loaded and rifles primed. The horses had been fed, watered, and were ready to gallop.

"An' jes ya remember, Bobby," Buck said to his son, "we're goin' after the strongbox—not to have us no shootin' party. Don't wanna kill nobody. Stage robbery's a small thing, but murder stirs up the hornets."

"Sure, Pop."

"Jes keep that ta mind," said Buck Haines.

And they prepared to ride.

▲

The drapes were now kept drawn in Anna Thursday's bedroom because her eyes could no longer tolerate sunlight. Thus, even in midday the room was dim.

In this gloom, Texas John stood next to her bed and held his sister's withered hand in his own. ". . . an' the doc says he can't do anythin' more, Sis. It don't look good."

Anna smiled weakly, her face like brittle parchment. "I know it's my time, John, and I'm ready to move on. I'm not afraid to die. I'm only afraid of what you'll do after I'm gone."

"There's no changin' my mind on that," he said. "I'm gonna give it all back and git that load off my shoulders."

"But what if they—"

"Hush!" he commanded. "I won't have you frettin' about me. I'm gonna be fine."

"But what about the Triple-Z?"

"I'll give up the ranch, too, if that's how the hand plays out."

"But all your work . . . your dreams . . ."

"Don't matter. There's a time ta clear the books an' start clean. When ya—" He hesitated, softening his tone. "When ya move on, I square my accounts. I can't keep pretendin' that the past never happened."

"You're a good man, John. After all these years there's no reason for you to suffer for what's long done and over."

"Nothin's over 'till I give it back," he said. "We both know that."

She sighed and settled deeper into the pillows. "I'm so tired now," she said, her words labored and weak. "I need to sleep, John." Her eyes fluttered closed.

When she was breathing evenly John Thursday stepped quietly from the dimness of the room. It would not be long now.

Not long at all.

▲

For the Haines gang, robbing the stage to Libertyville was child's play. They were well-practiced in the art of stage robbery and expected no trouble with this one.

"Here she comes," said Bobby, pulling a checkered bandana across his face. The other men did the same.

"Now!" shouted Buck—and the seven outlaws galloped out from a narrow cut in the canyon wall to confront the rattling coach as it rounded the long curve known as Devil's Twist.

The shotgun guard threw down his weapon and thrust both arms high as Jed Perkins, the stage driver, tossed away his Colt and also raised his gloved hands.

"Don't shoot, boys," said Perkins, nervously shifting his wad of tobacco from one cheek to the other. "We don't aim ta give ya no bother."

"That's what we like to hear," said Buck Haines. "Toss us down that strongbox."

Perkins did this.

Bobby blew off the lock with a single shot. "Well, lookee here!" he said as he held up a thick sheaf of green-backs.

Scooping up the money, Buck Haines swung his horse around. "Let's move out," he said to the others. "We got what we come fer."

"Wait up," said Bobby. "I wanna see what all's inside."

He stepped to the dust-filmed coach and pulled the door wide. He peered in at a young couple cowering back against the leather seat. The woman wore a linen travel duster and bonnet, while the man sported a derby hat, the glint of a gold watch chain peeping from under his vest.

"Git down from there," Bobby ordered. "Both a'ya!"

Hesitantly, the couple climbed from the coach and stood together in front of the open door. They looked thoroughly frightened.

"You two married?" asked Bobby.

"Yes," said the man. "And my wife is about to have our

child. We need to reach the doctor in Libertyville. Every minute counts."

The girl held both hands to the swell of her stomach. Her condition was obvious.

"C'mon, Bobby! We gotta ride!" shouted one of the outlaws, a horse-faced man called Ringo.

Buck Haines turned and viciously slashed him across the face with his leather riding quirt. "Didn't I tell ya never to use none'a our names!" he snarled. "Damn ya, next time ya ferget, I'll plant a slug in yer gut!"

"Sorry," muttered Ringo, as blood seeped from his cut cheek.

Buck gestured toward the coach. "If my boy wants to talk to these here folks, then we kin wait. Let him be."

Bobby was standing close to the pregnant woman. "Gonna have you a squallin' little snot-nosed brat, huh?"

"Please," begged the derby-hatted young husband. "You've got the money. Let the stage go on. My wife *must* have a doctor!"

Bobby Haines chuckled and kept his weapon leveled. "Let's have this first." He grabbed the gold chain and jerked the watch free.

"*Now* will you let us go?" asked the sweating man.

"Jes' shut yer yap," snapped the outlaw as he moved back to the girl. She was wearing a gold and amethyst necklace.

"That too," he said. "Gimme."

She put a protective hand to her neck. Haines slapped her hard, then grabbed the necklace and pulled it free. Staggering from the blow, she fell to the ground.

"You bastard!" shouted her husband. "I'll—"

He lunged forward. Haines raked the barrel of the heavy pistol across the young husband's skull, knocking him senseless.

"Enough!" his father ordered. "Git mounted an' let's ride."

Bobby stuffed the necklace and watch into his shirt pocket, then vaulted into the saddle of his pinto as the others spurred their horses into a quick gallop.

Soon they were gone, leaving a cloud of rapidly thinning dust to mark their passage.

⋏

From the high ridge overlooking Devil's Twist, Shan saw the coach below, motionless, the team horses fretting and stomping their hoofs in the day's heat. Three men were huddled over a woman lying in the roadway.

He'd been riding fenceline for John Thursday and had decided to allow Hellfire to have a free run; the horse had taken them to the high lip of Devil's Canyon. Now Shan jockeyed the big red stallion down a steeply-angled rock flume to the valley floor.

When he reached the stagecoach, Shan hailed the three men. They looked drawn and on the edge of desperation.

"This here lady's about ready to bust loose with a kid any second," Jed Perkins told him. "You ain't a doc by any chance, are ya?"

"No," said Shan, "but maybe I can help."

He quickly dismounted and knelt beside the young woman. She was clutching her distended stomach; her face muscles were stretched in pain. Closely-spaced spasms racked her body, causing animal sounds to come from her throat.

"This is my wife, Mae, and I'm Bill Thomas," said a young man about Shan's age. A bloodstained bandana was tied around his head. "We were robbed, and one of the thieves struck Mae. She fell and that put her into labor. None of us knows anything about delivering a baby."

"That's the God's truth!" muttered the shotgun guard. "What we need is a doc, only there ain't time to fetch one."

Shan waved them back and instructed Mae Thomas to

breathe "deep and slow," telling her that she and her baby were going to be fine. He removed the Disc from his belt pouch and made an adjustment. The silver began to glow a shimmering blue.

"What are you doing?" she gasped.

"Trust me," said Shan. He rearranged her skirt and then removed her petticoats, leaving her legs free. He began moving the Disc over her midsection in a slow, circular pattern while his other hand stroked her head in a soothing rhythm that visibly relaxed her.

Mae groaned softly. A final spasm—and an infant's pink head emerged from between her legs. Shan lifted the newborn male free of her body as easily as a cake is lifted from the oven. Shan asked the guard for his bolo tie, which he used to tie off the umbilical cord before severing this last physical connection between mother and child. The baby was now free, a separate human being.

"Lord a'mighty, she done it!" marveled Jed Perkins. "She done give birth!"

Shan checked the infant's mouth for obstructions, then gently slapped the child's buttocks until it began to cry. He carefully wrapped Mae's son in a discarded petticoat, then placed the child in her arms. Overcome with joy, she began crying.

"You have a healthy son, Mr. Thomas," he said to the stunned father. "And your wife will be fine."

The baby continued wailing as the adults around him smiled in relief.

⋏

At the Triple-Z, on the long wooden veranda, Texas John paced back and forth, scowling. He stopped to face Shan.

"An' yer dead sure the driver said the name was 'Bobby'?"

"That's what he told me," said Shan. "And the gang's

leader also called him 'son.' The driver was clear on what he heard."

"It's them, by hell!" exclaimed Thursday. "The Haines bunch. I never figgered they'd range this far south."

"You know them?" asked Shan.

Thursday's face tightened. "I know Buck Haines—an' he's as mean as a stepped-on rattler."

Shan stared at him. "Then you and Haines—"

"We tangled once," nodded Texas John. "Long time ago. It don't matter now. The thing is, he's back. An' there's no tellin' what he's upta."

"You're worried."

"Wouldn't anybody be, with the Haines gang in these parts? I jes hope they keep movin' is all."

Thursday's eyes were troubled, clouded with dark thoughts.

⋏

That night, at the square dance in town, Shan was startled to see Molly Robbins approaching him from across the plank floor. He was sitting on the sidelines with Texas John and Rebecca, watching the action as Molly came up to them.

"Howdy," said John. "Ya here with yer Pa?"

"No, Daddy's back at the store," she said. "I came with Tug Hollister, but he ran off to spark some widow lady visiting from Sweetwater." As she answered Thursday, her eyes remained on Shan.

"You're sure lookin' mighty nice tonight with your hair up like that," said Becky. "That a new party dress?"

Molly ran her fingers along the seam of her nipped-in bodice. "Yes. Came in from St. Louis last week on the stage. Ordered special."

"Well, you're pretty as a picture in it," nodded Becky. Then, to Shan: "Isn't she?"

"Yes, she is. I mean, you are." He met Molly's direct gaze.

"Ask her to dance," John urged. "You'd like to, wouldn't you, girl?"

"Yes, I would."

"I've never square-danced," said Shan.

"C'mon," said Molly, taking his hand. "I'll teach you."

On the floor, Shan discovered that square-dancing was most enjoyable. A quaint Western folkway that had much to recommend it. As they whirled through the steps, following the lively fiddle music and the directions of the caller, Molly told him she had forgiven him his "rudeness" at the store. Would he like to go riding with her tomorrow?

"It's my day off at the ranch. I'd be honored to ride with you, but please keep in mind what I said at the store. I know you don't understand right now, but please believe that I'm trying to avoid your being hurt later."

"I've decided to trust your good intentions. You're not like the other boys I know," she told him. "The way you talk is so . . . so different." She smiled. "And I never met anyone who couldn't square-dance."

"I'm from the city, remember?"

"Don't they dance in the city?"

"Not like this . . . not in the city I'm from."

Later, at the punch bowl, as Shan filled Molly's glass, she nodded toward Texas John and Becky who were sitting across the room. Their heads were close together and they were smiling into one another's eyes.

"They make a beautiful couple," Molly said.

"They do," said Shan. "And they're going to have five beautiful children together."

Molly blinked at him. "You say the strangest things!"

"It's a strange world," he said. "I suppose you could call me a fish out of water."

She didn't even *try* to understand what he meant by that.

᛭

Molly had packed a full picnic basket for their ride and it was now strapped to the saddle of her beloved "Whiskers," a spotted gelding she'd raised from a colt. Beside her, Shan was mounted on Hellfire.

When they reached a cluster of cottonwoods on the banks of a sunlit stream Molly suggested that they stop. "This is a lovely spot," she said. "Let's have our picnic here."

Shan readily agreed. "I've been thinking about your picnic lunch since we passed the road to Pecos," he confessed. "I'm ready to eat."

"You *do* have picnics where you come from?" she asked him as she spread a blanket over the grass.

"We have a large park," he said. "People go there to conduct what I suppose would correspond to a picnic."

She unpacked the wicker basket, which was filled with fried chicken, potato salad, fresh-baked bread, and chocolate cake. As each new dish was brought forth, Shan's eyes gleamed. "Everything looks so good," he said.

"What was your life like before you came to Libertyville?" she asked.

"Quite ordinary," he replied. "There's nothing very unusual about me."

"On the contrary," she said. "*Everything* about you is unusual. I don't think you're being quite honest with me."

Shan smiled. "I thought that was what got me into trouble with you in the first place—my honesty."

"I didn't mean it that way. I mean honest about who you really are."

"I'm Shan," he said. "And I work for John Thursday at the Triple-Z. There's little more."

Molly stared at him for a long moment. "I think there's a *lot* more."

"Maybe," he said. "But what there is, I can't tell you.

Instead, I want to hear about *you*. For instance, where did you grow up? Here? In Libertyville?"

"No. In Philadelphia. My father sent me to boarding school there. He was a drummer before he came West to open the store, so he couldn't take care of me."

"You mean he was a musician?"

She laughed. "No, although that's a funny thought. A drummer is a salesman. That's what he did, and he had to travel most of the year when he was doing it."

"And your mother?"

"She died before I was old enough to remember her," Molly replied.

"How did you like boarding school?"

"I *hated* it! I wanted to be with Daddy, but he said it was no life for a child." She sighed. "The only subject I really liked was French. Someday I hope to travel to Montreal so I can study the language. Eventually, I'd like to teach it."

"A worthy ambition," said Shan.

"My father wouldn't agree with you. He expects me to marry some cowpuncher here in Libertyville, raise a flock of kids, and then—with my husband—take over his store after he retires. But that's not the kind of life I want."

"Then keep your goal in mind," Shan told her. "Live your own life, not your father's. That's the wisest thing you can do, for everyone's sake."

The sky suddenly darkened and a gusting wind began to shake the trees.

Molly stood up, pointing. "Out on the plain," she said. "A *twister*! Really big one. And it's headed straight for town."

On the distant edge of the flat plain a long, quivering black ribbon had unfurled from sky to earth.

"You stay here," said Shan. "We're only two miles from Libertyville. I'll ride in and warn them."

"Can you make it in time?"

"Hellfire is fast," declared the young man. "I can make it."

"Then hurry!" she urged him. "I can't ride that fast. I'll wait here."

Shan was already mounted on the red stallion. Bending low over Hellfire's neck he urged the horse into a furious gallop in the direction of Libertyville.

Once he had cleared the woods and was beyond Molly's sight, however, Shan abruptly changed course, riding Hellfire straight into the tornado's path.

When he was close enough to feel the storm's savage force surging around him he raised the silver Disc and beamed it full at the howling funnel of primal energy.

The twister seemed to hesitate, as if considering its next move. Then—success!—it began to whirl away in a reverse direction toward the empty plains.

Shan returned the Disc to his belt, swung Hellfire around, and then headed back for the cottonwood grove by the stream.

Two grizzled hunters who had witnessed this amazing event from the porch of their cabin were awestruck.

"That there twister . . . it jes up an' turned tail like a whupped bobcat!" declared one.

"End'a the world's at hand fer sure, jes like the Good Book says," moaned the other. "We was saved by the grace a'God this time, but mebbe next time the Good Lord will see it different. We best do some prayin' now, Jeb."

The tornado continued on its new route. Now it was only a dim streak of black, fading to gray along the far horizon.

⋏

In Anna Thursday's bedroom the doctor murmured soothing words to his patient, repacked his medical bag, and met John Thursday in the outer hallway.

"Is she any better?" asked the rancher.

The doctor's face was grave as he shook his head. "You're going to lose her, John."

"How much longer?"

"Her heart is getting weaker. It'll give out, probably before next week."

"Is she in pain?"

"No, not now. Perhaps . . . in a couple of days."

"Thanks, Doc. I know ya done what ya could."

"I have indeed. Anna's a good woman. I just wish I could've saved her."

They shook hands and the doctor left the house.

Thursday entered Anna's room, saw that she was still awake, and sat down on the chair beside the bed.

In a quiet voice she asked him: "Have you changed your mind?"

"About what?"

"Don't play with me, John," she said, frowning at him. "About what you said you would do after I'm gone."

"I have to tell the truth," he said.

The finality of his statement silenced her. Anna knew that further argument would be futile. But there was one last thing she could do.

She asked her brother to bring the writing board to the bed, along with her stationery, pen, and ink.

"Who you goin' to write to?" he asked, not caring if he was trespassing on her personal business.

"Never you mind. Let me do what I have to do, John. It's going to be my last request."

Abashed and somewhat ashamed, he brought her the stationery and writing board, then left the room without another word.

Anna dipped a long pen into the ink pot and began to write . . .

Dear Aunt Hattie,

The Good Lord is about to call me home, but before I depart this Earth I must beg you to help my

dear brother—your only nephew, John. He is on the
verge of a very rash act which will surely result in
terrible consequences . . .

Breathing with difficulty, she continued on with the last
letter she would ever write.

▲

Afternoon along the sunswept expanse of the Rio Grande.

Shan and Texas John were watering their horses after
the day's roundup. Shan was kneeling at the bank, filling
his canteen when John nudged his shoulder, pointing.

A flimsy wooden raft, bearing three young children,
emerged from a bend of the river.

"Them's the Albernathy kids," exclaimed Thursday.
"Little Timmy an' his two sisters. They oughta be in
school!"

Shan grinned. "Didn't you ever play hookey?"

"Well, now that ya mention it . . ."

Timmy was handling the crude wooden oar, homemade
like the raft. He paddled while his two giggling sisters
urged him to go faster.

"They seem to be having a fine time," said Shan. He
took an apple from his pocket and held it out to Hellfire.
The horse snorted, snatched the apple from his master's
hand, and began chomping contentedly.

"Good boy," said Shan, rubbing the big stallion's satiny
muzzle.

"They'll be into white water a'fore they know it," said
John. "This here is a dangerous part of the river."

"How dangerous?"

"Waterfall's ahead. With sharp rocks. Big drop over
them falls. The raft'll break up fer sure."

The children were now out of sight around the next
bend.

"We'd better do something," said Shan, mounting Hellfire. "Get them off the river before they reach the falls."

"I'll toss 'em a rope an' we can pull 'em ashore," said Thursday, who had also mounted.

"Then let's go!"

By the time they caught up with the raft it was into a section of white-water rapids. A glancing blow against a boulder in mid-river knocked the oar from Timmy's hand. The three children were suddenly helpless in the surging grip of the river, with the raft twisting and spinning in the foaming current.

"They'll never be able ta grab no rope now," declared Thursday. "Takes all they got jes ta hang on."

"The falls," said Shan tensely. "How far?"

"Jus 'round the bend," said the rancher. "They'll be smashed to bits. I'm goin' in after 'em."

Texas John was stripping off his shirt when Shan stopped him. "Stay here! You can't fight that current. I'll handle this."

"Handle it *how*?"

"Watch me," he told the older man. Shan slipped the Disc from his belt pouch and made a quick adjustment. He swung around, facing the river.

Too late. The raft had vanished around the final bend which led to the falls.

With Thursday following, Shan rushed along the bank—to a high point of ground just above the raging waters. Below, the raft had almost reached the lip of the falls, poised for the long drop onto the rocks. All three of the children were screaming when Shan beamed the Disc.

The raft quivered, then lifted itself clear of the water, rising like a magic carpet with the children huddled in its center.

As Shan directed the Disc's beam the raft slowly descended, landing gently on the ground directly in front of Shan and a totally astonished John Thursday.

⋏

Back at the ranch Texas John took Shan into his private study, firmly closed the door, and told the young man to make himself comfortable because they had some serious talking to do.

Thursday sat down behind his desk while Shan took the chair facing it.

"All right, boy," said John, "jes how did ya pull off that stunt at the river? Are ya some kind'a miracle man?"

"No more than you are, John—but I have this."

And he placed the silver Disc on the desktop.

Thursday picked it up and turned it over in his hand.

"Got kinda like little buttons on the side," he said.

"Don't touch any of those," warned Shan. He reached out: "I'll take it back if you please."

The rancher handed over the Disc. "I saw ya use this thing at the river. Is this what moved the raft?"

"Yes," said Shan. "It allows me to suspend or reverse gravity, so I can control objects in space. Also, it can fire a laser beam that has immense power because it's so concentrated."

"Lay-sir?" John lowered his brows. "What in tarnation is a lay-sir?"

"I don't think you would be able to understand my explanation," Shan said.

"Try me, son."

"This device contains a crystal in which atoms, when stimulated by focused light waves, amplify and concentrate those waves, emitting them in a narrow, extremely intense power beam."

"Yer right," nodded John. "I don't understand a damn word."

"I used the Disc to restore Becky's mirror, tame Hellfire, knock off those tin cans, and deliver that punch in the barn when we were boxing. And then, of course, I used it to save the children."

"This . . . this silver doohickey . . . it done all that?"

"Yes," replied Shan. "And there's more."

"More?"

"I can focus body energy through my hands. We all have the power of touch, it's just a matter of knowing how to release it. Most people use only ten percent of their brain. Where I come from, we use over fifty percent."

"Hell, boy, where *do* you come from?"

"I can't reveal my place of origin at the moment—but I *can* tell you that I came here with a mission to perform."

"What kinda mission?"

"You'll find out at the proper time. And then I'll be able to tell you everything. For now, you'll simply have to trust me and know that I came here to help you."

"An' ya won't say what ya come here *fer*?"

"Not now. Not today. But soon."

"Well . . ." Thursday sighed, flattening his hands on the desk. "I been keepin' some secrets a'my own, so I kin see how a gent can't 'fess up ta everthin'. An' ya *did* save them Albernathy kids an' that's a fact. They woulda been dead by now, 'cept fer you. So I guess I'll jes hafta wait out the full truth."

"Thanks, John. I appreciate your trust."

The rancher chuckled. "Them Albernathys . . . they ain't gonna believe how ya saved their young'uns. They'll figger the kids made up the whole wild yarn. Can't blame 'em none. I know I'd never have believed it unless I seen it."

"There's one other thing," said Shan. "What you witnessed today . . . everything we talked about . . . you tell no one. Not Anna . . . not Becky . . . *no* one. Understood?"

"Understood," nodded John. "But I feel like I'm livin' some kinda dream an' I can't wake up."

Shan smiled. "No dream, John. It's all as real as the sun in the sky."

⚔

At the town post office in Hannibal, Missouri, all incoming letters and packages were sorted in a small room just behind the front service counter.

Postal clerk Arly Willows, a balding scarecrow of a fellow whose watery eyes blinked constantly behind bottle-thick glasses, emptied a canvas sack onto a wooden table and began sorting the day's mail.

A particular letter caught his attention. He plucked it from the stack, squinting to make out the wavery hand-scrawled words on the envelope:

Miss Hattie Grover
3337 Forest Avenue
Hannibal, Missouri

"I'll be damned!" muttered Arly. Looking over his shoulder to make certain he was unobserved, he stuffed the letter into his vest. Then he walked to the front of the office.

Portly Earl Gates, Hannibal's postmaster, had just finished waiting on a customer. He turned to his thin-faced employee.

"You look a bit odd, Arly," he said. "Something wrong?"

Willows took off his glasses and scrubbed at his eyes. "I think I've got the gripe coming on," he said. "Feeling kind of dizzy. I need to get home to bed."

"Well then, you trot right on," said Gates. "Got sick time coming as it is. I'll handle things here."

"Thank you, Mr. Gates. I'll do that," said Willows. "I'll just head on home."

But Arly Willows didn't head for his home. Instead, he walked briskly to the rail depot and boarded the next west-bound train.

The letter to Miss Hattie Grover was still in his vest.

▲

Becky O'Rourke ran a slow hand along the frame of her restored bar mirror and smiled fondly at Texas John.

"I'm *so* grateful to you for this," she said. "It's almost as nice as a marriage proposal."

"C'mon over here," he said, nodding toward a table at the rear of the saloon. It was early afternoon and the room was deserted. Even the barkeep dozed on his stool in the languorous heat of the day. A fly circled lazily in the air near the batwing doors.

Becky and John sat down at the table. He looked solemn and depressed.

"After Anna's gone," he said, "a lotta things are gonna change in my life."

"How do you mean, John?"

"All of yer questions about me are gonna be answered," he declared darkly. "But ya won't like what ya find out."

She reached over to take his hand. "Nothing I find out could affect the way I feel about you. I *love* you, John."

He bowed his head. "An' I love ya too, Becky—but sometimes love ain't enough."

"It's all we need," she said, pressing his hand. "You'll see."

He said nothing. The pain of what lay ahead caused him to close his eyes. There was a storm gathering in his life and it would likely destroy him.

And everything they had together.

▲

"I *knew* it'd come," smiled Buck Haines, holding the letter in his hand. "I figgered she *had* to contact ole Hattie sometime, an' you were right there, waitin' for it. Good work, Arl."

"Thanks, Buck." Willows was transformed; he had discarded his thick glasses and store-bought suit. Now he wore range gear, and a Colt was strapped to his thigh. "I aim ta put on some weight. Workin' as a skinny-ass postal clerk ain't my idea of the good life."

Buck gave him a gap-toothed smile. "Well, you're back with us now, me an' the boys, an' we're soon due fer a *real* good life, with enough money to buy all the women and whiskey in Texas."

He turned to the others, who were sprawled about the camp. "Arl here is what ya might call 'Fate's Messenger.' He brung this letter all the way from Missoura, an' by God, it tells me jes where to find Jack Oliver, damn his black soul!"

"What ya got agin' this Oliver fella?" asked Ringo.

Buck Haines drew his lips back in a bitter snarl. "We got us an ole score to settle, me an' Jack," he said. "He took somethin' away from me that I'm gonna git back. This letter tells me all I need to know, includin' what name he's been usin' all this time."

"Which is?" asked Cheyenne, a ferret-eyed half-breed with a knife scar running the length of his left cheek.

"Thursday," said the outlaw. "Texas John Thursday. An' as the Good Lord would have it, he's not more'n ten mile from this here camp. Got a spread outside Libertyville."

"Are we headin' there?" asked Little Charlie, a slope-jawed gunman with a patch over one eye.

"Not quite yet," said Haines. He nodded to his son. "Bobby, I got a job for ya."

Young Haines raised his head . . . waiting for orders.

▲

Shan was with Molly Robbins at the mercantile, helping her move some heavy grain sacks, when Bobby Haines dismounted outside and staggered through the door.

He banged a fist against the counter. "Service!" he shouted. "Where's that cute 'lil gal that sold me a shootin' iron?"

"I'm here," said Molly, wiping her hands on her apron as she approached the cash register. "How may I be of service?"

Haines leered at her, swaying back against the counter. He seemed to be very drunk. "Ya kin gimme a kiss ta start with!" And he reached for her.

The girl twisted away as Shan stepped between them. "Leave her alone."

"Stay outa this," warned Haines, drawing his Colt, "or I'll blow ya to hell!"

"Put up the gun," commanded a voice from the doorway.

Thursday was there, his rifle leveled at Bobby Haines.

Clumsily, Haines holstered the Colt, his face twisted with rage. "You talk big, mister—with a rifle in yer hands! Maybe you'd like to settle things another way."

"How?" asked Texas John.

"With *these!*" Haines raised his two fists.

"My pleasure," said Thursday. He put the rifle aside, walked up to Haines, and knocked him senseless with a single blow.

"Help me get this piece'a rotten dogmeat outa here," he said to Shan, who was grinning ear-to-ear.

"You sure settled things," the young man said as he helped John pick up the outlaw. Together, they dragged him to the door and tossed him into the street. Haines landed facedown in the wagon-rutted dirt. Coughing, with blood running from his nose, he sat up groggily.

"Here!" Molly threw his hat after him. "Don't forget this," she said. "Wouldn't want you to get sunstroke."

Haines stood up, glaring. A small crowd had gathered at the front of the store, staying well clear of the enraged gun-man.

"You, old man!" Haines pointed at John Thursday. "I'll be back, come sunup, but I won't be alone. I'll be with my Pa, Buck Haines, an' the rest of the boys. We're gonna burn this stinkin' town to the ground an' you along with it. That is, if ya got enough guts to face us!"

"So you're young Haines," said Thursday. "I shoulda guessed, what with ya bein' a bully an' a cheap braggart jes like yer Pa. You go tell him ta come on in. We'll deal with him an' his mangy crew the same way we dealt with you!"

"Oh, I'll tell him," said Haines as he mounted his horse. "Ya kin damn well be sure'a that."

And he rode off at a fast gallop.

Silently, the crowd watched him go.

▲

"You stay here, Molly," said Texas John. "Me an Shan hafta see the sheriff."

The office of Harrison Dobbs, sheriff of Libertyville, was six doors up from the mercantile store. When Shan and Thursday walked in they found the lawman hurriedly cleaning out his desk.

Dobbs was a small, stoop-shouldered man who affected a thick mustache which was carefully curled at each end. He attempted to compensate for his lack of height by wearing high-heeled boots. Now he was stuffing personal items into a green carpetbag.

"What's goin' on, Harry?" asked John Thursday.

"*Hell* is what's goin' on," he replied without looking up. "Come sunup, when the Haines gang gets here, this town is finished."

The rancher stared at him. "Ya mean ya ain't gonna be here ta face 'em?"

"Dang right I ain't," declared the little man. "An' any-body who does is gonna be fit for buryin'. Ya heard what young Haines said . . . they're gonna burn down the place."

"Not if we stand up to them," said Thursday.

Dobbs finished cleaning out his desk and closed the bag. "Lotta folks around here seem to think you oughta be sheriff—so *you* stand up to 'em. Me, I'm no fool. I'm ridin' out fer good."

And he left the office, moving quickly to his tethered mustang. Dobbs tied the carpetbag to the saddle, then mounted, turning to face them, reins in hand.

"My advice to ya both," said Harry Dobbs, "is to skedaddle outa town a'fore them Haines boys show up in the mornin'. By this time tomorrow, there won't *be* no Lib-ertyville."

And, in a drumming cloud of dust, he was gone.

⋏

At the outlaw camp Buck Haines greeted his son. "How'd it go, Bobby?"

Young Haines was grinning. "Jes like you said it would, Pa. Whole town knows we're comin' in. They'll scatter like chickens."

"Well, I jes bet ole Jack ain't one of 'em," said the elder Haines. "He knows we got a personal score to settle and he'll stick around to settle it. Meanin' he's gonna die."

"That old man's got no chance," agreed Bobby. "Ain't nobody faster with a six-gun than you. But why d'ya think he won't cut an' run?"

"Pride," said Buck. "His pride'll hold him there. In a way, he's gonna be killin' hisself."

"I wanta see it," said Bobby, excitement in his voice. "I wanna see you gun him down."

"You will," said his father. He turned to the others. "Git ready. We ride at sunup."

⬥

That night at the ranch, in Anna Thursday's candlelit bedroom, the dying woman pleaded with her brother.

"Please don't do what you're planning, John. They'll put you in jail and claim the ranch. Everything you've built up . . . it'll all be lost. Promise me you won't do it."

"That's a promise I can't make," said John softly. "After all these years, I gotta do what's right."

She nodded, knowing he was committed. Thursday leaned down to kiss her cheek.

"You been more than a sister ta me," he said. "Ya been a light ta guide me in this world. It's gonna be mighty dark without ya." Tears were rolling down his cheeks. "I'm gonna miss ya somethin' fierce, Sis. God, how I'm gonna miss ya!"

She smiled weakly. "I've had a good life, all told, and I'm ready to move on. But I want you to know . . . that no woman could have a finer brother." She drew in a long, shuddering breath. "Now send in Shan. I want to say something to the boy."

Her voice was barely above a whisper. As John walked from the room, he knew he was leaving her forever.

Within moments Shan was sitting in the chair by Anna's bed. His hand held hers; its warmth felt strong and calming to the dying woman.

"John won't talk to me about you," whispered Anna. "But I know you're real special. And I know you're going to be able to help my brother after I'm gone."

"You're right," said the young man. "I can help him."

"He's going to need you, son. Don't fail him . . . Just please don't fail him . . ."

Her voice caught, then she exhaled very slowly, and Anna Thursday closed her eyes for the last time.

⚓

Later, in his study with Shan, John talked about the good years with his sister at the ranch.

"She always backed me up, an' never laid no guilt on me fer what I was a'fore I bought this ranch," he said. "Anna was a rare one."

"She was indeed," agreed Shan.

"I done me some bad things in my young days," said Texas John.

Shan nodded. "Back when your name was Jack Oliver," he said. "Twenty years ago, when you robbed a government gold train with Buck Haines."

The rancher stared at him. "But how could ya—" Then he smiled. "I see. Anna told ya."

"No, she told me nothing about your past," Shan declared. "Not a word. Yet I know all about you. I can't reveal *how* I know—quite yet—but I know."

"By this time I oughta be usta yer big surprises," said Thursday. "Jes when willya be ready quit bein' so all fired mysterious?"

"Soon now," Shan said. "*Very* soon."

⚓

It was almost dawn. The eastern sky at the edge of the plains beyond Libertyville was no longer black; a pale gray luminescence had replaced the night's darkness.

Despite this very early hour the town's main street swarmed with activity. Store owners and private citizens were frantically loading wagons, carts, and carriages with supplies and personal goods. In front of the Greater Libertyville Bank the massive iron safe was dragged into the street by a team of horses where it was lifted, via a crude rope-pulley, into the bed of a heavy supply wagon.

The townspeople were desperate to clear out of Libertyville before the Haines gang arrived.

Inside the saloon, in the quiet of her upper living quarters, Becky O'Rourke was listening to John Thursday as he told her the full story of his past, when his name had been Jack Oliver and he'd ridden the outlaw trail.

"I was still crazy wild in them days," John admitted. "After me an' Buck pulled off the government train job, we had a fallin' out. He threatened to kill me—so I shot him an' rode off with the gold."

"What happened to it?" she asked. "Where's the gold now?"

"Where it's been hid all these years since I first come here," said Thursday. "It's buried next to the back wall of the old Spanish mission just outside town. Part of it went to buy my ranch an' the stock I needed. The rest is still buried out there.

"Reason I kept quiet fer so long was fer Anna's sake," he said. "I didn't want Sis thrown out homeless once I lost the ranch." He looked down. "An' I never told *you* none'a this, cuz I was ashamed'a what I'd been and done."

"I would have understood," she said. "I *do* understand. You're no outlaw, John."

"I was once, but I've lived with my guilt long enough. Now that Anna's gone, I'm turnin' myself in along with the gold. But first, I gotta *defend* it."

"What do you mean?"

"The ruckus with Bobby Haines was set up by Buck. He sent Bobby in ta act like he was drunk an' start a fight—all so's he could scare folks outa town by word'a the gang comin' in. An' it worked." Thursday pointed to the window. "Look out there on the street. Everybody's leavin'—just like Buck wanted."

"What about Sheriff Dobbs? Won't the sheriff be able to—"

"He was the first ta run!" declared Thursday. "An' now all the geese is followin' after him."

"Does Buck Haines know about the gold . . . about where it's hidden?"

"He knows *now*. Somehow, he found out. But he'll hafta kill me ta git it!"

"You can't face the whole Haines gang single-handed!"

"I'll have Shan with me." Thursday chuckled. "An' that boy knows a trick or two."

"I'll stay here and fight them with you," she declared. "I've got my sawed-off and I know how to use it."

"The *hell* you will!" John Thursday said, glaring at her.

Farther down the street, at the mercantile, Molly Robbins was saying good-bye to Shan as her father finished loading their supply wagon. They were heading East. Permanently.

"I've had me enough Wild West," Pete Robbins had declared. "I'll open me a store where things are civilized and outlaws don't go around burnin' down whole towns!"

"I'm proud to have known you," Shan told her. "Now it's time for you to go and live your life. I'm sorry, Molly, but there's no way that I can be a part of it."

"But I'll come back to you," she said, tears in her eyes.

"That's not possible," he told her. "I must go to a place you can never reach."

"But Shan—"

"When you get back East, go to Montreal, just like you planned. Perfect your French there. Become a teacher. Find a good man and get married. Have a family. Believe me, Molly, the good life you seek is waiting for you back East. And you *will* be happy, I promise."

He kissed her, then waved farewell as her father

whipped up the horses. The heavy supply wagon rolled down the street, diminishing with distance.

Shan did not move until it was out of sight.

Then he headed for O'Rourke's.

Becky and the bartender had taken down her antique mirror and it was now wrapped carefully in blankets. Along with Texas John, the three were loading it into a wagon in front of the saloon when Shan walked up to them.

"Becky refuses to go," Thursday told Shan. "If she stays, they'll kill her."

"I'll take care of it," Shan said quietly. "Just leave her to me."

∧

Sunup.

Buck Haines spun the cylinder of his long-barrel Colt, making sure the weapon was fully loaded. Slipping the gun back into its holster, he let his eyes range over the other seven outlaws who were standing near their saddled horses. Bobby, Ringo, Little Charlie, Arly Willows, Dex Givens, Cheyenne, and Laredo Slim.

"Sun's up," said Bobby.

Buck Haines smiled. "Gonna be a real treat, meetin' up with ole Jack Oliver again." His voice rose to a shout: "Let's ride!"

And the Haines gang swept away from their camp in a sudden thunder of hoofs.

Toward Libertyville.

∧

Shan and Becky sat inside the deserted saloon at a corner table. No, she is *not* going to run. She's not going to leave the man she loves. Since John is staying, so will she—and there's nothing Shan can do or say that will change her mind.

"You could die here," declared Shan.

"I can take care of myself. If I can run a saloon, I can handle a few scurvy outlaws."

Shan moved his chair close to hers and leaned in to look her right in the eyes. Then he reached out and touched her arm.

"You understand that you really should go," he said softly, stroking her arm. Gently, he moved his hand to the top of her head. Becky didn't flinch or resist; she looked deeply relaxed, curiously focused on hearing each of his words. His touch vibrated through her body with a pleasant sensation she had never felt before.

"You need to go," Shan said. "It's the right thing to do."

Becky thought carefully, then slowly nodded. "Yes," she repeated softly, ". . . the right thing to do."

Thursday walked up to their table.

"She's decided to leave," Shan told him.

"Yes." Becky stood up. "I'm ready."

She exited the saloon without another word and climbed into the high seat of the wagon. The bartender, holding the reins, looked surprised to see her.

"I'm leaving town," she told him. "It's the right thing to do."

The wagon pulled away. Shan and Texas John Thursday stood alone in the middle of Main Street in the pale light of a new day.

⋏

Buck Haines eased forward in the saddle, shading his eyes against the early-morning sun. His horse shifted restlessly as Haines scanned the dusty length of Main Street.

"Bare as a bone," he said to his son, who had reined up

his horse next to Buck's. "You done real good, Bobby. Ain't nary a soul left in town."

"What about Jack Oliver?" Bobby asked. "I thought you said he'd stay on."

"He'll show his face eventual," said Haines. "I'll have my chance to kill him."

"What now, Buck?" asked Laredo Slim, whose vast bulk belied his name. The horse he'd ridden into Libertyville was badly winded.

"You boys stay here an' burn this one-hoss cowtown flat to the ground. Teach folks not to mess with the Haines gang." He nodded toward his son. "Me an' Bobby, we got some business out at the mission. Meet us there when yer done with this place."

"We're gonna have us one high ole time," declared Ringo, grinning broadly. "I purely enjoy seein' things burn!"

"Won't be nothin' left but a pile'a ashes when we're done," said Dex Givens.

Buck smiled at Bobby. "Ready to be rich, boy?"

"Ain't never seen me no gold bars," said the young outlaw. "How many of 'em do you reckon is buried out there, Pa?"

"Lots," said Buck, gold hunger in his eyes.

And they spurred their horses into a gallop.

▲

The remaining six members of the gang dismounted in front of O'Rourke's saloon.

"Let's wet our whistles a'fore we set fire to the place," said Little Charlie. "A shame to waste free whiskey."

The others roared agreement, filing into the deserted saloon. Their boots rang like gunshots in the long room.

Cheyenne hopped over to the bar and brought forth a

quart of bourbon. He pulled the cork and took a healthy swig, then passed the bottle along to the others.

"I could use me one'a them fancy women right about now," said Ringo. "Drinkin' an' whorin' is what makes this ole world go round,"

"Shut yer hole," snapped Cheyenne. "We're here to do a job. Let's git to it."

When the six men left the saloon, their bellies glowing from a generous intake of bourbon, they encountered a slim-bodied young man standing in the middle of the street.

He stared at them, silent and unmoving.

From the high porch, the outlaws hesitated, grinning at one another.

"Looks like one'a the chickens forgot to run," said Laredo Slim.

"He must be loco," said Little Charlie. "How's he figger to stand up to us?"

"An' he ain't even packin' a gun," scoffed Ringo.

"You'd better climb on those horses and ride out," said Shan.

Ringo spat a thick wad of tobacco juice from the side of his mouth and glared at the youth. "An' what if we stay right here an' burn down this piss-ass town a'yours?"

"Then I'll be forced to stop you."

Ringo walked down the porch steps to his tethered mustang, removed a wooden torch tipped in black pitch, and struck a match to it. Instantly, the pitch ignited.

He raised the flaming torch in the air as the others joined him at the bottom of the porch. "An' jes how do ya aim to stop us, sonny?"

"I'll show you," said Shan.

He whipped up the Disc and beamed it at Ringo's right hand. The torch leaped from Ringo's fingers and landed on the outlaw's head.

Slapping wildly at his burning hair, Ringo yelled: "*Kill* him! Shoot the bastard!"

Shan felt a bullet from Little Charlie's Colt fan his cheek as he levitated the outlaw off the ground, then dumped him—sputtering and swearing—into a water-filled horse trough.

The youth whirled, then beamed the six-gun out of Laredo Slim's hand, caused the Colt to reverse itself in mid-air, then club its owner across the forehead, knocking him back onto the porch steps.

Cheyenne was next. He was deposited, head first, into a pile of horse dung, while Shan sent Dex Givens and Arly Willows sailing through the saloon window in a shower of broken glass.

All six outlaws ended up bundled together by a rope that seemed alive as it looped itself around them, tying its own knots.

Smiling, Shan replaced the Disc in his belt pouch.

"I'd like to know how ya done what ya done to us," said Little Charlie, still dripping from his dip in the trough.

"That's a bit complicated," said Shan. "I'd like to stay and have an enlightening chat with you boys, but right now I have another job to do."

He whistled sharply. Hellfire appeared from the rear of the saloon and trotted up to him.

"Yer the Devil hisself come to Earth, ain't ya?" murmured Ringo, staring up at Shan as the youth mounted Hellfire.

"I'm no devil," said Shan. "I'm just an ordinary fellow who happens to believe that rabid curs like the lot of you belong behind bars."

They glared at him and began twisting against their bonds.

"I ought to warn you: the more you struggle, the tighter that rope's going to get. So it's best to just settle down and wait. You'll be taken care of eventually."

Shan rode away, leaving the six frustrated outlaws writhing in the dust of the street.

▲

An ear-splitting roar, and the back wall of the old Spanish mission exploded into fragments of rock and clay. As the smoke cleared, Buck Haines crouched down to peer into the hole created by the blast of dynamite.

"D'ya see it, Pa?" asked Bobby, who was just behind him.

"Yeah . . . I *see* it, by God!" He stood up, smiling broadly. "Come here and look fer yerself."

Young Haines leaned in to savor the dull gleam of exposed gold, then let out a whoop. "We're *rich*, Pa! Jes like ya said we'd be!"

"Not quite," said a voice from the mission doorway. Texas John stepped out, a gun in each hand. "This gold belongs to the government, not to you. And that's where I'll be takin' it."

"The hell you will, old man!" shouted Bobby Haines, sweeping up his gun to fire at Thursday. His shot struck the tall rancher in the shoulder, causing him to drop his right Colt, but—triggering his left—he slammed Bobby into the dirt with a bullet through his head.

A death shot.

"Just you an' me now, Buck," he said tightly.

"I been waitin' twenty years ta kill ya," said Buck Haines. "An' by Christ, now I'm gonna do it!"

Twisting sideways, he fired directly at Thursday.

Texas John staggered under the bullet's impact. A sudden rush of blood darkened his chest. Willing strength into his right hand, he fired back twice at Haines, both of his bullets striking the outlaw.

Haines pitched forward with a startled grunt, rolling

over onto his back. His eyes popped wide as he stopped breathing.

Shan skidded Hellfire to a stop and leaped from the saddle to kneel beside Texas John. The older man was very close to death.

"Don't . . . let them take . . . the gold," he whispered, blood bubbling at his lips.

"I won't," Shan promised.

"And . . . tell Becky . . . that I . . ." The rancher's voice failed; his fingers clenched spastically, then totally relaxed.

Texas John Thursday was dead.

In the shocked silence of the moment Shan stood up. A soft wind blew the scents of sage and prairie grass into his nostrils and the morning sun lay hot on his shoulders.

He removed the Disc from his belt pouch, adjusted it, then beamed John Thursday's lifeless corpse.

A pulsing multicolored mist settled over the body. The bullet wounds began to close and the rancher's skin soon began to glow with an inner luminescence. Currents, like miniature bolts of lightning, crackled and sparked around him.

Shan put away the Disc and waited until John's eyes opened. The multicolored fire mist faded from his skin.

"Welcome back," said Shan.

Thursday sat up, puzzled. His fingers probed the wet spot on his clothes where his wound had been. He shook his head in confusion. "Can't figger it. I thought sure he got me."

"He did," nodded the youth. "Buck Haines killed you. He put a bullet in your chest and your heart stopped." Shan smiled. "I started it again."

John Thursday nodded, accepting the miracle. "I know now where ya come from, with all'a your powers. It's in the Bible, in Ezekiel . . . what it says in there about comin' to Earth in a chariot'a fire. Ole Zeke, he was talkin' about folks like you." He drew in a breath. "Yessir, I know where ya hail from. From Mars mebbe, or one'a them other planets in the sky at night."

"No," said Shan. "I'm from the same planet you are—this one. And the same state. I'm from Texas, John . . . *future* Texas, a hundred and fifty years from now."

With a helping hand from Shan, Thursday stood up, then sat down heavily on a section of ruined wall. He pulled out his kerchief and mopped his forehead. "Ya lost me, boy. How kin ya be from a place that ain't happened yet?"

Shan picked up a stick and drew two separate lines in the dust. "Think of time as a road," he said. "You are *here* on the road now, in 1910,"—and he poked the stick into the ground. "I'm farther along up *here*, in 2060." Again, he used the stick to indicate his position. "I traveled back, down the road, to where *you* are."

"But *how*? How'd ya git here?"

"In a ship. A Timeship. It carried me back to the Old West . . . *here*, to Texas, in the year 1910."

"I don't savvy any'a this, but supposin' it's a fact. Then I ask ya, why? What brung ya here?"

"*You* did," said Shan. "Where I came from, in 2060, our history has recorded that a reformed outlaw named Jack Oliver, generally known as Texas John Thursday, was shot to death by his former partner, Buck Haines, at the old Spanish mission outside Libertyville. The Haines gang escaped with a stolen government gold shipment after they burned the town.

"Since you didn't have any children, the family line ended with your death. Therefore, no one was able to stop the plague."

"What plague?"

"The one that killed my wife and my parents," said Shan. "A deadly supervirus that ravaged my world. I'm one of only a few survivors."

"But if all this is fact, what good can ya do comin' back to me?"

"By saving your life, I've been able to change the future," declared the youth. "Like switching a train to another track. Now you can marry Becky and have children. And *they* will have children.

"Your great-great-great grandson, Bennett Oliver, will become a brilliant scientist. He will develop a process that will annihilate the plague virus, and because of his work, millions of lives will be saved."

Texas John shook his head. "I can't marry Becky. When I turn in the gold, they'll take away my ranch and put me in prison fer the rest of my life."

"No. For saving Libertyville and returning the gold, the governor will grant you a full pardon. And you'll be able to keep your ranch."

"How do ya know that if it ain't happened yet?"

Shan smiled. "It's a matter of mathematics—the physics of action and reaction. There are many alternate futures. I simply activated another alternative."

John looked at Shan through narrowed eyes. "Sounds like a lotta hogwash to me."

Shan shrugged his shoulders. "You've seen what I've been able to do. You don't have to understand how it works."

"Ya saved my life, an' that's fer sure. So what can I do fer you by way'a thanks?"

Shan laughed. "I was hoping you'd ask something like that. I'd like to take a souvenir back with me. Your Hupmobile, if that's all right with you."

"You're welcome to it!" Thursday said enthusiastically. "Ya talk about the future. I kin tellya *one* thing fer damn sure—there ain't no future in these autee-mo-beels."

Shan smiled, but he didn't reply.

▲

Back at the ranch they entered the stable where John kept the Hupmobile. John cranked away, but the car wouldn't start.

"We have a problem," Shan announced. "The Timeship can't enter the past—your present, right now—unless the mathematical coordinates match precisely."

"Meanin' what?" asked Texas John.

"I'm supposed to meet the ship just beyond Libertyville, but we're running late. I could miss it."

"Then *you* crank!" Thursday said.

"Let's try this instead," said Shan, beaming the Disc at the car's hood.

Success! The engine burst into rumbling life.

"Hop in," said John, "an' we'll git this pesky critter on the road."

Tying Hellfire's reins to the back of the ponderous vehicle, Shan climbed into the high passenger seat next to Thursday.

"We're off!" declared John, and the big car began to roll.

⋏

As the Hupmobile bounced and rattled over the broken surface of the prairie Shan became apprehensive.

"Can't you get this car to move any faster?" he asked Thursday.

Texas John lowered his driving goggles to glare at his passenger. "Hell, no! We're doin' almost ten miles an hour as is, an' over this kinda ground, that's as fast as she can go."

"We're almost there," said Shan. He pointed ahead. "Turn right, just past that stand of rocks. There's a clearing on the far side. That's my pickup point."

Once the big machine had passed the rocks, Shan told Thursday to stop.

"This is the contact area," he said, stepping to the ground. He began checking the terrain, then groaned and slumped to his knees.

"What's wrong?" asked John from the driver's seat.

"It's too late," murmured Shan. "The ship has come and gone."

John got out to stand beside the younger man. There was a deep depression in the ground which was surrounded by charred sagebrush.

"Yep. Sure looks like *somethin'* landed here!"

"It's my fault," Shan said. "I should never have stopped for the car. If we'd come here straight from the mission, I would have met the ship."

"Mebbe it'll come back fer ya."

"Impossible," said Shan. "The space-time elements must match exactly to create a passageway for the ship to appear at this spot. It can't return again. Now, I'll have to die here."

"Die?" John stared at him. "Why can't ya stay on, go East, marry that sweet Molly Robbins, an' start a new life?"

"Because my body isn't vibrationally attuned to this century. My genetic structure will disintegrate. By your standards, I'm 175 years old. If I stay here, within another month my cells will begin to break down. Within weeks, I'll be dead."

He slumped to the ground now and sat cross-legged, his head bowed in a posture of defeat.

"I'm right sorry," said Thursday.

"At least I accomplished my mission," declared Shan in a subdued tone. "I saved your life, and the lives of all the people who would have been struck down by the plague. If I have to die here, it's been worth it."

Texas John looked skyward, shading his eyes against the sun glare.

"Somethin's *up* there," he said.

Shan raised his head as a vast humming surrounded them. A shimmering wheel of silver and gold was descending from the sky.

The Timeship!

⋏

". . . so when you altered the future by saving Jack Oliver's life, you created a new set of time-space coordinates," Captain Edwards was explaining to Shan. "I was able to reprogram the ship for a second entry." He shook hands with Shan. "Congratulations! Your mission has been a complete success."

The proud young man introduced him to the rancher whose life had been saved. The captain's grip was firm and resolute as he shook Thursday's hand.

John grinned. "Glad ta know ya. Never met me no spaceman a'fore."

"That machine you arrived in," said Captain Edwards to Shan. "What, exactly, *is* it?"

"A gas-powered 1909 Hupmobile, with an internal combustion engine," Shan told him. "And it's a gift from John. I'm taking it back with me."

"How very generous of you," Edwards said to the rancher. "Giving it up must be quite a sacrifice."

"A sacrifice it ain't!" muttered Thursday. "Be damn glad to git rid'a the thing. Never give me nothin' but grief."

The captain chuckled and turned back to Shan. "Ready to go?"

"In a minute. I still have something to tell John," he replied.

"Signal when you're ready," said Edwards. He shook the rancher's hand again. "I don't need to wish you luck, Mr. Thursday, because I know you're going to have a marvelous life. Been a pleasure meeting you."

"Obliged," nodded Thursday.

The sun-dazzled, silver-and-gold Timeship hovered silently in the sky just above them as the captain beamed himself aboard.

"There's one more thing you should know," Shan said to Thursday. "I *do* have a last name. In this new future we've created together, my father is Bennett Oliver. I'm Shan Oliver, your great-great-great-great-grandson."

"But I don't savvy—"

"It isn't necessary that you understand any of this," Shan told him. "Just accept it—and know that I love you . . . Grandpa."

The two men embraced. For the first time since Anna's death, tears filled John Thursday's eyes.

"You have a long, productive life ahead of you," said Shan Oliver. "You and Becky and your five children . . ."

The rancher found it hard to speak. "I dunno what to say . . . all ya done fer me . . . fer Libertyville . . . fer Becky . . . an' savin' all them folks in the future . . ."

"*You'll* be saving them," smiled Shan. "Your blood will flow into future generations. Because of you, my father will live to stop the plague."

They embraced again, then Shan climbed into the high seat of the Hupmobile. He raised a hand to signal the hovering craft.

A glowing red beam speared down from the underside of the Timeship to envelop car and driver.

The big Hupmobile wavered, then lifted from the ground and was smoothly beamed into the hovering ship.

Shan waved a final good-bye.

From the prairie, Texas John waved back. The ship's hold closed.

A rising hum. A flash of glowing metal.

The Timeship was gone.

John Thursday mounted Hellfire and began riding toward his future life under the vast Texas sky.

PEOPLE OF THE BLUE-GREEN WATER
John Tomerlin

JOHN TOMERLIN is another core member of the Group, and its only native-born Californian. He grew up in Los Angeles, and majored in Radio at the University of Southern California. After college he entered radio on a professional basis, writing copy, running a disc jockey show, handling newscasts, and functioning as a play-by-play sportscaster.

In the 1950s, when he was in the Group, John was a director at a Los Angeles advertising agency. His first novel (*Run From the Hunter*, 1957) was a collaboration with Charles Beaumont, written under the pen name of "Keith Grantland." John went on to write nine more novels, including a Grand Prix racing epic, *Challenge the Wind*, which he researched in Europe (where he lived for a year with his wife, Wilma).

A long-time technical editor with *Road & Track*, John has competed in many races, winning a slalom championship in the 1980s. Enjoying his hobbies of golf, skating, and bridge, Tomerlin has been an active pilot, flying his plane around the country on various writing assignments. (His daughter, Erin, is also a pilot and flight instructor.)

Tomerlin has some three dozen teleplays to his credit, and has sold short fiction to several markets, including *Playboy*. The story he chose to write for this book is an outdoor character study in the tradition of Hemingway's "Big, Two-Hearted River," with its wilderness locale superbly rendered.

In this neatly-crafted tale we witness the rite-of-passage transition from boy to man.

W.F.N.

The sun broke above the rim of the Coconino Plateau, filtering down through scattered clouds to the road and the parking area below. A shaft of light picked out a small black van parked near the entrance to the Hualapai trailhead—it glanced through the windshield and dazzled one of the van's occupants awake. He swore and turned his head away. A moment later he rose stiffly on one arm and shook the shoulder of the man next to him.

"Hey, you awake? Time to get moving."

"God, already?" Terry said. He was several years younger than Con and different enough in appearance that people seldom guessed they were brothers. "Feels like I only got to sleep an hour ago."

"About that," Con said. They'd taken turns driving all night from Phoenix to the reservation, with Terry drawing the rough and narrow 68-mile run over Indian Route 18. "You can nap after we get there."

The two men slid out through the side door of the van, still mostly dressed but searching along the sides of the mattress for boots and jackets. The van was rigged for sleeping with room for two adults in back and a shelf above the front seat large enough for a child. Terry leaned forward and thumped the bottom of the ledge to wake his son. "Hey, Erik, rise and shine!"

"No!" the boy said.

Breakfast was cereal and milk with no sugar, and no coffee. Con had arranged the trip and bought their supplies, and didn't want to waste time unpacking the campstove or food. "It'll be hot by the time we get to the bottom," he said, handing out rolls of toilet paper. "Better piss or take a dump if you need it. Won't be another chance for a while."

There were patches of creosote bush growing close to the road, but no real privacy, and Terry intercepted a look of dismay on his son's face. The boy had refused his cereal saying it tasted yucky without sugar, and Terry wondered, not the first time, if it had been a mistake to bring him. When Erik complained of the weight of his pack Terry transferred some of the load to his before they set out.

The path down the cliff face was steep, but wide and smooth, with a mortared stone wall and viewpoints at some of the switchbacks. It was meant to accommodate horses, which could be rented from the resident Havasu Indians by those who preferred to ride. Though Con had considered this option, in the end he'd decided against it, preferring the experience of the surroundings at ground level. The guidebooks rated the eight miles to Supai village (two more to the actual campsite) "very strenuous," but his younger brother was up to it, he thought. As for his nephew, the kid was almost eleven, and still a bit of a wimp; he could use some toughening up.

The boy had run ahead, excited by the ease of the descent and the view of the canyon below. When Con caught up he said, "Better take it easy, Erik. You're going to need all that energy later."

They descended 800 feet to broad flat hardpan at the base of the cliff, then continued on a slight downslope between walls of red sandstone. It was cool, still in shadow, and at first they made good time; later, where the land leveled out and the canyon walls began to recede they emerged into sunlight, and had to stop to remove their jackets. They drank from their canteens before going on.

Gradually the canyon floor turned green around them. There were cottonwoods and box elders and willows, the vegetation heaviest on their right. After walking for an hour they began to hear the sound of running water: a stream hidden in the trees.

"I'm tired," Erik announced. "My feet hurt."

"Let's take a break," Con said.

They left the trail and walked toward the sound of the water; they sat on rocks beside the stream where Terry helped his son remove his left boot. He inspected the reddened areas on the ball of Erik's foot and heel. "Have I got a blister?" the boy asked querulously.

"I don't see anything." Terry could feel the heat beneath both spots.

"Where the hell did you get these?" Con asked, picking up the boot.

"At the shoe store. They weren't cheap."

"They're crap. I told you to go to a sporting goods place, didn't I?"

Terry felt defensive. His own boots, bought for the first hike he'd taken with his brother, years ago, were extremely comfortable. "I guess I made a mistake."

"What am I gonna do?" Erik whined. "I can't walk."

"Well, you can't stay here, either," Con said. He got a packet of moleskin from the first-aid kit, cut centerholes and taped them in place. "A little blister isn't going to kill you," he said.

They went on more slowly then, stopping often to rest and drink; Erik limped in a way that made his father feel guilty. He'd already taken over the rest of the boy's pack; there was no more he could do for him.

Con offered both of them advice: to minimize effort, lift the leg at the knee and let your foot come down flat, "The way cows and horses do it." During the next hour, this seemed to help.

When at last they reached the Indian village—a few sagging shacks and a corral, empty at the moment—they stopped to get supplies. There wasn't much to buy other than canned goods and a few candy bars, which Con added to their stores. "Only a couple more miles," he told them.

It seemed farther, the final hundred yards ascending though scree, where the footing was treacherous. Erik had stopped complaining but Terry had seen tears on the boy's cheeks and knew he'd been crying; he thought he might have to carry him into camp—if he had enough strength left to get that far himself.

He was still worrying when they reached the top of the hill, and all three stopped to stare. Ahead lay a flat table of land, longer than it was wide, confined on the left by a low sandstone ridge and on the right by forest. As they moved into the clearing they became aware of the roar of water, and looked back and to the right to see a cataract gushing from a notch in the cliff. Its waters lunged forth in a twisting white-edged ribbon that crashed down a hundred feet or more to a deep blue pool, from there hurrying out by way of a series of travertine terraces that lapped down to smaller pools.

"Golly!" Erik said, precisely eloquent.

Con led them to the first large masses of foliage, clumps of hackberry and wild grape just a few yards from the tree-shaded stream. He stopped in a small clearing where there was a picnic table made of heavy, dark-stained planks. He shrugged out of his backpack, laid it on the table, and peered farther down the creek. "I think we got the whole damn place to ourselves," he said, sounding pleased.

While his brother unpacked, Terry examined Erik's feet, finding whitish spots the size of quarters on both of them. The blisters had already started to fill with liquid. He got tennis shoes from the boy's pack and gave them to him to wear.

Con made lunch—tuna spread on slices of the white bread he'd bought at the Indian store—and afterwards they changed into swimming trunks and went down to the stream. Only then did they realize how fortunate their choice of campsites had been: right next to one of the travertine formations, a spillway that directed water from the stream into their very own swimming pool. Con jumped in, surfaced, and announced the water "cold, but not bad . . . In fact, great!"

His brother followed and then the boy who sucked his breath in sharply when he touched the emerald-green water. Con climbed to the top of the travertine and slid down the natural spillway, landing in the deepest part of the pool. Even here it was so clear that the marble-smooth bottom was perfectly visible.

"Look!" Terry said, pointing upstream at the waterfall,

entirely revealed where they stood, "this place is like something you'd see on a postcard."

Erik shrieked, and scrambled onto the bank. "Something's down there!" he shouted. "I felt it!"

They looked.

Something was . . . A cloud of tiny fish, the largest no more than an inch, their bodies nearly transparent. They darted away at any movement but returned immediately to butt against the men's toes when they stayed still.

"I think the little bastards are trying to eat us."

"If they were bigger, they probably could," Terry said.

"If they were bigger we'd fry some of 'em."

Erik didn't come back in the water.

⚑

The late-afternoon sun made toweling off unnecessary and by the time they walked the few steps back to camp they were almost dry. The two men changed into pants and canvas shoes while the boy fell onto his sleeping bag and closed his eyes.

"He's pretty worn out," Terry said.

"Let him rest. How about we walk down a ways, see if anyone else is here?"

As near as they could discover, no one was.

It was late September, still warm, but the summer crowds were gone. Con had planned it this way, talking Terry into allowing his son to miss a few days of school so they'd have as few people around as possible.

The brothers hadn't spent a lot of time together while growing up; the difference in their ages had been one barrier, their parents' divorce another. When he'd gone away to college Terry had stayed with their mother, getting the short end of the deal, in his opinion. She hadn't really known how to cope with the needs of a teenage boy. Con thought he could have done more if he'd stayed around; he worried that he should have.

"Come on," he said, "I'll show you something. Not too tired are you?"

The camping area ran on another hundred yards before the floor of the canyon narrowed and the trail disappeared into thick forest. The path descended gradually through the trees while the stream itself cut downwards even more sharply, at the same time angling away from them. Con led them along the trail until they began to hear the sound of another waterfall; after a few more minutes they came to the edge of a steep drop overlooking a lower canyon and saw a waterfall larger and higher than the one above their campsite. As they stood looking windborne mist brushed their faces.

"Is this the end of the trail?" Terry asked.

Con shook his head and pointed; not far from their feet was what looked to be a small seam or notch in the embankment. Pieces of iron pipe or spikes were driven into the rocks at varying angles—less a set of handholds than random opportunities for support.

"You mean you go down *that?*"

"If you're headed for the Colorado River, you do. Want to try it?"

"How far's the river?"

"About ten miles; I just mean do you want to try the steps."

"What steps?"

Con laughed and moved to the edge. "If you're worried, I'll go first."

The older man turned his back to the abyss and put a foot down to feel for the first spike. There was a length of braided wire attached to a rusted staple, apparently meant for a handhold, but rusted and broken off after a few inches. Con felt for the next foothold then changed his mind and pulled himself up.

"Take too long to go down and come up again," he said. "But I'll wait if you want to go."

It was almost, if not quite, a dare; the kind his older brother often threw at him when they were younger. He wanted to surprise Con by doing it, but when he approached the edge and looked again at the distance to the bottom and the skewed pieces of pipe meant to support his weight, he knew he couldn't. "I guess you're right, we should be getting back."

"Not scared, are you?"

"Maybe we can come here tomorrow and both go down."

"Now you're talking," Con said, turning and starting up the trail.

But Terry was sure his brother was as reluctant to make the climb as he was.

Erik was awake when they got to camp. "Where *were* you?" he asked querulously. "I looked *everywhere!*"

Terry told him about the other waterfall, repeating what Con had said on the way back: "It's called 'Mooney Falls,' because that was the name of the man who discovered it."

"The Indians might argue with you, there," Con said as he started to prepare dinner.

"Well, the first white man. It's a lot higher than our falls," he said. "In fact, Mooney fell and was killed trying to get down them."

"Wow, I wish I could see it."

"Maybe you will tomorrow."

Con served them chipped beef on toast with peas and carrots, all but the bread vacuum-preserved, and a chocolate pudding made with dried milk. The coffee, made with water from "their" stream, was excellent. Even Erik, who was usually finicky about food, cleaned his plate. Then he said "goodnight" and curled up in his sleeping bag.

Since returning to camp the brothers had been sipping from flasks and chasing it with water dipped from the stream: "Bourbon and branch," Con called it, "with *real* branch water." Now, he got out a bottle of Chivas and added it to their coffee. "This is the life," he said. "Only thing we're missing is a real campfire."

The gas lantern percolating at the end of the table seemed a good-enough substitute. "Pop would have liked this," Terry said, watching a moth butt against the lantern. "Did you ever bring him?"

"Here? No. Nothing to catch or kill."

"Yeah, he liked that."

"He liked this, too," Con said, putting more scotch in their cups.

"He was a tough old bird . . ."

"Tough enough on me, at times . . ."

"You got that right. Me, too."

After a silence Terry said, "Be nice to be able to stay here a few days, wouldn't it?"

"I wish I could, but duty calls."

"I'm kind of worried about—" He tilted his head toward Erik's bedroll.

Con shrugged. "They go through phases. He'll be okay when he's a little older."

"Well, yeah—but I mean going back tomorrow. It's uphill, and that cliff at the end will be rough, especially in the afternoon heat. I don't know if he can make it."

Con said nothing.

"I thought it might be a good idea to go to the village tomorrow, see if I can rent a horse for him. What do you think?"

"I guess. If they have any. I think they move 'em up to the plateau at the end of the season."

"Well, I'm going . . . You were right about the damn boots, I should have listened to you."

"You should have."

Erik's feet looked better the following morning. The

blisters had shrunk without breaking, and Con thought fresh moleskin would keep them from getting too bad.

"I want to see about a horse, anyway," Terry said.

Con decided to accompany him, leaving Erik to watch the camp; they left after breakfast, promising the boy they'd be back in a couple of hours.

When they were gone the boy looked around for something to do. His father had made him promise not to go swimming when no one was there. Not that he wanted to. He reread some of the comics he'd brought with him before growing bored and putting them aside; he remembered what his father and uncle had said about Mooney Falls and wished he could see them. The camp should be safe enough for a while, and no one had told him he couldn't go for a walk . . .

He passed a dozen or more unoccupied tables before he reached the trail leading into the woods. It was cooler in the treeshade and very peaceful and somehow the silence of the place added to his confidence; by the time he started hearing the falls, he'd gone much farther than expected.

But when he saw them at last he was glad he'd come. They were even bigger than he'd imagined and louder, and at the bottom where a cloud of mist arose from a wide blue pool arose a perfect rainbow. He gazed at the flourish of color a moment or two, then made up his mind, and started down the cliffside using the metal hand- and footholds.

It was hard work and some of the rungs moved slightly when he put weight on them, but if they'd held his father and uncle all right he wasn't worried they'd hold him. Moments later he put his foot on the last spike and felt it give way under him; he let go of his handhold and dropped to the ground, landing on a carpet of leaves, shaken but in one piece.

When he stood up and looked around, he could no longer see the rainbow. When he looked back the way he'd come, and realized he'd have to climb up the cliffside in order to get home, he felt terror.

He spent some time searching for an alternate route but soon saw this was useless. From here the trail led deeper into the forest and held still greater terror. He began to cry: silently at first, then with stifled sobs. He stumbled back to the notch of the cliff, tried jumping halfheartedly at the lowest of the remaining spikes, but couldn't reach it. He sank down with his back to the slope, shaking with fear and praying someone would come to look for him soon.

The sibilant pounding of water was the only sound he heard. The forest itself seemed to have grown very still. He listened for birds but heard none. A cloud passed over the sun, turning the air chill, and when the sun reappeared a man was standing on the other bank of the stream, looking at him.

The man wore a hat with the brim turned down and sweat stains around the band; a denim jacket and pants, both faded near white, and raveled at the cuffs. His skin was the color of dried beef, deeply wrinkled at eyes and mouth, cheeks furrowed as though by claws. The braid of hair across his shoulder was streaked with gray. Erik knew at once this was an Indian, but could tell nothing else about him, least of all his intentions. He wanted to ask for help but was afraid to speak a word.

For a while the Indian merely stared, eyes shifting from the ground to the embankment, then back to the boy. When he finally moved it was to kneel beside the streambed and reach into it, feeling for something.

Erik tensed for flight.

The Indian rose again holding a stone the size of a grapefruit; he raised it a little, balancing it in his palm—a gesture that seemed less a threat than a kind of offer—then dropped it on the ground. Erik watched the rock roll toward the water and stop, and when he looked up again the Indian was no longer there.

The boy remained motionless. His fingers had closed on the metal spike he'd dislodged during his descent—the only possible weapon at hand—and now he looked at it, then got up and waded across the stream to where the rock had fallen. He picked it up and came back, found the seam in the sandstone where the spike had been, and drove it back in place. When he tested the step it bore his weight easily.

⋏

Con and Terry returned to camp to find Erik already packed and ready to leave. The father was angry and apologetic: "I'm sorry, son. They didn't have any horses to rent—or anyway said they didn't." He said to Con, "That bastard could have found us one if he wanted."

"I dunno. The corral was empty."

"You know damn well there's *one* horse left somewhere in the damn valley. He almost laughed at me—spoiled-rotten savage!"

Con shrugged. "No use crying about it. We'd better get started if we're going to get back before dark."

He began making up their backpacks, loading as much of the weight into his and Terry's as he could. There was less to carry without the food and liquor they'd consumed. Terry knelt beside his son and put a hand on his shoulder. "Listen, now, we'll take our time . . . It's still early, so we can stop whenever we want. Or whenever you need to. If you think you can't make it all the way up to the top of the plateau, well—I'll just go find help. What do you think?"

Erik thought he'd do just fine.

C.O.D.—CORPSE ON DELIVERY
Robert Bloch

ROBERT BLOCH, despite his many awards for a multitude of works, will always be known as the author of *Psycho*. This despite twenty-five other novels and more than 350 short stories (gathered in no less than fifty published collections). His classic short, "Yours Truly, Jack the Ripper," has been selected for countless anthologies worldwide.

Bob's script writing career didn't begin until he moved from Illinois to Southern California in 1959. He had sold film rights on *Psycho* to Alfred Hitchcock that same year for $9,500 (his Estate, represented by his widow, Elly Bloch, was paid $50,000 for the 1998 remake), and due to this Bob was able to write and sell a dozen screenplays and more than forty teleplays, including several to *Alfred Hitchcock Presents* and *The Hitchcock Hour*.

Born in Chicago, Bob was an avid horror fan, selling his first pro story to *Weird Tales* when he was just seventeen. His idol was H.P. Lovecraft, who exerted a heavy influence on Bloch's work. An equally rabid fan of the "Silents," Bob could answer any question regarding even the most obscure silent film. A vigorous supporter of small press publications, he contributed an ocean of words to amateur fanzines. He was also into radio drama, writing scripts for his own show (*Stay Tuned for Terror)* in the mid-1940s.

The thing most people remember about Robert Bloch was his personal warmth and outrageous wit (Bob loved puns). A number of his loyal friends expressed their affection for him in a memorial volume edited by Richard Matheson following Bob's death in 1994.

The story chosen for *California Sorcery* is pure pulp nostalgia, dating back to the 1940s where it was originally printed in the lurid pages of *Detective Tales*. It's super hard-boiled, a typical but little-known example of Bob's work in those early pre-*Psycho* days when he was churning out shock fiction for a wide variety of markets.

W.F.N.

When I came in, the living room was empty. I set the trunk down in the middle of the rug and lay down next to it.

I was too bushed to move. I lit a cigarette and panted on it. My coat was sweated under the arms, so I took it off and used it for a pillow.

After a while I got up and went over to the window. I pulled back the shade and looked across the street to the cigar store. That's where I figured he'd be, if he'd picked me up again.

He was there, all right. Just loitering in the doorway with a waiting-for-a-streetcar look. Well, maybe he thought it was going over. It might have, if I lost my nose. But outside of that, I can smell a shamus a mile off—and cheap dicks like Logan I can smell from here to Hoboken.

I peeked just long enough to make sure he wasn't going to move for a bit. Because while he was playing cigar-store Indian, I had work to do.

I walked back, doused my cigarette, took another look at the trunk on the floor, and headed for the bedroom. Sure enough, Mae was asleep in there. She was lying on her stomach with her kimono all tangled up under her. Quite a dish, all right. But this was no time for sentiment.

I reached down and slapped her in a likely spot. She snorted and opened her eyes.

"Hello, honey. When'd you get in?"

"Little while ago. Figured I'd let you rest. You don't know it, but you got a long stretch ahead of you."

"Huh?"

"Rise and shine, baby. You're pulling out of this dump."

She sat up and stared at me, pushing her hair out of her eyes.

"What's cooking, Tony?"

I smiled. "Plenty. It's all lined up. You're taking a little trip, starting tonight. Chicago."

"Alone, you mean?"

I nodded.

She got that sulky look. "What's the big idea? You trying to pull a fast one?"

"Come here, baby," I said.

I pulled her off the bed and over to the window. You could see the cigar store from here, too. Logan was still standing in the doorway, trying to look inconspicuous. His feet stuck out a mile.

I pushed the curtains back and pointed him out to her.

"Copper?"

I shrugged. "Logan. He's been tailing me all over town today. I shook him for a little while, but he must have picked me up again. He doesn't know enough to put the finger on me yet, but he sure as hell won't like it if he sees us scramming out of town together. That's why you're going alone."

She gave me one of those searching looks. I didn't mind. When it came to reading my mind, Mae needed glasses.

"What about you?" she asked. "How do I know you aren't pulling a fast one?"

I heaved a sigh. "I can't figure this, baby. We hook up together. We plan the slickest heist you ever saw. You case the job for me, but I pull it off alone. Why? Just so they can't pin anything on you if something goes wrong."

She didn't say anything.

"I plant the ice in a safe place until we can turn it into cash," I went on. "Then I run around town brushing dicks off the trail. Now we're being tagged. So what do I do? Before I get the dough, I take all kinds of chances just to figure a way to get you out of town ahead of me, in the clear. And then you ask me if I'm pulling a fast one!"

I sighed, just for emphasis.

"Aw, gee, Tony. You know I trust you."

"You better trust me," I said. "You're getting on a train tonight. Alone. Logan may tail us, but he'll stick to me. Tomorrow, sometime, I'll manage to shake him. Then I'll get the cash. It's coming through; don't worry about that."

"Honest?"

"Sure." I grinned. "I saw Fat Frisco today. He's made a connection."

"How much?"

"Eighteen."

Her eyes got wide.

"Eighteen grand?"

I nodded. "In cash. Strictly. Three days from now I'm joining you in Chi with the folding. After that we're hitting for the big time. Okay?"

"Okay," she said. But she didn't sound as if she meant it.

I grabbed her by the shoulders.

"Look, Mae. You're dumb. Suppose I don't show up? What then? You know all about the job, don't you? You know just how I stuck up the joint—you ought to, because you used to work there. You got the time, the details, everything. You even know I planted the ice with Fat Frisco. So if I don't show up, you run to the law and sing. Do you think I'd turn a canary like you loose ahead of me if I didn't intend to play it square? Look at your hand, baby—you've got aces."

She grabbed me and kissed me. I could tell that she was sold, all right. We fooled around for a minute and then I pushed her away.

"Better start packing," I said. "The train leaves at eight."

"Packing?" she said. "What'll I pack in?"

"I got it all fixed," I told her. "Brought you a trunk."

She followed me into the living room and I pulled down the shades. It was getting dark outside and I figured the bright lights from the living room would dazzle Logan's eyes. When I turned them on, Mae got a load of the baggage.

"Where did you get that crummy outfit?" she complained "It's second-hand."

"I know it. I'm sorry, baby. I told you how Logan's been sniffing my heels all day. I didn't dare shake him to go into a luggage store, or he'd get panicky. Had to ditch him down along Fourteenth and duck into Fat Frisco's. He gave me the trunk. It was the best he had."

She looked at the big green old-fashioned trunk and shook her head.

"After all," I said. "What does it matter? After you hit Chi and I come out, you'll get the damnedest set of luggage you ever laid eyes on. Airplane luggage, baby. From now on we travel in style."

"Sure, Tony. It's all right."

"That's a good girl. Well, snap into it. I'm going out and have a drink. It's been a tough day."

I went into the kitchen and poured a shot. I needed it. After I got it down I figured I needed another, so I took it. Then I began to sweat, so I had a third one.

That did it.

I reached down for a pile of old newspapers. Mae was always after me to throw them out, but I'd kept saving them. I knew they'd come in handy at a time like this.

I put them under my arm and walked back into the living room.

Mae had opened the trunk, but she wasn't packing yet. She just stood there looking sick.

"Brought you some papers to line the bottom with," I said. "Keep your clothes clean."

"Oh, honey, I don't like this. Going away and leaving you all alone with that dick following you."

"Cheer up. It's just for a few days."

I patted her shoulder.

"But it's such a long trip. I don't like long trips, Tony."

I stood behind her and breathed down her neck. It made the little blonde curls jump up and down.

"Well, it's just one long trip you've got to take," I told her. "We all have to take things as they come."

"Did you get my ticket?" she asked.

"Yeah," I said. "I got your ticket. Lucky you reminded me. Here you are, going away on a trip and I almost forgot to give you your ticket. Here it is."

I reached under the bundle of newspapers and gave Mae her ticket.

A hatchet in the back of the neck.

▲

It was funny about those newspapers. They'd helped me all the way through.

Reading a story in one of them about a murderer had given me the idea in the first place.

Carrying them in when I talked to Mae helped to hide the hatchet I used.

And now they kept the blood off the rug.

It took me quite a long time to do what I had to do, in order to fit Mae into that trunk. A couple of times I stopped and went out for a drink. The sweat just poured off me. Even though the hatchet was plenty sharp, I had to work. There were five separate jobs to do before I got her to fit the way I wanted. Sort of like a jigsaw puzzle, except for the thumping.

I hoped Mrs. Callahan downstairs wouldn't notice the noise. But after some of the drunken brawls Mae and I used to throw, she ought to be used to it. Besides, this was the last time I'd be bothering her.

When I was all finished, I used the newspapers again, this time to pack around Mae inside the trunk. I should have used salt, I guess, but it didn't matter. She wasn't going on a very long trip, after all, and the newspapers would keep her in pretty good shape. Damned good shape for the shape she was in.

Just for good luck I went through the bureau drawers and dumped in all of her clothes I could find. I wrapped dresses and blouses around each loose part and then put more newspapers over the top. That made it perfect.

I threw the hatchet in, slammed down the top, and locked the trunk tight.

After that I took one more drink, a double shot this time, and stepped over to the window. Sure enough, Old Faithful was still doing sentry duty.

I looked at my watch. A little after eight now. I had to get moving.

I went into the bedroom and looked around for a clean shirt. There was a pile of stuff in the top drawer—mostly a lot of bills, unopened. Mae's work. I always gave her enough to pay the bills, but she couldn't be bothered.

Well, it didn't matter. Another day or so in this town and after that they could all whistle. Bill collectors, coppers, the whole pack.

I found a white shirt from the laundry, right next to Mae's purse. She wouldn't be needing that anymore. I opened it and looked for loose change.

She had it, all right. A wad of small bills, not exactly big enough to choke a horse but plenty to choke a Shetland pony.

One hundred and eighty-eight bucks, I counted. Plus— a ticket to Palm Beach dated for just two days ago.

That set me back on my heels a little.

No wonder she wasn't paying bills! Holding out a roll and buying a ticket to Palm Beach—it was as plain as the nose on what used to be her face.

Evidently I'd done the right thing just in time. No wonder she wasn't sold on the idea of blowing for Chicago. She had her own plans. Probably meant to squeal on me and get a cut for the return of the ice. Only thing holding her up was she didn't know where I'd planted the stuff.

I may have felt a little sorry for her, particularly while I was doing some of the messier work with the hatchet, but I didn't anymore.

She got what was coming to her, all right. Got it in the neck.

I put the bills and the ticket in my pants pocket and then slipped into the new shirt. I chose a tie, went in the closet and got my sports jacket, turned out the bedroom light and walked back into the living room.

Eight-thirty.

I hoped it wasn't too late. But the Ace Express ad in the phone book said "Night or Day Service," and I hoped they meant it.

I dialed their number.

"Hello? Ace Express? This is Mr. Anthony Carello, four-one-six-three, Hyde Mount Avenue. Apartment twenty-five. Got it?"

The voice on the other end got it.

"I want you to pick up a trunk over here right away. Yes, a trunk. It goes to Mr. Sid Frisco. Frisco, F-r-i-s-c-o, one-eight-one-eight Fourteenth Street. That's right. Frisco's Auction Shop. Collect. He's expecting it before eleven tonight. Yes. What's in it? Oh . . . books. Books. Uh-huh. Tell you what you do. I won't be here when you come. I'll leave it sitting right in the front room. You can get the passkey from my landlady downstairs. Apartment one. Mrs. Callahan. Right? Thank you."

I hung up.

You could bet I wouldn't be here. That was part of the gag. My cue was to scram out now and let Logan follow me. Then he wouldn't be around to see the trunk when it came down.

Eight forty-five. Almost time to go.

I had it all timed down to the split second, almost. You got to do it that way in this business. Nothing can go haywire, or the whole thing falls apart.

This was a perfect setup.

I'd send the body to Fat Frisco in the trunk. He was wise, of course. He'd promised to get rid of it for me in a hurry.

That's why I liked old Frisco—he was so good at getting rid of stuff. Anything from hot ice to cold meat.

I couldn't take a crazy chance and dump the body myself. That's the mistake the guy made I read about in the paper. He sent his trunk off in care of General Delivery or something. And sure enough, it turned up.

But I was sending it to Frisco. He'd quicklime it in the cellar of his auction joint. He'd quicklime anything for a cut of eighteen thousand bucks.

Tomorrow he'd pick up the ice and give me the cash. By tomorrow night, if I ditched Logan, I could hit out of town. Maybe I could use Mae's ticket to Palm Beach. Thoughtful of her to pick it up for me.

By the time Logan found out I was gone for good, there would be no loose ends. The trunk would be gone, Mae would be gone, I would be gone. If Logan investigated, he'd find out that Mae had worked for the jeweler. And since she wasn't around, he'd probably figure she had copped the ice in the first place.

Neat, very neat. Now I'd go out, get Logan to follow me, and then ditch him. I just wanted him at my heels long enough to get the trunk away during his absence.

▲

Five to nine. Time to go.

I pushed the trunk next to the door where they couldn't miss it. They'd get the passkey from old lady Callahan downstairs.

I could have left my key, but I knew what that meant. The old dame might come up and sniff around. It wouldn't be smart.

It was cold when I hit the street. Logan saw me and

drifted along behind as I walked toward the corner, slowly. He wasn't taking any chances of losing me.

I grinned.

The next hour was just good clean fun. I took a taxi, rode on the subway, ducked down an alley. Logan had an interesting time, but I finally got tired. Fun is fun, but there's a limit. Besides, I had a heavy date.

I ditched Logan uptown in a bar I knew. It had a long back corridor leading to the washroom. What Logan didn't know is that a side door led out to the street again.

I took the side door, and ten minutes later I was in the Ace of Clubs, watching Connie in the floor show.

Connie did one of those military numbers, wearing a big fur hat. Shako, they call it. And she certainly knew how to shake.

After her act was over, she headed back to her dressing room. I followed.

I didn't bother to knock, just walked right in. She turned, and when she saw me she made a big red "O" with her mouth.

"Tony," she said. "You've come back." She put her hands on my shoulders. "Remember what I said, Tony. Nothing doing until you get rid of that woman."

"I remember." I kissed her. "And—I got rid of her. For good."

"Honest?"

"Cross my heart. From now on, it's just you and me, kid."

I walked over to the dressing table and picked up her big fur shako. I reached inside the lining and pulled out a lot of stuff that gleamed and glittered. It was the ice, of course. I'd planted the jewels here for safekeeping a week ago.

"Tony! Where did *that* come from?"

So I told her. Not about Mae, of course—I just explained that Mae had gone away forever. But I gave her the pitch on the jewels. We'd get the money tomorrow and head for Florida.

Connie clung to me. She got powder all over my lapels, but I didn't care. "Darling, you're wonderful," she whispered.

That was the start of a very big evening.

But the next morning. . . .

▲

The next morning I came walking up to Fat Frisco's auction joint, very fast, and almost bumped into a man in the doorway.

It was Logan. He stood there, big as life, pretending to read a paper. His big face was blank and his puffy eyelids only flickered as I brushed past him.

This was bad. He must have been nosing around trying to pick up my trail and found out I visited Fat Frisco recently. So he was hanging around here on the chance I'd show.

Well, his dumb hunch paid dividends.

Now I couldn't head for the back room and see Frisco. Not with Logan tagging me.

I decided to stall. The easiest way was to sit down and make like an auction hound.

It was almost noon, and the joint was crowded with live ones. I never figured the deal that gets them into these places, but they come. There was a bunch of women and a lot of old whiskers in the dump, and I noticed one or two quaint faces in the lot—Frisco's shills, of course, planted to heist the bidding. The auctioneer was up on the platform, spieling. He was a tall skinny wallio with a smooth line. Rico Zucconi—one of Frisco's boys. He had on a morning coat and his hair was plastered down. He looked like a waiter in a clip joint, but he could make with the tongue.

I sat there listening to him raffle off a grandfather's clock—a genuine antique that Frisco probably made over in Jersey—and he raised the ante on bidding to $145.

Easy dough. But then, that's what Fat Frisco liked. Easy dough.

I looked around for him out of the corner of my eye, but couldn't spot him. Instead, I spotted somebody else.

Logan.

The big dick was sitting two rows behind me. He still looked half asleep, but when I gave him the eye, his cigarette flared up and I knew he was breathing hard.

I didn't breathe so easy myself.

I had to see Frisco, get the dough, and catch the night train with Connie. But I didn't have any extra ticket for Logan.

It was a bad spot. I turned my head back to the auction platform and sat half-listening to Rico Zucconi's patter.

Then it was as if somebody had stepped up the volume on me. All at once his voice came booming out.

"And now we come to Lot Four-fifty-six. Lot Four-fifty-six, ladeez an' gen'mum, consistin' of one trunk, locked and sealed, contents unknown. To be sold for storage charges . . ."

I looked at Lot 456. It was a big secondhand green trunk, all right. Rico Zucconi hadn't lied about that. But he did lie when he said the contents were unknown.

I knew what was in that trunk.

Mae was!

No, there was no mistake about it. I saw the trunk I'd brought home last night—sitting up there on the platform, waiting to be auctioned off right now!

Zucconi was giving with the heat.

"A sporting proposition," he said. "Who knows what this trunk contains? Clothing, bonds, jewelry—even cash. There is no key. The lucky owner can break the seal himself. All right, what am I offered for this trunk, contents absolutely unknown—what am I offered for this treasure chest? Who has the feeling that this is his lucky day?"

"Ten dollars!" yelled a voice.

I looked around, gulped. It was my voice that yelled.

Zucconi spotted me, gave me a grin. "Gen'mum bids ten dollars! A ridiculous offer! Think of it, friends, this trunk may be worth a fortune—"

He was telling me!

"Fifteen!"

The bid came from behind me. Two rows behind me. From—Logan.

He wasn't playing possum anymore. He was sitting up straight, staring right at the trunk.

"Twenty!" I snapped.

"Twenty-five!" Logan again.

Zucconi was a little confused, but happy about the whole thing.

"Twenty-five from the sporting gentleman—a man who knows a good thing when he sees it!"

I could tell Zucconi was excited, because he remembered to pronounce that "t" in "gentleman." Well, he wasn't the only one who was excited.

"Thirty!" I yelled.

"Forty."

"Fifty!"

When I said it, sweat ran into my mouth. I just couldn't figure it out. I sent the trunk to Frisco. Now he was auctioning it off. What was this—a double-cross?

"Seventy-five" said the voice behind me. And Zucconi was chanting, "Seventy-five once, seventy-five twice—"

"One hundred!" I said, but my throat choked up, so that it was only a gasp. I put air into my lungs to shout, but before the words came out, Zucconi had done it.

". . . seventy-five three times, and—sold!"

Logan got up and walked briskly down the aisle.

I couldn't scream now, either—because there was
something new in my throat. My heart.

Logan walked down the aisle to the side of the platform
and slipped bills to Zucconi's assistant at a little table. He
didn't wait for a receipt.

Zucconi was working on Lot 457, and nobody bothered
to watch Logan when he took out his pocketknife and
began to pry the lid off the trunk.

That is, nobody watched him except me. I watched
from way over next to the door. I should have run, but I
had to look. I had to.

Logan was prying at the lock, and he was so excited the
knife kept slipping. I didn't blame him—I was excited,
too.

Then at last the lid gave, and there was a loud creak,
and the trunk opened.

Logan looked down inside it. I couldn't see his face.

All at once he slammed the lid back down with all his
might. He shrugged, and walked up the aisle toward me. I
didn't run, just waited. I put my hands behind me, holding
the blackjack very tight.

Logan drew abreast of me, but he didn't stop. He didn't
even look at me. He just walked straight out of the store
and disappeared down the street.

I went down that aisle in five steps and tore the lid off
the trunk.

It was full of old books.

▲

It's too bad there were no track officials around to watch
me. I broke the world's record for the one-hundred-yard
dash, getting into Frisco's back room.

Fat Frisco was hunched over his desk. He didn't look so
hot to me, because he resembled a big fat killer shark.

Then he smiled, and that was better. He still looked like a killer shark, but a happy killer shark.

I didn't return his smile. I grabbed him by the nearest roll of fat on his neck and pulled him to his feet.

"All right," I said. "Spit it out. Where's the body?"

"Body? What body, Tony?"

I shook him into quivering blubber. "I sent it to you in the trunk. I know you got it, because you just auctioned the trunk off now."

"I never got any trunk with a body in it, Tony. So help me—"

He was going to need help before I got through with him. The help of a licensed embalmer. Two kills come as easy as one.

"Cut it. I saw the trunk auctioned off out there. The big green trunk I bought from you yesterday to hide Mae's body in. I had the express company deliver it last night to you here and—"

"We didn't get any trunks in." He blinked his eyes and shook. I helped him shake a little.

"Now I understand," Frisco wheezed. "That trunk I sold you yesterday was part of a job lot I bought. All green, all alike. I filled the rest with junk: old books and stuff. You saw one of them out on the platform. But I didn't get any trunk by express from you."

I dropped Frisco in a hurry and picked up the phone.

What Ace Express had to tell me didn't help much. Sure, they called for my trunk. But the landlady was out. Nobody there to let them in. They figured on picking it up again this noon—

"Cancel the order!" I yelled and hung up, sweating.

This was sweet. Very sweet. The trunk was still sitting in my apartment. We still had to get it out without Logan seeing it.

I explained matters to Fat Frisco. He shrugged.

"What can I do?" he said.

"Plenty. That is, if you're interested in these items."

I fished the ice out of my inside pocket. It made a very pretty glitter on his desk. But it had to go some to match the glitter in Fat Frisco's eyes.

"Well, I'll be damned!" he whispered.

Why should I contradict him? It seemed like a pretty sure prediction.

"All right," I snapped. "Where's the moola?"

He opened a drawer in his desk. When I saw the big bills, my eyes made the glitter unanimous.

"Everything's okay, then?" he asked. "It's a deal?"

"Just one little detail left. You have to help me dispose of that body. But fast."

He started to shrug again, but I was tired of that routine. I picked up the jewelry, and let him grab my arm.

"All right, Tony. I've got it figured. We can get the body ourselves. Right now. We'll take my truck. Pick up the trunk and bring it back here."

"What about Logan?"

"You'll be inside the truck, won't you?" Frisco reminded me. "And he won't pay any attention to my truck pulling out."

Frisco was right, it turned out. Because when we drove out of the alley ten minutes later, Logan wasn't around to pay attention. I couldn't spot him anywhere on the street.

I got a little happier as we drove along. I was beginning to figure things straight, now. There was nothing to worry about.

Logan didn't know about a body. He didn't know there *was* a body. The dumb shamus was just tagging me until he could spot those jewels. When I bid on the trunk, he figured the ice was inside—so he outbid me. After he saw what he'd bought, he went back to headquarters to sulk.

Well, by the time he got over his little pet, it would be too late. Quicklime would have the body, Frisco would have the ice, and I would have my eighteen grand and a ticket south for Connie and me.

It was perfect. When we went through the hall and upstairs without meeting anybody, it was still perfect.

I opened the door of the apartment and walked in. The trunk still stood in the center of the rug, lid down. That was perfect, too.

"Everything set?" Frisco asked.

"I'll make sure," I told him. I took a quick look around the place. Nothing had been disturbed. We were clear.

We lifted the heavy trunk and carried it down to the truck. I slid it in back and then climbed in next to Frisco. The motor started.

I looked at the street ahead and smiled into the bright sunshine. It looked so pretty—I couldn't understand how all at once everything turned black.

▲

I can't understand it even now, when I'm sitting here, with the D.A.'s reporter taking the whole confession down in shorthand.

Of course, Logan is here too, and he explained a lot.

He said he didn't get suspicious at all until he saw me bidding on that trunk at the auction. He figured the jewels were planted there, and he was disappointed, of course.

But when he marched out, he got to thinking. Guess he'd read about the trunk murders, too, in his day.

Because he started calling the express companies in town—and when he hit the Ace Express, it was the tip-off. So he beat it over to my place and found the stuff.

They had already picked Mae up—a lot less of her than I'd once picked up—when Frisco and I arrived.

Then we came, carried the trunk out to the truck, put it in, and started away.

That's when Logan sapped us, of course. And here we are.

Still, it bothers me. How could Logan sneak up behind and knock me over the head? I know for a fact he wasn't hiding outside, and he wasn't crouching down in back of the truck when I put the trunk in. I know, because I looked.

I just asked Logan that question, and he told me.

I might have known the answer.

He was hiding inside the trunk.

THE WAY OF A MAN WITH A MAID

Ray Russell

RAY RUSSELL became an "Official" member of the Group in 1960, when he left his job as fiction editor of *Playboy* in Chicago to move to Los Angeles with his wife, Ada Beth, and their two children. He intended to write for motion pictures and did, in fact, script several, beginning with *Mr. Sardonicas* (based on his classic Gothic novella), but his first love was prose fiction. He had eight novels published, along with nine collections of shorter works, and his horror novel, *Incubus*, was a best-selling paperback.

The story that follows is excerpted from an unpublished novel-length manuscript called *The Mountebank's Mistress*, set in the 1800s. "The Way of a Man with a Maid" is a chapter title. Unhappily, this may be Russell's final piece of hitherto-unprinted fiction. As this book went to press, Ray died following a decade-long series of strokes.

Therefore, "The Way of a Man with a Maid" becomes all the more valuable, reminding us of Ray's period expertise, bawdy sense of fun, and unquestioned writing talent. Although he produced reams of crime fiction, fantasy, and SF, this present tale is a full-bodied Victorian Romance with all the trimmings. The tale is narrated by Lady Rachel Paige in the form of a personal memoir. In it she describes, in wicked, often hilarious detail, her wedding night—which is followed by a spirited account of her passionate love affair with a famous British actor, climaxed in a scene of betrayal and dramatic confrontation.

Here, then, a farewell performance from a man whose contributions to imaginative literature have always been richly rewarding.

W.K.S.

I am split in two, and have been so from my birth. My left eye is bright blue, a gift from my father, and my right eye is deep brown, a hue bestowed upon it by my umber-eyed mother. This kind of aberration, I have been told, is not as

uncommon as one might think. Some have said that my
light left eye is twinkling and saucy, and my dark right eye
sombre and grave. One man called them sun and shadow.
Others have seen in my ocular discrepancy a sign of a divided character, of duplicity, inconsistency, inconstancy.
The curious thing is that many people do not notice this
anomaly at all, or notice it only after they have been ac-
quainted with me for a considerable span of time. This
may speak ill of their powers of observation, but I prefer to
believe that it means my condition is not disfiguring, and
perhaps not even especially distinctive. In all other ways, I
am reasonably symmetrical from head to toe.

Indeed, *so* symmetrical am I that I can perform most
manual functions, including writing, with either hand and
with equal dexterity—although I must own that passages
set down with my left hand appear to have been written by
another person. Perhaps they are: perhaps they are written
by a hidden self, an unborn twin, a *gauche* Rachel, a
Rachel "sinister" in the heraldic meaning of the word? In
any case, you take my meaning about being split in two.

My earliest memory is that of dipping a biscuit into a
cup of milk to soften it for my presumably toothless gums,
and discovering to my disappointment that the milk was all
gone and the cup empty. I wept with rage and dashed the
cup to the floor. How old I was, I do not know, but I think
I was not yet one year of age. What a silly picture for the
mind to trap and retain. Do memories hold hidden meanings, as dreams are reputed to do? Sometime I shall have
to ask my brother Wilfrid's sister-in-law, who is said to
possess powers of divination.

Indeed, she even has a small reputation as a sibyl. The
year after Wilfrid married Melissa Worthing, daughter of
the Bishop of Hans Town, there was a grand gathering of
the Summerfield and Worthing families at Wilfrid's new
house in Berkeley Square. Melissa's elder sister, Esmeralda, a widow whose slain husband had been a gypsy, pro-

vided diversion amongst the ladies when we were all gossiping in our nightdresses in Melissa's sitting-room, just before retiring. She demonstrated the art of pedomancy—a curious practise which is exactly like palm-reading, but performed with the sole of the foot. I, unshod for bed, was her subject.

Esmeralda bade me sit on a chair. She perched on an ottoman and took my bare foot in her hand. I remember that her touch tickled and I uttered an involuntary giggle. "Silence," she said, and peered intently at my naked sole. (At my naked *soul*, as well, perhaps!)

At length, she spoke: "You have two daughters, Rachel." I nodded. (Everybody knew *that*.) "Your next child will be a son."

I was delighted to hear this. "Are you quite sure?" I asked. "My husband and I almost have resigned ourselves to producing nothing but girls. Even the stillborn baby of his first wife was a female. How can you be so certain?"

"Because your love will be keen," she said.

I wondered: can an unprecedented keenness of love, a summit of rapture higher than ever it had been before, truly result in the birth of a man-child? Was that her meaning? If so, what an old wives' tale, I thought. But I said nothing, and merely put on my slipper. Now, of course, I understand her words.

It is difficult for me to believe, but next year I shall be fully a half-century old! Whither has my time fled? It seems but yesterday that I was in the spring of my girlhood; and the bright summer of my life still glows warmly in my memory. The brisk winds of autumn followed all too soon; and now I sniff the snow and sleet and bitter cold of the winter that has come upon me. To every thing there is a season, we are taught, but the seasons of my life have come and gone with cruel swiftness, and ahead of me lie the mysterious climate and unknown seasons of that other sphere to which I must repair in what will seem to be the twinkling of an eye. For, as the clock of mortal life ticks ever later, the hours and minutes—yea, the very seconds— grow ever shorter.

When I have finished writing this secret account, it shall be thrice-sealed and put into the hands of my solicitor with instructions that it may not be opened and read until—at the earliest—I and my offspring have ceased to inhabit this world.

Those offspring are still, at the time of this writing, young. None of them has, as yet, given me grandchildren. It will be many years before such grandchildren (by then well into middle age, no doubt) may read these disclosures by a long dead grandmother. Such a wide chasm of time will not likely be spanned by a bridge of embarrassment. The follies of our parents' parents are a source of humor, not humiliation.

Why is she writing at all?

I hear your question, my dear descendants, and I will answer it:

I am writing because I must. I am writing because I may not speak. I am writing because silence is torture to me, and with this pen-point I physick myself and lance a flaming boil.

I am writing in the hope that a glorious episode of my life may not die when I die, and that the storms and sorrows and searing, soaring joys of a great, if guilty, love may not be banished forever from human memory as if that love never had flowered in my breast.

And I write to say, to you who read these words, that love is a precious treasure, worth any cost; that you must never spurn it; that you must seek it, and seize it, and grasp it greedily for as long as you can. You must break any rule and pay any price for it. As a wise woman once said to me: Lie, cheat, hurt if you must, but sink deep into love; cover yourself with it, if only for a year, a day, an hour. For life is death without it.

⟡

I was born in Suffolk in 1784, the fifth of my parents' six children, and christened Rachel, after an ancestor of my father's. His name was Barnaby Summerfield. My mother was the former Phoebe Fanshaw. I have two brothers, both older than I: Roger (born 1769) and Wilfrid (1778); and a younger sister, Hannah (born 1788). Two other children, Philip and Christopher, died in the years of their births (1772 and 1775). I lived in Suffolk with my parents until I was married.

I first met Sir Peregrine Paige late in the summer of 1806 when my mother, moved by his loneliness, invited him to be our dinner guest. I was then twenty-two and he was thirty-three, the eldest of three children. He came from a very old Suffolk family, but was not rich, having only his house and the income from some land on which tenants resided. He was reputed to be looking for a wealthy wife and a large dowry; in return he offered his ancient lineage and the prestige of his baronetcy. His father was the late Sir Edmund Paige, a bit of a spendthrift and scoundrel, we'd heard, who'd claimed that the baronetcy could be traced all the way back to those first baronets of all, created by James I ostensibly to install "a new Dignitie between Barons and Knights," but in truth to raise money for the crown by the sale of such titles. Sir Peregrine's ancestor, Jonathan Paige, received his "new Dignitie" in 1616, and died in the same year of "a marvellous Distemper, come on him by reason of a surfeit of Sack." Shakespeare also died in that year.

I thought Sir Peregrine to be a striking figure of a man, despite—or possibly because of—the eleven years' advantage he had of me. He was quite tall, slender as a birch branch, and of fair complexion, with pale green eyes. Moreover, he appeared to be worldly and all-knowing.

⋏

Nearly a year passed before Sir Peregrine began courting
me in earnest; and that courtship was a formal, stately pro-
cedure that occupied the better part of yet another year.

In the early summer of 1808, almost two years after our
first meeting, we were married in my parents' house. No
member of his family was present, for both of his parents
were dead, and two younger siblings, Pendragon and Mor-
gan, had long since quit England to dwell in foreign
climes.

Almost immediately, we came to London to set up residence in a handsome new edifice in Duchess Street,
Cavendish Square. Peregrine said that he did not want us
to live in his Suffolk house, which had been the scene of
Drusilla's—his first wife's—death. "Let us make a fresh
start" were his words, and my large dowry made the fresh
start possible. Hannah was consumed by envy, of course,
for to live in London was her notion of Paradise.

Our house was done in the latest style. The excessive
wood carving of the last century was but little in evidence.
The doorways throughout, for example, reflected the
newer taste. Gone were the old architectural overdoors and
broken pediments: these had given way to simple six-panel
mahogany doors in plain frames. Our walls were just flat
plaster surfaces, most of them painted, some covered with
wallpapers and Pompeian decorations. Large mirrors
graced many of the walls. As for colors, the rooms were
done in subtle tones: maroon, yellow, fawn, lilac, pea-
green, light blue, cream, pale terra cotta, Chinese pink,
buff, and the like. The old-style mantels of carved wood
were absent: ours were of marble: black with gold trimming, mostly, but here and there white, grey, or rose marble were used. These mantels were in the classic spirit,
unblemished by overmuch ornamentation, and most of

them had free-standing columns with Doric or Ionic capitals. The whole effect might be summed up in the word "austere"—a reflection and expression, I have no doubt, of Peregrine's character.

An even sharper reflection of Peregrine could be seen in one of the most important rooms in the house: his study. This was fitted out with his desk, his maps, his endless shelves of books in many languages, including Greek. "This," he once said, taking down one volume of a many-volumed work in that ancient tongue, "is my Bible, so to speak. *The History of the Peloponnesian War*, by Thucydides, a great historian whom I revere above all others."

The staff of our house was headed up by two treasures Peregrine had brought with him from his former residence in Suffolk: the indispensable butler, Higgins, and Mrs. Forbes, a young woman of unparalleled culinary talent.

A wedding trip to the Continent was deemed inadvisable by my husband. "The time is out of joint," he said, opening one of the many maps of which he was fond. "There is strife on the Iberian Peninsula, and I feel certain that Wellesley must soon lead an expedition into Portugal. Bonaparte's damnable influence in the Mediterranean; his deliberate attempt to destroy English trade there; our reprisals against the goods and ships of Tuscany, Naples, and whatnot, make it unwise to travel to Italy. France, of course, is our enemy. Switzerland holds no interest for me. Your father's homeland, Austria, would be an embarrassing place to visit, I think, after her ignominious defeat at Austerlitz obliged her to withdraw from the war, her tail between her legs, as it were . . ."

("But that was two—almost two and a half—years ago," I said to myself, wondering if Peregrine had a simple aversion to travel, belying one of the meanings of his Christian name?)

". . . And so," he concluded, after naming several other European nations, "we must postpone our wedding trip until things are more settled, and content ourselves with England for the present. Unless," he added as he folded up his map of the Continent, "you wish to journey through Scotland or Ireland?"

"Ireland is reputed to be infested with French agents," I replied, "stirring up discontent against us. I should not feel safe there now. As for Scotland, I have seen it and, what is worse, heard it—that is to say, heard bagpipes. I did not enjoy their sound."

"It has been truly said," Peregrine pointed out, "that the definition of a gentleman is one who can play the bagpipes—but does not."

"Of course," I said, "there is Wales . . ."

"That is an exotic land," he replied, "inhabited chiefly by a strange, one might say Oriental, race. They are short of stature, swarthy of countenance, and are supposed to have come from the deserts of the East, from Araby and Egypt. Their faces resemble those on Assyrian stones."

"But surely some Welshmen are as tall and fair as you?"

"They are the Celts," he informed me, "who represent a higher stage in the development of civilization. But I fear that they are among the minority in Wales."

"You are so learned, Peregrine!" I said admiringly.

⋏

Our nuptial night took place in the Duchess Street house. It was preceded by a short though serious speech by my lord and master:

"No doubt your mother has told you some of what you may expect as a wife," he said, "but I fear that she, with that delicacy we cherish in ladies, may have employed euphemism and circumlocution; and these may have left certain matters somewhat clouded in your perception."

"Certain matters?"

"Certain physiological matters. It will not have escaped

your notice that men are not in all regards the same as women . . ."

"Sometimes," I said, "they seem almost to be members of an alien race, like the inhabitants of Wales."

"That is understandable. The beard, the deep voice, the lack of that . . . er . . . fullness that distinguishes the bosoms of your sex—all these declare us to be different. And yet, my dear Rachel, I must tell you that these differences, as great as they are, you must consider trifling, when measured against the most important difference of all."

He paused, and poured himself a glass of barley water. I declined his offer of a drink, and urged him to go on.

"I have spoken," he continued, "of a fullness which men lack and which women possess. There is, if I may put it in this way, another fullness—which *women* lack and which *men* possess; an amplitude, a generosity of natural endowment in a place where women are favoured with only an aperture, niche, or indentation."

"How curious," I said.

"This . . . masculine fullness," he went on, "is fashioned by our Creator in such a manner that it may be . . . accommodated . . . by the corresponding feminine part."

"Like a sword and a sheath?"

"Precisely," he whispered, and sipped his barley water. "Remarkable."

"The coming together of . . . of sword and sheath . . . is the principal event of the wedding night," said Peregrine. "It is the act which, if bride and groom are blest, may, with the passage of time, result in the birth of children. It is known as the connubial union, the carnal congress, and sometimes as the conjugal privilege or marital duty."

"Is it also known," I asked, "as 'fucking?' For I have overheard simple country folk use that word when referring to an act similar to that which you have described."

He cleared his throat. "It is a word I should not like to hear from your lips again, Madam."

"I am so sorry, Peregrine: have I been naughty?"

He took my hand and patted it. "It is your innocence that is at fault," he said. "Your innocence, which is also your most valued treasure. Words of that kind are common currency in soldiers' camps and in certain disorderly houses, but no lady may utter them—and, to my mind, no true gentleman."

"I will never utter that word again," I promised him. "But you have alluded to other words 'of that kind,' and I fear that I may, in my innocence, utter *them*. Will you, perhaps, write down for me on a sheet of paper a list of them, together with their meanings, so that I may be sure to avoid them?"

"That will not, I think, be necessary," he assured me.

The reader will have guessed, perhaps, that although I came a virgin to my husband's bed, I was not quite so innocent as he thought me to be. One cannot be raised up in the country, and see how bulls disport themselves amongst cows; stallions amongst mares; indeed, dogs amongst bitches—and remain entirely in ignorance of what is involved in what Scripture calls the way of a man with a maid.

⚊

I was instructed by Peregrine, shortly thereafter, to prepare myself for retiring. "I will join you anon," he promised.

Mamma had given me a nightdress made of the most becoming white silk, trimmed with rose-coloured lace. I wore this, and climbed into the four-post bed, under the counterpane, to await my bridegroom.

Whilst I waited, I looked back on his courtship and on our long period of engagement. He had been attentive, solicitous, chivalrous; a model of courtesy. Not once had he overstepped the bounds of decent behavior, or taken unseemly advantage of me by stealing kisses or placing his hands upon me. He had, after a time, taken my hand in his, it is true; and had on more than one occasion kissed *it*; and had searched my eyes beseechingly; but had done no more than that. This plenitude of gentlemanly conduct was not what I had led myself to expect of an ardent swain and I surmised that it was his age that had cooled his youthful embers—for he was fully thirty-five years old by the time we were married.

The bedroom door opened, and Peregrine entered the room. He wore a sumptuous sashed dressing-gown over a long linen nightshirt, and on his head was a nightcap with a tassel at its lop-sided apex. He approached the bed and sat upon it. "Do not be afraid," he said solemnly.

"I am not afraid, Peregrine," I said.

He stood up, removed his dressing-gown, folded it, and placed it neatly on a nearby chair. Then, turning down the counterpane, he climbed into the bed and lay next to me, staring straight up at the canopy of our bed.

After a moment, I said, "Peregrine?"

"Yes, my dear?"

"Must you wear that cap? It *is* summer."

He removed it and held it in his hand. He cleared his throat, as if he were about to speak, but he said nothing.

After a moment of silence, I decided to take the initiative, and so I turned over and lay on my stomach.

"What are you doing?" he asked.

"Nothing," I replied. "Merely . . . making myself ready . . ."

"Ready?"

"For the coming together you spoke of. The sword and the sheath . . ."

"In *that* position?"

"Is it incorrect? When I have seen bulls and cows . . ."

"My *dear* Rachel . . ."

"And stallions and mares, and dogs and—"

"What is proper for beasts," he said, "is not proper for men and women. We are not beasts, my love."

"Then . . ."

"We are distinguished from the beasts," he said, "not only by our outward appearances, and the superiority of our minds, and by our immortal souls. We are distinguished by this, as well: that, of all God's creatures, we alone come together in the act of procreation face to face."

"Oh, good!" I said. "That is ever so much more jolly."

"I hardly think that 'jolly' is the appropriate word," he responded. "The act is too sacred to be called that. But certainly it is more pleasant to face one's beloved partner during the union, than to—than to—emulate the brute beasts."

"That is what I meant."

I had got off my stomach by this time, and was lying on my side, facing him. Another moment passed, and I said, "Peregrine dear . . . I feel a curious prodding through my nightdress. Can it be that masculine endowment of which you spoke?"

"Yes," he said hoarsely.

"Shall I remove my nightdress?"

"That will not be necessary," he assured me. "There is no need to offend your maiden's modesty. It will suffice if you will merely . . . raise it . . . hitch it up, as it were, to a point above . . . above your . . . waist."

"Very well. There."

"Thank you. That will do nicely."

I could tell that he, under the counterpane, was hitching up his nightshirt.

"Goodness," I said, "that feels to be quite an 'amplitude,' indeed." His part had brushed against me and I was surprised at its adamantine solidity. It felt like one of the large beef-joint bones we used to fling to our mastiff, Nero, at home. "May I see it?" I asked.

"I think not," he said. "It is no object of beauty. The sight of it would disgust you, I fear."

"If you say so, Peregrine. Would it be all right if I touched it?"

"I would voice no objection," he replied in a whisper.

"Heavens!" I said, marvelling at what my fingers encountered. "This is, in truth, a mighty weapon, a true Excalibur! Can my poor little scabbard accommodate it?"

He said, "There may be, at first, some difficulty, but you have my word that, with patience and perseverance on both sides, there will be accommodation and to spare."

"I must place my faith in you, Peregrine, for you have the benefit of experience in this matter."

"Thank you, my dear," he said gratefully. "And now, if you would assist me by . . . separating your limbs? . . ."

"Like this?"

"No, not your arms. Your—ah, yes, excellent."

"Gracious!" I exclaimed a moment later. "I feel distinctly uncomfortable. Are you sure that you are doing it correctly?"

"Trust me," he murmured in my ear.

"Gracious!" I said again.

Before too long a span of time had been spent, Peregrine shuddered and gasped; then rolled his weight off me and lay at my side, staring up at the canopy again.

I dared not speak. He was so silent. I sensed that he was displeased with me. But, after some moments, I took courage and said in a small voice:

"I'm sorry, Peregrine."

Still gazing at the canopy, he blinked and said, "Sorry?"

"You must be patient with me," I pleaded. "I am a green girl. I have had no experience. I am ignorant and awkward, and I know that I have been a disappointment to you, but . . ."

He turned to me. "A disappointment?" he said. "My dear love, you are everything that a man could ever desire in a wife."

"Oh, Peregrine, I am *so* glad."

He put his nightcap on his head again, and soon he was asleep.

It took me longer to fall asleep. Before I did so, I asked myself if I had been foolish to have expected something more, something higher, something sublime on my wedding night.

Nine months later, on the tenth of April, 1809, our first daughter, Constance, was born.

⋏

[Rachel falls deeply under the spell of stage actor Edmund Kean and begins a tumultuous affair. Russell had chosen a real-life lover for his fictional heroine. Edmund Keen (who died in 1833) was lauded for his brilliantly-realized Shakespearean roles as Shylock, Iago, Lear, and Richard III. He was (and is) considered to be one of England's greatest actors.]

⋏

How shall I write of love? The body's thirst and slaking I can set down well enough, but the soul of love, the sublime and disembodied spirit of it—these elude my pen like quicksilver. They need, for their conveyance, the winds of vaulting Pegasus; they cry for Byron, Shelley, Keats, the radiant poets of my youth—all gone at the time of this writing, long dead, alas, cut down still young, their singing silenced in mid-song.

As I sit here at my desk, the mantle of my nearing-fifty years heavy on me, the darker strands amongst my tresses outnumbered by the grey, I see again across the wide abyss of time that purple couch; I feel the richness of its velvet against my naked back; I hear the crackling of the fire in that room; I smell the mingled essences of our bodies; I taste the flavor of his skin.

What is glory? What is grace? How are they defined? I know that I have felt them, been embraced by them, and have been lifted high by them to within the reach of Heaven. At almost the age of thirty, after nearly six years of marriage and the bearing of two children, I first felt love—roaring love—mountainous love—love that knew not shame nor limit.

We devoured each other like hungry cannibals in those furious first minutes of tumbling and grappling. We rolled off the couch, onto the carpet. It was over, in a withering blast, before it began. Then we set about the slow and patient replenishing of powers; his adoration of my every inch, and mine of his. My shoes and stockings he at last removed, and flung aside. I stript him of every thread he wore. We stroked and plumbed and kneaded—this in hot lust certainly, but as if seeking love, as well, searching it out, rooting it out, delving for rare new nuggets of love: for sweet new morsels of love: Where may we find thee, love? in this crevasse? on this hummock? . . . Where may we taste thee? in this tender bud? this swollen fruit?

We disported ourselves like beasts, like angels, like children. We were innocent, we were knowing; we were conventional, we were innovative; we were obvious, we were subtle. We were not fastidious.

For to be fastidious is to offend Nature by shrinking from it in disgust. In this way, we insult God, saying: Lord, Thy works are not dainty enough for my exquisite sensibilities; Thy creations oft are gross and coarse, or flecked with slime, or scaly, or hairy, or pungent with indelicate musk.

If one would praise the Almighty, one must then revel in His works, and take them whole, adore their very grossness, savour the oozing quiddity of that slime of which He seems to be inordinately fond. Love is not nice. God's love assuredly is not; and human love, its copy, must not presume to be.

In words, my lover praised the beauty of my every part; yes, even those that surely could have had no beauty in them he found in some wise dear and precious. A little hidden tea-rose he declared the buried button of my after passage, if you please!—for nothing about me was vile to him, no place ugly or forbidden.

We traveled far together, exploring wild, uncharted continents (*in*continents!) of passion—and if the reader will be tolerant and excuse the extravagance of my figures (they match the extravagance of my love), I will risk saying that we traversed lush, steaming, tropic forests . . . swam rapids . . . climbed awesome, craggy ranges . . . endured simooms and savageries . . . were shaken to our bones by mighty earthquakes . . . and returned at last to safe harbor in that house in Cecil Street, the drawing-room of that house, the carpet—magic carpet!—of that room, clinging naked to each other for protection.

The fire, untended for hours, had gone out. We did not heed the cold. I was a creature of all feeling, with not a reasonable thought in my mind. My home, my husband, my children, my very name did not exist for me: all that existed, all that mattered in the world was that moment, that man, that miracle.

"I'd best be going," I said in a whisper.

"Must you?"

"It grows late."

"Time is a tyrant. It is the enemy of love."

"I have a household in my care; a husband and children in my stewardship." He groaned at the mention of them.

"When may we meet again, Rachel?"

I should have said—I wanted to say—Never, my darling! Never, my love! This precious time has been a dream; this lapse has been a glorious mistake; it must never happen again. But I could not make my lips utter those words.

I said, "I do not know."

"You will be at the theatre to-night?"

"Yes."

"Come to my dressing-room after the performance."

"I will be with my husband and our friends . . ."

"Bring them. I must *see* you, at least, even if I may not touch you; love you in silence, if not in deed. You *will* come? Say that you will!"

I nodded.

He seized my hand and kissed it. "Ah, bless you, Rachel!"

"But when we, *if* we may be alone again, I cannot say . . ."

" '*If?*' That word is like a knife, stabbing my heart!"

"We have done wrong."

"Nothing so blest with joy can be wrong."

"It will be difficult . . ."

"We will manage. Love will prod our brains—you will see!—and we'll devise such strategies, such devices! . . ."

"Such deceptions," I said ruefully.

"Why, what of that, my love? They will but add a sauce to our delights."

"You *are* a pagan, Edmund," I said.

"Perhaps I am," he owned. "If to love love and feel no guilt at loving love be pagan—then I am a pagan for a certainty."

He sprang to his feet—naked as a babe!—and, with arms outstretched and with the full theatrical power of his cold-coarsened voice, declaimed:

". . . Great God! I'd rather be
A Pagan suckled in a creed outworn;
So might I, standing on this pleasant lea,
Have glimpses that would make me less forlorn;
Have sight of Proteus rising from the sea;
Or hear old Triton blow his wreathèd horn!"

In that splendid instant, it seemed that he was a faun from some Garden long before the Fall, a sinless, child-like thing that did not need the tears of Christ to wash him white as snow.

The instant passed; he smiled shyly. "Wordsworth is not my favorite poet," he said, "but *those* lines speak to my soul. They are rather fine."

He sneezed violently. "You'd best put on your clothes," I said, "or you will make your cold worse than it is."

Before he put on his stockings, I embraced and kissed his dear legs, and ran my fingers over what I had not, in love's frenzy, marked before: the scars of old wounds or welts.

"My dear, what are these?" I asked, kissing them.

"From the irons," he said simply.

"Irons? You wore *irons?*" I saw him as a prisoner in gaol, loaded down with fetters.

"Until I was seven," he told me, "to cure a crookedness of the knees. Day-irons and night-irons. The night-irons were the worst."

"You poor darling."

"It was long ago."

He put on his stockings, hiding the pitiable weals. I, too, began to dress. "I have lost a shoe," I announced, after I had put on everything else.

"Only a shoe?" he said. "I have lost my heart."

We searched for the shoe together, on our hands and knees, peering under the purple couch, under chairs, tables, the pianoforte, laughing, embracing, kissing. We found it at last, lying on its side on top of the mantelpiece, whence it had been flung by Edmund in his witless, blind desire.

▲

[Rachel eventually discovers that Edmund is also bedding down a certain "Mrs. Cox," and confronts them in this highly-charged climax.]

⟡

When I burst into the bedroom, Edmund and Mrs. Cox were, as I had expected them to be, naked abed, *in flagrante delicto*.

"What the devil?!" he cried.

"Bloody hell," she said. "Who is this woman, Mr. Kean? Is she your wife?"

"Shut up, you old whore!" I snarled at her. Turning to Edmund, I said, "Sir: I wish you joy of your new, if aging, mattress—forgive me, I meant *maîtresse*—whose name, I am told, is, with apt plurality, *Cox*; and who, no doubt, if she were to have as many of them protruding *out* of her as have been plunged *into* her during the course of her long, *long* life, would be a prodigy to affright the eye. You will remember, surely, the line in *Hamlet* about the quills upon the fretful potpentine."

"What impudence!" said Mrs. Cox.

"Rachel—" he started to say, but in that instant I pulled Peregrine's pistol from my hand-bag. I was thankful that I had become, in the early days of our courtship, an expert at shooting it, hitting the mark nine out of ten times. Dropping my hand-bag to the floor, I held the pistol in both hands and pointed it in the direction of the bed.

"My God!" said Edmund. "Take care with that thing!"

"*You* take care," I retorted, "lest Mrs. Cox, and you, become the butt of pamphlet-writers' doggerel—for her Christian name lends itself to several unfortunate rhymes, such as: A certain woman known as Charlotte . . ." I fired off the pistol with a *bang!*—blowing off the brass ball at one of the bed's four corners. "Whose many sins have stained her scarlet . . ." *Bang!* and another was blown off. "Is *keen* to bed an actor varlet . . ." *Bang!* went the third. "To whom she lewdly plays the harlot!" And *bang!* went the fourth and last brass ball, clattering to the attic floor.

By this time, in a wise panic, both Edmund and Mrs. Cox had scrambled, naked, under the bed, from whence I now saw him peering.

"For the love of God, Rachel!" he cried. "Would you murder us?"

I replied, "Murder a whoreson bastard and his decrepit old strumpet? Go to the gallows for such low creatures? Neither of you is worth it! But be grateful, you miserable mountebank, that the only balls I shot off were *brass* ones!"

Feeling positively splendid—for the discharging of that pistol had also discharged the greatest portion of my rage (no wonder that men love shooting!)—I turned and left the attic, walked out of the inn, straight into the waiting hackney coach, and was home before Peregrine returned. I replaced the antique pistol in his desk, then ascended to my sitting-room to await dinner and to contemplate the condition of my spirit.

I determined that I was hurt, but not mortally wounded. Had I been younger and less seasoned by life, I might have thought it the end of the world; but as it was, I uttered a sigh of regret and a prayer of thanks for the joy our love had brought me and for the closing of that cherished interlude.

Yes, I was strangely thankful to Mrs. Cox for bringing the episode to an end. Without her intervention I never should have had the strength to stop seeing Edmund. The risk of discovery would have grown greater (what a narrow escape I'd had from the blackmailing Mr. Rankwort!); the shame of scandal would have dangled over our heads like a blade, and eventually that blade would have fallen. Our love was destined to die some time; let it die now, I told myself, quickly and cleanly, not by long, protracted torment. I was no green girl, and harbored no illusions about eternal love. It was Edmund, my dear dreamer, who was nourished by such fancies. They were sweet, his illusions; they were noble; and for as long as I live I will re-member his words—"Our love will outlive these bodies. It will outlive the stars. It is a jewel that will be gathered up and treasured by the angels through all eternity"—and I will remember, too, with a pang, that even whilst I admired those pretty sentiments, I never believed them, not even in the moment that he spoke them. And so I turned that lovely page in the album of my life, and resumed my duties as a wife and mother.

HUNGRY ALICE
Jerry Sohl

JERRY SOHL grew up in Chicago where he attended Central College. He worked as a news reporter, photographer, telegraph editor, and feature writer until joining the service in World War II as part of the Army Airways Communication System. Married during wartime, he fathered a son and two daughters. He and his wife Jean now live in Thousand Oaks, in the Conejo Valley of California.

Jerry is the author of some twenty-five novels, most in the SF genre (such as *Costigan's Needle* and *Night Slaves*). His mainstream novels include *The Lemon Eaters* and *The Spun Sugar Hole*.

In the 1950s, living in California, Sohl became an early member of the Group. He was active as a scriptwriter, with three of his screenplays produced as well as a host of teleplays for such shows as *Naked City*, *Route 66*, *The Outer Limits*, and *The Twilight Zone*. Affable, pragmatic, with an easygoing personality, Jerry is also a talented piano player and an expert on chess and bridge (having written books on both).

"Hungry Alice," the story he provides for this anthology, reminds us that he also wrote scripts for *Star Trek*. It deliberately harks back to the "what-kind-of-place-is-this?" stories of Robert Sheckley and Philip K. Dick from the 1950s. A nostalgic SF adventure.

Ever been chased through deep space by a planet? After you've read "Hungry Alice" the question won't seem so bizarre.

W.F.N.

I t was on Specialist Cray Beeley's watch that the *Firestorm*'s Object Alarm went off, filling the cabin with a strident, raucous blast and flashing red lights. Nervous and exhausted, Beeley joined the other Deep Space Sounders at their detectors to pinpoint the object on their grid screens at 7934.

Was it the *EX241*, the ship they'd been searching for?
Most likely not . . .

Their shift was ending, and Beeley and others of the
Firestorm crew were weary from having monitored endless alarms with no Positives to report. Beeley hoped for
another Not There, and didn't feel guilty about it. He
needed sleep.

But this one *was* different, faint but definitely there.
"Duty's End," as one wag dubbed the object located at
7934, and cracked that it wouldn't be until 7934 AD that
they were likely to find it. Since nothing had been detected
by other Searcher ships since the start of the hunt for the
vessel, *Firestorm* was given permission to zero in on the
area.

Kamon Sigurtu, the only female on the roster, said,
"We'll find it before lunch, if we're lucky, given a few par-
secs either way. Right, fellas?"

The truth was, objects retrieved from or found in space
had their ident signals encoded and sometimes took
months to work out; some rogue Searchers considered
them fair game. Therefore, speed was essential.

They would find the object as long as it emitted a signal. When it did not, they would have to rely on last reported positions, which could be time-consuming.

Captain Grisky had read a message labeled "Secret" in
his orders from Fifth Collective Matrix, the most recent fu-
sion of world states. It proclaimed the existence of another
life-form somewhere in this galaxy, and to beware of it.

For all his years with the Searchers, Grisky had seen no
reason to be paranoid about possibilities of extraterrestrial
life.

In fact, when he thought about it, he found space in-
comprehensible, more vast and mysterious the longer he
served with the Searchers. The captain never liked uncer-
tainties, especially those beyond his own galaxy, yet here

they were moving again toward one, if this was indeed a Possible and not another stellar phantom.

After a course correction, he headed the *Firestorm* straight for the coded grid site and hoped for the best. Space offered many inextricable puzzles. Lights, shadows, life and inert matter that imitated life; he'd seen many of the possibilities, and all were different. *Homo sapiens* vs. whatever else had pushed itself into existence out there. He'd see, and so would his crew, what new horror—or beauty—awaited them.

As the hours passed, the signal grew stronger and stronger, until at last crewman Templer was able to take off his listening gear and announce, "It *is* the ship we've been looking for, Captain." He brought the tapes to the Bridge and placed them before Grisky. "The signal's so clear now we can make out the ship's serial number. It's the *EX241*, all right."

This was one of the few times Templer saw Grisky pleased about something.

"The *EX241* used to be a fighting ship before she was converted to a Searcher," said the captain. "Rouhard Hafner's her captain now. Hell of a good man, Hafner. Shared a few jaunts with him. You talk to him yet?"

"We've tried, Captain, but there's no answer."

"No answer?" Grisky squinted at him. "What the hell's that supposed to mean?"

"They've turned their sound scope in our direction, but have nothing to say."

"Maybe they're listening," Grisky said, leaning back in his captain's chair to consider it. "If they are, then they're still alive, and that's good news. Hafner has his reasons for what he does. Let's move to full power, see what the situation is."

They were nearing their objective, a planet so small it was not even indicated on any of their star charts. The *EX241* was grounded there. Perhaps a crash. No way to tell as yet. At first, because it was green, they thought it must be a planet of water or its equivalent, but when they saw gradations of green they were puzzled. A solid world of nothing but plants?

They were struck by the brilliance of shifting colors. The green became magenta, and other hues played before them, swirling, eddying, all beautifully iridescent.

Grisky shook his head. "By God, I've never seen anything like this." His hard voice was edged with respect.

"Awesome," Sigurtu said in a whispery small voice.

The planet faded to its original green. There was something ominous about it.

When they were near enough, Grisky had the *Firestorm* put into orbit about the mystery planet, which now looked like a striated green marble shooter surrounded by three moons.

"Well, there's certainly vegetation," Beeley declared, using the big scope. "In fact, looks like that's *all* there is."

"Can't have plants without water," Grisky said. "You see any?"

"I see what *looks* like water, sir, but I don't think it is." Beeley relinquished the scope.

The captain took it, moved it this way and that. "Damned strange. Where's the ship? I don't see it."

Crewman Brian said: "She's still giving off the signal, so she's gotta be down there." His eyes flicked to the signal's depth gauge, then the wall computer. "Left vector's 270 meters, the right is—" he squinted for a clearer reading.

"Vector sum is 35," Sigurtu said. "We need to slow down, Captain. The ship's below us. I don't know how far below."

Grisky gave the order, then turned to Sigurtu.

"We'll need to use one of the pods, Captain," she declared.

"Right. I'll want two Searchers aboard a pod to have a look-see down there, and another manned pod standing by. Sigurtu and Beeley in the first pod. Jenniken and Birknick in the second, if we need it."

⋏

The first pod was released from the *Firestorm*.

In the small craft, Sigurtu and Beeley approached the surface of the green mass slowly, cautiously. At first, the planet seemed pure ocean, but that was an illusion. There was no water, but a kind of oil beneath the surface of what looked like growing bamboo.

On the *Firestorm*, Crewman Kranshaw grunted, glancing at the monitor where colors swirled around the descending pod.

Grisky said, "What's wrong, Kranshaw?"

"It's Alice," Kranshaw said to the captain, and seeing he didn't understand, added, "*Alice in Wonderland*, sir." Kranshaw turned away from the screen. "I think we should call it Alice, Captain."

⋏

On Pod One, Beeley was having difficulty steering through the forest of giant bamboo-like plants that swayed in an unsettling rhythm around them.

"What are these things?" Sigurtu asked as she worked to help Beeley at the helm.

"Like bamboo . . . Stems are divided into nodes . . . See? . . . they're called internodes . . . just like the ones we have on Earth."

They hit one rod squarely and the shock was intense.

Grisky's voice crackled over the monitor. "You okay?"

"Hit a bamboo tree," Beeley said. "Found out they don't break."

"Something's going on," said Grisky. "Your picture's become brighter."

"It's brighter, all right," Sigurtu said, steadying herself. "Don't know why."

After a long moment Beeley said, "It's getting pretty hot down here, Captain, and according to my readout the planet's atmosphere is breathable." He asked permission to open one of the hatches.

"The temperature outside is hotter than the Sahara," Grisky replied. "And the humidity is as high as it gets. So that's a negative. You read me, Beeley?"

"Aye, sir."

Now they touched down on Alice, and through the viewscreen they could see the colossus that was the *EX241*. Long and sleek, lying on its side on the ground, its main hatch yawning open.

"It's the *EX241*. We've found her, sir."

"Any sign of Hafner?" asked the captain.

"No, sir," replied Beeley. "But *something* is happening."

Beeley and Sigurtu saw several figures come surging out of the ship's open hatch. Crewmen from the ship—wearing what appeared to be green clothing; even their *skin* was green. But as the figures swarmed closer it became obvious that the green was actually a growth, cloaking their bodies like cheese mold.

A man's head appeared beyond the heavy glass of the viewscreen. His dull green face was . . . surrounded by chunky, cilia-like hair. It was Captain Hafner. He beat at the glass fiercely with his fists, his face gone dog mad. Behind him, the enormous green bamboo trees were in motion—moving toward the pod.

Inside the *Firestorm*, Grisky jerked around to the big screen.

*He was seeing something alive in space. He had no time
to try to work out how it came to be or what its purpose in
the universe was. But it was about to enfold the pod.*

Beeley reacted to the captain's harsh voice: "Emergency! Up and out of there as fast as you can make it."

"It's the equivalent of a Venus's flytrap," Sigurtu declared, as she watched the swaying trees advance in a men-
acing green wave.

They *had* to lift off. Now!

Grisky watched the pod rise, shooting upward, dimpled
by collisions with the trees, but thank God whole. Safe and
whole.

He tersely gave the order that opened the pod bay.

Alice had obviously not expected this maneuver. Too
late, she turned to intercept.

Grisky was faster. As soon as the pod bay light indicated "closed," the *Firestorm* was on her way out, velocity
increasing exponentially.

They had no time to relax.

Alice was angry, beginning her own acceleration.

⋏

She was incredibly fast. Coming like a vast green God. Almost on them, her hungry petals extended, ready to engulf
them as she had engulfed Hafner's ship.

But Grisky was well armed. Perhaps Alice had never
encountered an attack vessel.

The captain threw everything he had at her.

The explosion was awesome. She was blasted, torn
apart . . . reduced to space detritus, fading through green to
black.

⋏

In his encrypted dispatch to the Fifth Matrix, Captain Grisky recounted the engagement and advised that all units be warned to avoid area 7934.

Later, on the Captain's Bridge, his thoughts turned dark . . . thoughts about Hafner and the lost crew of *EX241*. Good men and true, every one.

And he thought about possible space seeds from the explosion . . . forever strewn through the galaxy. Was it possible for them to grow, reproduce . . .

. . . into other hungry Alices?

THE WIND BLOWS FREE
Chad Oliver

SYMMES CHADWICK OLIVER, or "Big Chad" as we called him, was a core member of the Group from early 1953, when he was living with his wife, Beje, in Los Angeles and attending UCLA, into the summer of 1955, when he returned to his beloved Texas. (He'd grown up there and had his home in Austin, where he taught Anthropology until his death in August of 1993.)

Chad was tall and muscular, with a disarming grin, a dry yet antic sense of humor, and an enormous capacity for work. For many years he managed to combine his full schedule as an award-winning teacher at the University of Texas at Austin with a multitude of duties as Chairman of the Department of Anthropology. He was also a loving family man, an expert on jazz (hosting his own radio show in the 1950s), and a dedicated trout fisherman. Yet, in spite of all this, Chad found time to turn out nine novels, a textbook, and some seventy high-quality short stories and novelettes.

A staunch science fiction fan from early boyhood, Chad gained an enviable reputation for his beautifully-crafted anthropological SF in such novels as *Shadows in the Sun*, *The Winds of Time*, and *The Shores of Another Sea*. (He was also a noted writer of historical Westerns.) Chad's understanding of various cultures, both Earthly and alien, made his fiction unique in the genre.

His novelette, "The Wind Blows Free," is a prime example. One of my special favorites among his many fine tales, I included it in my anthology *A Sea of Space* in 1970. Here Oliver deals with the culture inside the metal walls of a great starship, spinning out his narrative to a most surprising climax. You'll have fun reading this one from Big Chad.

I'm sure he had fun writing it.

W.F.N.

Have you ever heard, with your ears or with your soul, the far wind that stirs the world? Have you ever felt the deep beat of the sea, the sea that is the heart of the Earth?

Samuel Kingsley had never known these things.

That may have been his trouble.

Samuel Kingsley was born with a fever in his bones and a fire in his blood. As a baby, he was difficult. His parents had to work to keep their initial joy from changing into impatient anger. Sam screamed, fought his food, clawed at his bed. He seldom smiled, and he was not affectionate.

He was bright enough, of course, or he would have been destroyed.

His childhood was little better, a stubborn series of scrapes and bruises and general mayhem. Sam was big for his age, and strong. He walked his own path and fought discipline like a wild stallion. He had no friends.

Sam was, in short, a maverick. He was unbranded. He should never have happened where he did, and when he did. But he was there, emphatically there, like a burr in the hide of a long-complacent animal.

He got into his first serious trouble when he was sixteen.

It was the day of his first big dance. He had to get dressed up in his best synthetic blue suit, which he detested, and the whole thing was very formal and proper, despite the fact that there were only twelve boys and girls of eligible age. The girls were poised and full of giggles, and the boys were shy, big-footed and gawky.

Sam liked the girls fine, but dancing bored him stiff.

And he wasn't shy.

When he was discovered to be absent from the dance, and it was noticed that a girl named Susan Merrill was also missing, the police were called. They found the two youngsters in one of the dark forbidden corridors. Susan, a blonde of pleasant proportions for her age, was unhurt but hysterical. Sam was defiant.

He knew that he had broken not one law but two. The black tunnels, those mysterious caves that burrowed into the hidden recesses of the Ship, were taboo except to older crewmen. And it was unheard of for a boy and a girl to be alone together before they were married.

Sam didn't care. He had acted on impulse and had no regrets.

Because he was so young, and because the Council still did not know quite what to make of him, Sam got off with a very light sentence. He was confined to his house for a solid year, and denied all privileges. His parents made it as rough on him as they could, but he was used to that.

He did his lessons contemptuously. When he could sneak out at night, he did so. The lights were low at night, and he could prowl the black caves all the way to the locked doors that sealed the people from the rest of the Ship. If he was unable to get out of the house, he read books he had stolen. Like most boys, he liked best the ones he was not supposed to read.

Sam liked sex in his books, because he was healthy and had a normal curiosity. And something in him responded to stories of rebels, to tales of men who struck out on their own. He dreamed of clipper ships, their sails taut against the wind. He dreamed of setting out into a green wilderness, with only a gun for company.

There were no seas on the Ship.

There was no wilderness.

And he had been taught that guns were evil. Not as evil, perhaps, as that greater evil no one talked about, but evil nonetheless.

At night, lying in his bed, he would slam his big fist into the plastic of his wall in an agony of frustration and bitterness, slam it until the blood smeared his knuckles and he could taste it in his mouth.

He knew tears, and the terrible loneliness of a boy who was out of step. No one ever heard him sobbing into the coldness and the silence of the long nights, and no one would have understood.

▲

By his eighteenth year, Sam had grown big and rawboned. Even his size was against him. He stood a rangy six-foot-four, and weighed better than two hundred pounds. His hair was black and untidy, and his eyes were dark. He was not a handsome man, but he had a strength in him, a power you could feel.

Sam was marked by his body. At eighteen, he was by far the biggest man on the Ship. He stood out like a pine in a forest of ferns, and he accentuated the difference by walking proudly erect, with his head thrown back.

He was a solitary animal, and therefore suspect. He was lonely, a man born out of his time, but he made no advances to others.

Since he was legally an adult, he had to take part in the annual observance of Heritage Day, on the eighth of February.

Bob Thomas came to get him.

Bob was the natural leader of his age group. He was a pleasant-looking boy, with an easy manner and an unforced politeness that endeared him to his elders. He was the sort that accepted life as he found it, growing up to embody the ideals and traditions of his culture. He would have done well in Greece, or in Rome, or in England in her days of glory. He did well on the Ship. In time, he would make the Control Room. It was as inevitable for him as breathing.

"Ready for the big deal, Sam?"

"Sure."

"We'll pick up the others and get on down, okay? I

think we ought to be a little early; shows the big boys we're on the ball."

"OK, Bob." Sam found it impossible to dislike Bob, although hate came easily to him. Bob was independent enough to be a man in his right, but he kept his independence within approved bounds. He even had a sense of humor. And Bob was big enough to put up a scrap. Sam respected strength as he respected few other things. He and Bob had fought it out once, and Sam had been hard-pressed to win. Much to his surprise, Bob had not reported him, and had even lied about the bruises on his face.

As a matter of fact, Bob was the closest thing to a friend he had ever had. There had been a few girls, but that was different.

They walked down the street, actually a sort of catwalk, past the rows of identical cabins that people called houses. Their footsteps echoed hollowly in the great chamber. Above and below them, huge metal girders spanned the belly of the Ship. The slope of the Ship's gray walls was their heaven and their earth, as though they lived inside a vast bowl. Branching off from the main street, smaller catwalks led to dark passages—corridors to the Control Room, to the engine room, the hydroponics chamber. Some of them even went Outside, or so it was rumored. Only the specially selected members of the Crew could use *any* of these passages; there were others that were taboo to all. And there were legends, myths, about things that lived in some of those black caves . . .

The Show was in the central square. It was a perfectly ordinary tri-di theater, and today it was even more solemn than usual. Men in full-dress uniforms stood in a double column through which they had to march. The priest blessed them before they took their seats. Patriotic music flowed from the speakers.

It was all fairly impressive, Sam supposed, but he was not moved. Of course, this was the first time he had been permitted inside the Show on Heritage Day, but he expected nothing more than a mild anticlimax. After all, it was no secret what went on in there. He had had it drummed into him as far back as he could remember.

Still, it ought to be more interesting than the usual pallid fare.

He took his seat in the front row with the others of his age group. Bob had the aisle seat, of course, and Sam found himself next to Susan Merrill. He grinned at her broadly and she flushed and kept her eyes on the screen.

There were blessings and speeches galore. Even old Captain Fondren made a speech, and the new Navigator was presented to much applause.

Sam endured it all.

Then the lights dimmed and the screen glowed.

The character of the music changed sharply. It was grim, threatening, with an insistent beat that thumped you in the chest.

Sam was suddenly conscious that he was very close to the screen.

In spite of himself, he tensed, waiting.

The palms of his hands began to sweat.

It started with a vicious abruptness, slamming him back into his seat.

▲

Sound that was more than sound, sound that tore at you with a solid physical impact. Light that was more than light, light that seared your eyeballs with a flash that mocked the sun.

Sam screamed with the rest, and his voice was less than nothing. He closed his eyes, and the brilliance hammered through his eyelids. He trembled violently. He had no mind, no spirit, no personality. He wasn't Sam Kingsley, he wasn't anybody. He was just a spot of horror in a maelstrom of violence, trying to hang on, trying to ride it out.

The ripping, screeching roar ceased.

The dead silence flowed in with a shock of its own.

Sam opened his eyes. At first, he couldn't see. There was only a voice, speaking into the emptiness.

The voice said: *This is Earth. This was your planet. Look at it now.*

Sam looked, his heart thudding like a wild thing in his chest.

He saw desolation, and death, and worse than death. He saw great cities gutted, their buildings shattered, their streets ripped like tissue paper. Black windows stared at him with cold stone eyes. A few figures that might have been human stumbled through the ruins, clawing at their faces, their shredded clothes, their blistered bodies.

He saw a land that had been green, and was green no more. A sere, scorched desert where nothing lived, where the very idea of life was blasphemy. No trees, no water, no crops.

Nothing.

A red sun glared in a murky sky.

He saw people. He saw men, women, and children: all dead or dying. A man, his naked body swollen with blisters, leaping into a swimming pool, holding himself under, gulping at the water like a fish from a nightmare sea. A blind woman sitting in what had once been an automobile, trying to feed a baby that could no longer move.

Sam could not watch it all. He was sick and dizzy. He could not think.

The voice was still speaking: *This is what a war did to your world. This is what hydrogen bombs and cobalt bombs and germ bombs did to your world. This is what people like you did to their own world when they couldn't grow up in time.*

There was more.

There was enough so that it rammed its message into your insides. No man could sit through this and ever forget it. Sam felt himself scaled down to size, and he discovered that there were bigger things than Sam Kingsley in the universe. This is not a discovery that any young man makes with pleasure, and it was doubly difficult for Sam.

But you cannot argue with obliteration.

The voice said: *These are the other planets that make up your solar system. These are the worlds we explored before the end came. These are the worlds we could reach.*

Sam knew of these worlds, knew them from the history books. But he saw them now as though for the first time, saw them through a mist of despair.

The wind-whipped sea of sand that was Mars.

The violet desolation that was Venus.

The frozen forbidding hell that was Saturn.

All of them.

Hopeless.

There was nowhere in our solar system that could shelter us. Our own world was dying. We did what we could.

We built the Ships.

The Ships filled the screen, immense towers of metal, standing like colossal silver tombstones in the graveyard of the world. Of course, most of them had been built long before the last poisoning of the Earth. They had been designed for man's greatest adventure, the exploration of the stars. They were not fundamentally different from the spaceships that had touched down on the planets of the solar system. Unhappily, no faster-than-light drive had been invented, in the nick of time or otherwise, and although men were working on the secrets of prolonged suspended animation, this had not as yet proved practical.

In any event, the problem was academic.

The Ships *had* to go.

They were planned to be entirely self-sufficient. Green plants in great hydroponic tanks provided the air, synthetic foods nourished in chemical vats supplied the means of support, and an entire Ship formed a balanced ecological system that would maintain life for generations—provided the population remained stable.

To Sam, it was a strange thing indeed to see a Ship from the *outside*. The Ship had always been a curved horizon of gray metal walls, a tangle of catwalks, a cluster of houses and tanks and sealed corridors that were dark caves of mystery. From the outside, it was a thing of beauty, but not the home he had always known.

Where sunlight and air and rolling land surrounded the Ship on the screen, there was now only the stardusted infinity of space, an emptiness more hostile to life than the polluted world the Ship had left behind. Sam had never seen that dark sea he sailed, but he had grown up with the ever-present knowledge of its existence. For the people of the Ship, the Outside was death itself. At night, when the lights were low, you would lie in your bed and feel that strangest of seas lapping at the walls of your room, those icy waves seeping into your head and your nerves and your blood . . .

The voice said: *You are all the passengers on a Ship. You who hear my voice may be the only human beings left; each Ship follows a different course. It may take centuries before you reach a world you can live on, circling a sun I cannot even imagine. You may never find it. But remember your Heritage! Remember that you are men, and remember what happened to men on Earth! You must begin again, you children of Earth. And you must be careful, you must be wise. If ever you find hate in your hearts, remember, remember . . .*

And it happened again.

The light that was beyond light, the blasting roar that was a crazed river of sound. The twisted cities, the poisoned air, the shrieks of the ruined and the maimed . . .

The screen darkened.

The lights in the Show came on again.

There was a terrible silence, for what was there to say? Sam kept his eyes straight ahead, afraid somehow to look around him.

Captain Fondren walked up to the stage, his body bent with years, his hair gray and lifeless.

"This is your Heritage," he said slowly, speaking the ancient ritual. "We all have a sacred trust to preserve what we can. All who hear my voice are adults, members of the people. You will conduct yourselves accordingly throughout your lives. We dare not fail. It is my duty to inform you that this Ship has now been in space for three hundred and ninety-seven years. I ask you to join me in prayer."

He paused, his old eyes looking far beyond the ship.

The Lord is my shepherd . . ."

The ancient words filled the chamber. It was one of those rare moments when mumbled phrases and familiar rituals suddenly become charged with meaning. The words were strong words, but Sam could hardly hear them.

Three hundred and ninety-seven years, he thought. *Three hundred and ninety-seven years.*

If they had not found what they sought in all that time, they would never find it.

The voyage would never end.

The Ship was all there was.

▲

Sam was impressed by Heritage Day, impressed and scared. For the first time in his life, he began to understand the Ship and the people who lived in it.

His people were a frightened people, a refugee people. They were conservative and cautious because they were trying to survive. They were existing in a kind of cultural suspended animation, just hanging on between disaster and a new beginning.

The words of his parents meant a little more now.

"Sam, Sam, why can't you be like the other little boys? Why do you always want to be getting into trouble? Now, do your homework and we'll have a nice synthesteak for you when you're through." That was Mom, a colorless, shapeless woman, going through the motions of life without ever really living.

And Dad, a big man like Sam, somehow tragic, somehow defeated before he had ever gone into battle. *"You can't change the world, son. The rules are there for a reason. You've got to do your part, son, whether you like it or not."*

Sam tried.

He told himself that he had been a fool. He was to live in the Ship, and he had only one life to live. Who was he to think he was better than other people?

He was assigned work in the main hydroponics chamber, and he learned his job dutifully. He forced himself to be interested in the growing plants and in the chemicals in which they grew. He regulated the sunlamps and adjusted the chemical flows with precision. He grew to like the fresh air of the chamber and looked forward to going to work every morning. At least, the hydroponics chamber was green, it was alive. The dead air piped in from the rest of the Ship depressed him, and going home at night was not pleasant.

And yet, Sam was not happy. He tried to be like the others, but he found no magic switch that would shut off his mind. If only the air would *move* more, if only it would flow in something different from its orderly, measured channels! If only the wind would blow, if only he could have clouds and storms and rivers of rain!

Sam still dreamed at night, and that was fatal.

He did not marry, and that added to his discontent. There were times when his body seethed as though with fever, times when the thoughts of women were like a sickness in his stomach. He tried to fall into what the people called love, but he could not. He would try one girl and then another, and each time something within him would rebel.

"Sam, try to be nice like the others . . ."

"Sam, you mustn't say such things, they're wicked . . ."

"Sam, you're so silly . . ."

For five years, Sam worked in the hydroponics chamber at the same job. He did it well. He did it better than it had ever been done before.

But he was not promoted.

No one ever sounded him out about joining the Crew, not even Bob.

The other men of his own age moved on up the scale. Every one of them was a member of the Crew. Sam stayed in the hydroponics chamber, and after five years he knew he was stuck there for life. The Council didn't trust him, would never trust him. His crime was that he was different, and on the Ship that was the worst crime of all.

One evening, when he was working late with the plants, he looked up to see Ralph Holbrook watching him. Ralph was the same age as Sam; they had gone through the ceremony of Heritage Day together. Ralph had been a timid boy, but he was cocky now in his new uniform.

He was also a little drunk.

"Still at it, eh, Sam?"

"Looks that way."

"Like your work?"

"Can't complain."

"You'd *better* like it, Sam boy."

Sam turned and faced him. "Meaning?"

"You know what I mean! You used to think you were really something, didn't you? Picking on everybody, swaggering around like you owned the Ship. Where are you now, Sam boy? Where are you now?"

Sam felt the old anger surging up within him. He

clenched his big fists, bowed his neck. His eyes narrowed. "Take it easy, Ralph. I don't want to hurt you."

Ralph laughed. "Still think you're tough, Sam boy? Still think you can be a big man with your fists? Come on, Sam! Try something!"

Sam took a step forward, his heart pounding. He could beat Ralph to a pulp, and he knew it.

But he stopped.

Striking a member of the Crew?

He didn't dare.

"Run along, Ralph," he said quietly. "Mommy's probably waiting up for you."

Ralph Holbrook stepped in and slapped his face with the palm of his hand.

Sam didn't move.

Ralph laughed again, turned, and walked proudly out of the chamber.

Sam's face was expressionless.

He turned back to his work, did what he had to do, and left the hydroponics room. The dead air clogged his nostrils as he walked.

There was no outward sign that anything had changed. He was just the same Sam Kingsley, big and awkward and alone walking home from work, his footsteps trailing him with empty echoes.

But Sam had been pushed over the threshold.

He had not made the decision; it had been made for him.

The gray hopeless monotony of his life had been nibbling away at him for a long time. The future stretched away before him like a featureless plain, without life, without color, without purpose.

He was caught in an alien world, trapped in a Ship in the deeps of space. There was nothing in that orderly world for him, nothing but an existence that was less than life.

Very well.

He had tried to live by their rules, and had failed.

From now on, he would make his own rules.

His step quickened, he was more alert than he had been in years. All his life he had been fascinated by those dark tunnels that burrowed away into the depths of the Ship. Those forbidden caves were the only frontiers he had. High officers of the Crew were the only people who were ever permitted in most of them, and it was clear by now that Sam would never be a member of the Crew.

He had no real plan. He simply knew that he had to do something, and there was only one place to start.

He ate a hearty meal and took a nap.

For once, his sleep was untroubled.

He woke up four hours later, stuffed his pockets with food, and tested his tubelight. He slipped out of the house into the gloom of the sleeping Ship.

His feet were sure beneath him, and there was nothing clumsy about him now. Like a shadow, he moved across a little-used catwalk that spanned the black belly of the Ship.

A dark tunnel loomed before him.

A faintly glowing sign said: AUTHORIZED PERSONNEL ONLY.

Sam smiled and stepped into the cave of night.

▲

He took off his shoes, careful to make no sounds that might be overheard. It was pitch dark in the corridor, but he was afraid to use his tubelight yet. Looking back over his shoulder, he could see the tunnel entrance framed by the Ship's night lights.

He moved along as fast as he dared, the fingers of his left hand lightly touching the wall to guide him. The passage seemed straight as a needle, and progress was not difficult. Nevertheless, he felt a nervousness he couldn't shake off. From his earliest childhood, he had been told never to go into one of those corridors, told of horrible things that lurked there, waiting.

He fancied that he was old enough now to discount such nursery tales, but just the same . . .

Something cold hit him in the face.

Sam ducked, fell flat on the floor. He stifled a scream, then managed a feeble grin as he realized what had happened. He had run into a door. He risked the light, and in its pencil beam he saw that the door was an ordinary metal one, sealing off the passage. There was another sign on it: KEEP OUT.

Sam tried the door.

It was unlocked.

He swung it open, stepped through, and closed it again behind him. He blinked his eyes. This tunnel was larger, and the lights were still on. It had a well-used air about it. He hesitated, figuring out his position. If he turned left, he would wind up back at the town where the people lived. If he turned right, he would be moving toward the bow of the Ship, toward the Control Room.

Sam went right.

He almost ran along, his shoes dangling around his neck. He felt the cold sweat on his body, the anxious thudding of his heart. It was all so simple, so like a dream, hurrying down this silent passage, the Ship around him like a monstrous beast, waiting, waiting . . .

What would they do to him if they caught him here? He tried not to think about it. He just kept going as fast as he could, his shoes bruising his chest, the tubelight gripped in his hand as though it were a weapon . . .

He rounded a turn, and stopped as though he had slammed into a wall. He held his breath, his lungs straining, the sweat dripping down his sides in icy streams.

There were two Crewmen in the corridor.

The two men were seated at a small table, playing cards. One man was facing Sam, but his eyes were on the cards in his hand. Just beyond the table, there was a blaze of light from the open door of the Control Room.

Sam stood stock-still. He was afraid to move, and afraid *not* to move. Almost involuntarily, he retreated back around the turn. He leaned against the wall, gasping with the effort to breathe silently.

Guards! Here, in the middle of the night. Why?

Had they seen him, caught just a flicker of movement? They would surely have spotted him if they had been alert, but why should they be alert? The Ship was run with the precision of a clock; people were *never* where they shouldn't be.

Still . . .

He tried to hold his breath, tried to listen.

Voices.

They *had* seen him!

"You're just jumpy. I didn't hear anything."

"I tell you, there was something there."

"You just don't like your hand." Laughter. "Did it have two heads, or three?"

"OK, OK. Maybe I'm crazy. But I'm going to have a look." A chair scraped across a metallic floor.

Run!

Sam sprinted down the tunnel, heedless of the noise, as fast as he could go. The passage was hideously straight, there was no place to hide. He damned himself for a fool, but it was too late now. If he could just find a pool of shadow, a curve in the corridor, anything . . .

"Hey!"

They had seen him.

Sam redoubled his efforts. He determined not to panic. He mustn't let himself go, he had to think . . .

The guards couldn't have recognized him, not at that distance. He could outrun them, he was certain of that. If he could get back to that branching passage, he could slip into the sleeping town and nobody would ever be the wiser.

He tossed a glance back over his shoulder, and his heart sank at what he saw. The guards had stopped, and were using a wall phone to call ahead.

Sam slowed his pace, fighting for breath. There was just one question he had to answer: could he reach that cutoff tunnel before the Crewmen from town got there from the other end? He wanted to think that he could, but he had to admit that the odds were against it. He still had too far to go. And even if he did, the others were not fools. They would know about that cutoff, would be waiting at the other end.

No, that was out.

There was only one thing to do, and he did it.

The next door he came to, he stopped. He fumbled open the catch, swung the door open, and slipped inside. At first he was blind; there was no light at all. He switched on his tubelight, closed the door, and bolted it shut.

He made himself take the time to put on his shoes. His lungs ached in his chest, and the air in the passage was stale and dead. He held the light in front of him, and tried to run. He soon slowed to a fast walk.

He listened carefully, but heard no sounds of pursuit.

The corridor was different from the others. It seemed older somehow, and he had the eerie feeling that no man had walked these floors for centuries. There were oil slicks on the walls, and the floor was gritty.

Sam kept going.

He came to another door that sealed off the passage. There was a sign on it, but it was streaked and dirty; he couldn't read it. He fumbled the catch open, shoved on the door.

It didn't open.

Sam bit his lip. He backed off, took a deep breath, and threw his shoulder into the door. It gave a little. He hit it again, and yet again. It swung open with a rasping screech. He squeezed through and shut it again behind him. The bolt stuck and he couldn't throw it.

He flashed the light around. The corridor was smaller now; his head almost scraped the ceiling. The air was so flat he could hardly breathe it. There was a layer of fine white dust on the floor. When he took a step, the stuff puffed up in a cloud, stinging his eyes and his nostrils.

Sam hesitated, doubting himself. He could still go back. It would be rough, but they probably wouldn't kill him. A little conditioning in the surgery, that was all, and he would be the most placid man on the Ship. He shuddered.

There was a chance, just a chance, that this tunnel might eventually take him back to the town, back to some forgotten entrance. He still had perhaps five hours before morning, and he would not be missed until then.

He smiled sourly. He had only intended to do a little exploring this first night; he had fully expected to be back at work tomorrow. Now he was trapped, cut off, and he would probably never be able to go back to the life he had known.

Well, it was a small loss.

Sam took a bar of food out of his pocket and wolfed it down. He felt a little better, but he was desperately thirsty. If there were ever a next time, he would bring water and forget about the food.

Of course, there wasn't going to *be* any next time.

Not for him.

He steadied himself and flashed the light around again. There was nothing to see. The black cave stretched away as far as the light could penetrate. The fine dust on the floor was white, like the snow he had seen in pictures.

There was just one way to go.

Sam moved forward at a fast walk, the dust puffing up around him until he could hardly see. He moved on, his mind frozen hard against the terror that seeped in around him, walking down a silent tunnel to nowhere.

▲

He kept it up for two hours, and then he couldn't take it any longer. The clouds of dust hung in the stale air like smoke, and his throat was raw and burning.

He had seen nothing.

He had heard nothing, save for the *pad-pad-pad* of his own feet.

The tunnel had twisted and curved until he didn't have the faintest idea where he was. There had been other corridors branching off from the one he was in, but he had been afraid to try them. This way, he could at least retrace his steps if he had to. He had a childish, irrational fear of getting lost, even though he now had no home to go back to.

But he *had* to get out of the dust.

He came to a door in the wall and forced it open. He went through and closed it quickly behind him. He stood very still, trying not to stir up the dust.

He flashed the light around him.

For one awful moment, he thought all the stories he had heard about *things* that lived in the forbidden caves were true. He was in a room, not a tunnel, and the walls were lined with grotesque figures—big bulging caricatures of men, with glassy faces and swollen arms and legs.

But the things were not alive.

They had never been alive.

Gingerly, Sam stepped over and touched one. It was made of some kind of smooth stuff that reminded him of pottery, and it glistened dully in the light.

How long had it been since this lost chamber had seen a light? A hundred years? Two hundred? Three?

He tapped the thing with his fingernail. It gave off only a faint click, although he knew that it was hollow. He looked around him, estimating rapidly. There must have been at least fifty of the weird figures in the chamber with him.

He knew what they were, and it came as something of a shock when he realized that he had never actually seen one of them before.

Spacesuits.

He was in a storeroom full of spacesuits.

Strange, half-formed thoughts began to well up in his mind. He hardly knew what to make of them, and for a moment he feared he might be going mad. *Funny I've never seen a spacesuit before. Funny none of us were given training in their use. Funny no one has ever had to go Outside for repairs.*

Or were they a carefully guarded secret, one of the privileges of the Crew?

But what was all this secrecy *for*, anyhow?

The puzzle of the midnight guards at the Control Room door came back to plague him. Sure, it wouldn't do to have women and kids and questionable characters like himself swarming over the place, getting in the way. But guards in the middle of the night seemed a bit excessive.

What were they hiding in the Control Room?

What was there they did not dare let anyone see until they knew they could trust him absolutely?

In fact, now that he thought about it, there was one question that might be asked about a lot of things on the Ship.

It was a deadly question, a question that had toppled empires.

Why?

The unvoiced word vibrated against his brain, and there was no answer to it.

He looked more closely at the spacesuit in front of him. The thing had a thin film of dust on it. He heaved on it, turned it around. There were two oxygen tanks clamped to its back. He found the switch that activated the air supply and threw it.

Nothing happened.

He picked up the heavy helmet, pressed it to his ear. He heard nothing. He sniffed at it, and the air was as dead as ever. There was no oxygen coming through.

Surely, in a ship in space, it would only be common sense to keep the spacesuits ready for action. He shook his head. Of course, there must be others somewhere, but still . . .

He replaced the helmet and chewed on another food bar. He hated to go back into the dust-laden corridor, but he couldn't stay here. He had only a few hours left before the working day began.

A plan?

He had no plan. He thought vaguely that there might be a lifeboat of some sort on the Ship, but it would be pure accident if he found it. Even if he did locate it, it would do him no good. He had had no training in operating a ship in space, and he knew enough about spaceships to be certain that he couldn't just pile into one and go blasting merrily on his way.

In any event, where could he go?

One notion did occur to him. Unless there was no rhyme or reason at all to the plan to the Ship, there must have been a purpose in locating the storeroom where it was.

And there was just one such purpose that he could think of.

He opened the door again, coughing as the dust hit him. He listened carefully, but the corridor was utterly silent. It stretched on before him, a dead and lifeless thing, heavy with the weight of centuries.

Sam moved on, trying not to give way to despair.

Pad-pad-pad.

The fine white dust swirled and eddied in the old, stale air.

The pencil of light stabbed through the gloom, becoming a solid bar of silver radiance as it knifed through the glittering clouds of dust.

His throat was so dry he could no longer swallow, and he thought of the clean, fresh air of the hydroponics room with hopeless longing.

Pad-pad-pad.

His shoes kicked something on the floor, and he looked down. There was a heap of something there, white as the dust that covered it.

Bones.

Bones, and a shrunken skin as dry as old paper. A human skull gaped at him with something that had once been eyes. He knelt and touched the thing. The skin crumbled at the slightest pressure.

Sam looked at the pitiful remnants that had long ago walked and breathed and loved. He felt no horror, only an odd surge of sympathy and relief. He was not the first, after all! He was not the only man who had gotten out of line.

How many others had there been?

He waved a friendly greeting at the pile of bones.

I wish I could have known you, he thought. *We might have done something, together. I might have had someone to talk to. We could have been friends, you and I.*

He stepped over the bones, being careful not to disturb them, and walked on.

Within half an hour, he came to the end of the tunnel.

A door sealed the passage before him, but this was no ordinary door. This was a massive metal thing set into the very side of the Ship itself.

A faded sign read: DANGER. LOCK FOUR. DANGER.

Sam stared at the gleaming metal. Involuntarily, he

backed away. He had come to the end of his world. Beyond that door, he knew, was the chamber of an airlock. And on the other side of the airlock . . .

Outside.

Deep space.

The End.

Sam sat down in the dust, his head in his hands. He didn't try to kid himself. He was through. This was all there was. He had no choice now. He could only retrace his steps along that dead tunnel, go back and give himself up.

And then?

He shivered, and the blood ran cold in his veins.

No, no. I won't give up. I can't. Not yet.

He got to his feet, trembling.

He forced himself to walk up to the airlock door. He reached out and touched it. It felt icy, or was that just his imagination?

He wasn't thinking; he was beyond that. He only knew that the Ship and everything in it had become horrible to him, unbearable. Maybe there was a workable spacesuit inside the lock, maybe he could go Outside and drift forever among the stars . . .

It would be a cleaner death than the thing that waited for him at the other end of the tunnel.

He reached out and gripped the wheel in the middle of the lock.

He wrenched it, hard.

It stuck at first, then began to turn.

Instantly, the corridor exploded into sound.

A siren screamed, rising and falling, screeching through the Ship.

The noise deafened him after the hours of silence. He covered his ears and the siren wailed in his brain.

Oh God, they've got it wired. They know where I am. They'll come after me, kill me . . .

Sam didn't want to die. Opening the inner door of the

airlock had been a gesture, nothing more. Faced with the reality of death, he had only one instinctive thought:

Hide!

Get away!

He ran back into the tunnel.

He ran blindly, bruising himself against the walls, a mindless body fleeing through a nightmare cave of arid white clouds and the insistent fury of the siren's scream.

⋏

With numbing abruptness, Sam Kingsley heard a human voice.

Human?

It was screeching so that he could hardly tell, screeching a single mad high-pitched note over and over again. How could he hear it over the wail of the siren? He shook his head wildly, like an animal.

The siren had stopped.

He stuffed his big fist into his own mouth, biting down on the knuckles. The screaming voice that might have been human turned into a strangled gurgle.

It was his own voice.

He sobbed, and the sound was shatteringly loud in the sudden silence. His ears were ringing, his body was wet with sweat. The dust in his lungs made him cough, but he didn't have enough air to cough . . .

He stumbled over the skeleton in the corridor, scattering the bones. He tried to keep running, but he was staggering now.

Hide!

Get away!

If he could just reach that storeroom, get in there with the spacesuits, there might be a chance, a prayer . . .

No.

It was too late.

He heard voices ahead of him in the corridor, brushing noises, the tread of feet.

"Kingsley!" The shout was strangely muffled. "Kingsley! We know you're in there! Stay where you are. Don't try to fight. We won't hurt you. Kingsley! Can you hear me?"

Sam collapsed on the floor, his face in the dust, gasping for breath. He didn't answer, he *couldn't* answer. He stayed there in a huddle, unable to think, beyond even despair, the blood roaring in his ears.

The lights in the ancient tunnel came on, blinding him, searing whitely into his brain.

The footsteps came closer, closer . . .

There. He saw a shoe, right in front of his eyes.

Voices. "Is he dead?" "No such luck." "He's too tough to kill."

A foot nudged his battered shoulder, none too gently.

"Come on, Sam boy. Get up."

It was like awakening after a too-long sleep. He had to swim back toward awareness, pulling his way through dense layers of stifling fog. Every bone in his body hurt. He rolled over very slowly.

He struggled to his knees.

The foot hit him again. It wasn't a hard kick, but it didn't have to be. Sam went down, his mouth in the dust.

"Come on, Sam boy. Stop playing around."

"That's enough of that, Ralph. Let him alone."

Sam tried it again. He got to his knees, waited. Nothing happened. He pulled himself erect. His vision cleared.

There were three of them in the corridor with him. They were all Crewmen, and they all had face masks on to protect them from the dust. He recognized Ralph Holbrook by his voice. The men all had canteens clipped to their belts.

"Water," he said. His voice was a dry croak.

The men were ghostly in the white light. One of them shook his head. "No water, Kingsley. Not until we get you back where you belong. After that, you can have all the water you want."

"Water," he said again. His throat was on fire.

"Sorry, Sam boy."

Holbrook moved a little. Sam could hear the water gurgling in his canteen.

"Let's go, Kingsley," said the man who had spoken before. He sounded almost bored. "It's a long walk back."

Sam stared at the canteen on Holbrook's belt with raw, red eyes. He stood absolutely motionless, and then something snapped inside him. It was like a dam bursting, a dam he had held in check all his life. His eyes brightened, and a terrible icy strength flowed into his exhausted body.

He stood up straight, his head almost touching the roof of the tunnel. His huge frame seemed to swell until he filled the corridor. His hair was white with dust, but his eyes were black coals in the light. He clenched his bleeding fists and his lips drew back from his teeth.

Suddenly, he was very calm, very sure.

He stood there like a rock.

He was through running.

And then, for the first time in his life, Sam Kingsley really got mad.

▲

He took one quick step forward and caught Holbrook's tunic in his fist. Holbrook's eyes widened and a curious noise came out of his mouth. Sam yanked, and the fabric ripped.

Off balance, Holbrook started to fall on his face.

Sam brought his beefy right fist up from his knees and sent it crunching into Holbrook's jaw. Something broke; the jaw went flabby. Quite coldly, Sam drove a piston left into Holbrook's stomach, and then caught him with another right to the side of the head as the man crumpled at his feet.

Silently, he went after the others.

The corridor was so narrow that the two Crewmen got in each other's way. With icy deliberation, Sam held them off with a jabbing left hand, throwing his right with merciless precision.

The first man kicked at him frantically. Sam caught the foot, twisted it with a wrenching jolt. The man screamed. Sam picked him up by the feet and smacked his head against the tunnel wall.

The last Crewman turned to run.

Sam reached out his long left arm, caught his shoulder, spun him around. The man slashed out with something that glittered and Sam felt a hot wetness in his chest. He narrowed his black eyes, slammed his right into the man's face with all his strength. He followed it up relentlessly, slugging the man back down the corridor. The man fell, staggered to his feet again.

Sam let him have it.

It was all over.

Sam felt a small warm glow of satisfaction deep within himself, and that was all. He stood quietly for a moment, gasping for breath in the dust-choked air, and then he reached down and unhooked the man's canteen. He lifted it to his lips and forced himself to sip the water slowly, letting it trickle down until nausea made him stop. Then he found one of the face masks that was still relatively intact and pulled it over his face.

Air!

Clean, filtered air!

He breathed deeply, luxuriating in the stuff. He filled his lungs with it, tasting it, loving it. His chest worked like a bellows until the oxygen made him dizzy and he had to slow down.

He examined his chest. It was slippery with blood,

blood furred now with sticky dust, but it was not a deep
cut. In any event, he wasn't worried about it. There was no
time left for worry.

Sam knew that he had killed the man he had slammed
against the corridor wall. He knew it without looking, and
he felt no remorse. It was simply another item to be added
to the list, and it made his position more serious than ever.
It made his position completely hopeless.

He laughed, shortly.

The hell with it, gentlemen! I'll cheat you yet!

There was no point in trying to reach the storeroom. It
might gain him an hour or two, nothing more. And they
would be after him very soon now, many of them, far more
than he could ever handle.

There was just one thing left to do.

Sam turned, picked his way over the prone bodies, and
went back the way he had come. It was easier with the
lights on, easier with decent air in his lungs, easier now
that he wasn't burning up with thirst. But as he walked the
reaction caught up with him, the adrenaline of battle faded,
and his legs wobbled precariously.

He almost made it before he fell down, and then he just
crawled the rest of the way.

The faded sign was the same: DANGER. LOCK
FOUR. DANGER.

The massive metal door still gleamed in the very side of
the Ship. Beyond that airlock . . .

Well, no matter. He was through, either way.

He pulled himself to his feet, grasped the wheel in the
middle of the great door, twisted it.

The siren exploded into fury again, but this time he was
ready for it. He ignored the bedlam, kept on turning the
wheel. It came more easily now, loosening up, it was spinning . . .

There was a rasping creak he could hear above the
siren's scream.

Sam's hand dropped from the cold metal wheel. In spite of himself, he backed away, holding his breath.

The airlock door opened with a hiss.

▲

At that precise moment, he heard a chorus of cries that cut through the racket of the siren. A glance down the tunnel showed a troop of Crewmen advancing through the smokelike dust.

Sam waved his hand at them tauntingly.

Without hesitation, he stepped through the airlock door. He found himself in a small metal chamber. Remembering the films he had seen, he jabbed a green button on a wall panel. The great door through which he had come hissed shut again, just before the others reached it.

That door could not be opened again from the Ship as long as he was inside the airlock.

He looked around him. There was little to see. The lock was a small one, perhaps ten feet square. It had been painted a dull gray, but the paint had peeled and cracked, showing the dark metal beneath.

The chamber was quite empty.

There was no providential spacesuit.

Sam stepped across to the circular portal at the far end of the airlock. He touched it with his finger. It felt cold. Just to the right of the portal there was another panel. The panel had a red button set into it.

Sam reached out to press the button.

His finger trembled so violently that he missed it altogether.

It was all very well to make up your mind to do something that went against your very soul. It was all very well to be convinced that you were going to do it. It was all very well to *try* to do it.

But beyond this last door was Outside.

Outside the Ship.

Outside the world.

Outside, past the sandy beaches of a warm and tiny island, out into the vastnesses of a desolate sea, cold and empty beyond belief. Out into space itself, out into a nightmare death that had haunted you from childhood . . .

A hollow clanging filled the chamber.

The Crewmen were trying to batter the inner door down.

Sam took a deep breath, and held it. He pressed the red button. He felt a cool current against his body as air began to cycle.

The circular portal creaked and hissed.

It began to open.

Sam closed his eyes, held his breath with manic ferocity.

He counted to ten.

He squared his shoulders and walked forward. He walked through the port. He was Outside . . .

He began to fall.

God, can I have guessed right, why don't I explode, why can't I feel anything . . .

He hit something with a numbing crash. The something gave under the impact; it was flexible. It ripped at his arms and legs as he fell . . .

Then it stopped.

It was over.

Sam couldn't hold his breath any longer. His lungs were bursting, his eyes bulging from their sockets. He opened his mouth, gasped, swallowed.

Air!

The face mask could only filter air; there had to be air there in the first place. And that meant . . .

Sam opened his eyes.

Green.

Yellow.

Red.

Colors! A riot of colors! He had never seen such colors; they stunned his eyes. He looked up, past a tangle of green. Light! Bright, golden light.

A sun.

Sam reached up, ripped off his face mask.

An avalanche of smells almost smothered him. It was like his hydroponics room, but magnified a million times. He smelled green growing things, flowers, trees . . .

Life.

He had been living in a dead world, a counterfeit world, and here was the real thing, dazzling, incredible, wonderful, overpowering. A gentle breeze ruffled the leaves over his head, a sweet living breeze he could taste in his mouth.

Sam tried his body gingerly. No bones were broken, as far as he could tell. He reached out and pulled the sticky green vines apart, making a hole. He began to inch along painfully, like a worm, sucking in the earth-moist air as he went. He forced his way through a tangled miracle of underbrush for some twenty long minutes, and then he found himself in a small clearing.

There was water in the clearing, a little spring bubbling up from an outcropping of glistening black rocks. Sam stared at it; it seemed to him that he had never seen anything so beautiful. Tiny brown rootlets trailed down into the pale water. There were clean white pebbles on the bottom, all worn and smooth. He could see the pebbles in exact detail, almost as though the water magnified them, but when he thrust his arm into the spring he could not reach bottom.

Sam cupped the cold water in his dirty hands and drank it. He had never tasted water so sweet, so charged with vitality.

He stood up on shaking legs. He looked back the way he had come.

He saw a sight he would never forget.

There was the Ship, the mighty Ship, rearing its bulk toward an electric blue sky. There was the Ship, the world he had known, and it was a dead thing, a defeated thing.

Its once-bright sides were dull with rust and corrosion. Its once-powerful jets were buried in dirt and brambles. Its once-proud outline was blurred by the tangled green ropes of creepers and vines.

There was the Ship, there was his world: buried beneath the decay and the growth of centuries.

The Ship had landed; that was obvious enough. It had touched down long ago, generations ago. It had found the world it had sought, the world that might give his people another chance.

The great journey had ended hundreds of years ago.

And the passengers?

They had stayed in the Ship.

They had been afraid to come out.

They had built their little safe sterile society in their metal tube of a world, and they had been afraid to start again. They remembered what had happened on Earth; they were never allowed to forget. A lifetime of warnings buzzed through Sam's brain:

"You must be careful, you must be wise . . ."

"Take no chances . . ."

"Careful—careful . . ."

Sam had known, somehow. A part of him had always known. *This* was the secret the Crewmen hid from their people. *This* was why the useless control room was guarded, even in the midnight hours. *This* was why the Crewmen had to be selected so carefully. *This* was why they had feared him, hated him, stifled him.

Sam felt the warm sun on his neck, tasted the living air in his mouth, smelled the breeze that had kissed the flowers and the trees and the blue vault of the skies.

And he threw back his head and laughed, laughed with the sheer blind exultation of being alive.

He flopped down on the ground by the bubbling spring, pillowed his head in his arms, and was asleep in seconds.

▲

When Sam woke up, the world was dark around him—dark and yet shot with a luminous gray that told him that dawn was near. He had no idea how long he had slept, since he did not know the planet's period of rotation, but he felt rested and ready to go.

He was cold, and his body was stiff and sore. The ground that had seemed so warm in the sunlight was chill and damp now, and there were tiny beads of moisture on the grass stems. The stars were fading as light seeped over the horizon, but they still dusted the heavens with their glory.

He drank some more water, but it failed to fill the emptiness that gnawed inside him. He searched his pockets, but he had no food left. He stood there and shivered, half-smiling at his own plight.

He didn't know how to build a fire.

He didn't know what berries or nuts were safe to eat.

He had no weapons.

He listened, almost holding his breath. He heard the world around him, the world he could not see. He heard sounds he had never heard on the Ship; the very air was filled with rustlings and sighings and a vague thump as something heavy moved in the brush.

Sam stood quietly, watching the sunrise. He felt as though he were just being born, coming forth as a man after an eternity of not-life inside a great metal egg . . .

The sun came up slowly, taking its own sweet time, doing the job right. It bathed the world in soft pastels, in rose and soft yellow and rich brown. It warmed the ground, the leaves, the grasses. It rolled into the sky, almost timidly, and looked down on itself, smiling into the chuckles of the spring.

Sam looked again at the Ship. It was a sad thing in the sunlight, a tragic thing. It looked like the tombstone placed over the grave of a giant. It was hard to believe that people lived and loved and died within those metal walls; it was as if the ancient Egyptians of Earth had sealed their society inside a vast pyramid, trying to preserve it for the ages . . .

Sam felt no anger now, not even triumph. The green world around him was too big for that. Instead, watching that rusting hulk being strangled in the patient coils of the vines, he felt the beginnings of compassion, of understanding.

I'll be back, he thought. *One day I'll be back.*

And then the irony of it welled up within him. *O my people! The door was always open to you, the door into sunlight and warmth and life. The door was always open, if you only had the courage to walk through it!*

He turned and set out toward a low range of bluish hills, still half-hidden by mist. He was desperately hungry, with no way of getting food, but happiness was in him like a song. He *knew* he was on the threshold of a new life, he *knew* that more miracles waited for him beneath that alien, golden sun. He had only to keep going, to walk far enough and long enough . . .

He smelled the smoke first.

He was walking through a clump of tall, cool trees, relishing the spongy softness of the leaves on the forest floor. He caught a whiff of wood smoke, heavy and pungent with the tang of broiling meat. He walked faster, almost running, trailing the smoke.

He came to the edge of a sea of grass, a rolling meadow of green. He saw the orange fire at the very edge of the timber, blazing up with sap-rich hissings and cracklings. He smelled the dripping meat hanging over the flames . . .

He saw the men, three of them, standing around the fire. Big men, men his own size, their muscles as golden as the sun in the sky. They saw him, smiled at him, waved to him.

Sam waved back. He knew there was nothing to fear here, and hurried toward the fire with a steady, eager step. He walked proudly, his head erect, his heart full.

And Sam Kingsley heard at last that far, free wind that stirs the world. He felt within him the deep beat of a living sea, and knew that he had found peace at the end of his journey, a peace as bright with promise as the morning sun.

DIFFERENT

Charles E. Fritch

CHARLES E. FRITCH and I worked side by side in the 1950s as job interviewers at the State Department of Employment in Inglewood, California. We both yearned to write full-time, but we had bills to pay. (I was able to quit in April of 1956, and have been a full-time pro ever since.)

An ex-paratrooper from upstate New York, Chuck served in Europe with the 11th Airborne. Stationed in California prior to going overseas, he liked the area, and returned to Los Angeles after obtaining a major in Psychology from Utica College of Syracuse University.

Fritch became an early member of the Group in the mid-1950s, and in his quiet, laid-back way was more of an observer than a loud-shouting participant in our all-night sessions. But he was as dedicated as any one of us.

Chuck began selling his work in 1951, placing dozens of short tales in markets from *Astounding* to *The Magazine of Fantasy and Science Fiction*. (The best of these were collected in his *Crazy, Mixed-Up Planet*.) Chuck's most famous SF story is the often-anthologized "Big, Wide, Wonderful World," which is actually a Group story set in the future. It earned a well-deserved slot in *The Year's Best Horror Stories*.

As an editor/publisher, Chuck launched the fantasy magazine, *Gamma*, in 1963, along with *Chase*, a crime publication. This led into his editing *Mike Shayne's Mystery Magazine* for a number of years. With his wife, Shirley, he continues to live in Southern California.

In "Different," Fritch contributes a new story with a lemon-twist ending that reflects his wry outlook on society.

W.F.N.

With one manly swing of the machete Johnny sliced off his mother's head and sent it rolling down the incline. The woman had been in the middle of telling him to go fetch some firewood, and now her mouth kept going even though her entire head had detached from her body. With a wry smile Johnny watched the head roll down the hill and come to an abrupt rest against a rock, its face obviously annoyed at the interruption.

"You shouldn't have done that, Johnny," his mother's head said sternly.

"Shut up, old woman," Johnny told her.

"Who's gonna fix your supper now, Johnny?" the woman's head asked. "Who's gonna mend your clothes? Who's—"

"I can do all that stuff myself," Johnny snapped. "I don't need you. Now be quiet, or I'll stuff your head down the well."

Johnny's mother shut up. She didn't want her head stuffed down the well. She eyed her body lying crumpled a short distance away and wondered if she'd be able to roll her head back up the hill to get to the rest of her. She certainly couldn't depend on Johnny in his present mood.

Of course her body was perfectly capable of getting up and walking over to her head, but without a brain to guide it, it would probably just lie there in the dirt letting the ants crawl over it and once in a while scratching instinctively at the occasional bug bites.

Feeling hungry, Johnny went into the house to check the fridge for food, and he nearly stepped on his father. Without a skeleton to hold his body upright the man was oozing along the floor like some flesh-colored amoeba. Johnny thought this was pretty disgusting, but he never said anything for fear of offending the old man, who would undoubtedly be quick to remind him that he (the father) was the normal one and his ungrateful son was not. What he should do, Johnny decided, was stuff his father in a big jar so he wouldn't be underfoot all the time.

"Have you seen your ma, Johnny?" the old man wheezed.

"She's in the yard," Johnny told him. "I got mad and chopped her head off."

"Chopped her head off," his father echoed. "You shouldn't have done that, Johnny."

"Oh for—" Johnny was annoyed again. His mother had said exactly the same thing. Maybe he would put the old man in a jar, after all.

Rummaging in the fridge, he found a big jar half-filled with pickles. He dumped the pickles in the sink, rinsed out the jar with warm water. Before his father could protest, Johnny scooped him up and stuffed him in the jar. It was a big jar, and his father was a small man, but Johnny still had trouble getting the jar top on securely. One of his father's eyes peered reproachfully at him from inside the jar. Under the eye, a twisted mouth said in a muffled tone, "I don't like it in here, Johnny. Let me out!"

Ignoring the old man's plaintive complaint, Johnny picked up a pickle from the sink and thoughtfully nibbled at it. "Johnny, stop that!" a female voice shrilled from between his teeth.

Johnny yanked the pickle from his mouth and threw it back into the sink, where it changed its shape and color and became his four-inch-tall sister.

"What a dumb thing to do," he exclaimed—"turn yourself into a pickle."

"Don't call me dumb," his sister advised. "After all, I'm not the abnormal one in this family. And what's this about you chopping off Ma's head again? I swear, Johnny, sometimes—"

Johnny was not in the mood for another lecture. Besides, he didn't like being constantly reminded of his abnormality. "Sometimes you sound just like Ma yourself," he accused. Angrily, he quickly stuffed his sister down the sink drain, turned on the water, and flicked the garbage disposal button.

"Have a nice trip," Johnny called after her.

"Johnnnnnnnyyyyy . . ." Her voice faded through distant plumbing and into the cesspool.

Frankly, Johnny was tired of his whole family. He was the only one of them who was different, and he didn't like being different. He was tired of the farm, too, with nothing to do but milk the chickens and gather the cow eggs. He'd been on the farm long enough. He craved thrills, excitement, adventure—and that's when he turned his thoughts once more to the Big City.

With all the people living there, he might be able to find others like himself, people whose heads or arms didn't fall off at the slightest provocation, who didn't slither around on the floor like some slimy microbe, who didn't change herself into pickles and Lord knew what else.

Sure, why not? No time like the present. He who hesitates—and so forth.

Johnny picked up the pickle jar containing his father and put it in the fridge, paying no attention to the old man's muffled protests. He went outside, where he discovered his mother trying to roll her head uphill to her body in vain because her nose had become accidentally impaled on a twig. He pulled the twig from her nose.

"Thanks, son," she said.

"You're welcome, Mom," Johnny said. "I'm going to the Big City. Dad's in the fridge and Sis is in the cesspool."

Picking up her head, he walked up the hill and placed it on her body.

"You're a good boy, Johnny," his mother told him.

"I try," Johnny said.

His mother was lying, of course, just to make him feel good. Johnny knew he should have tried harder to be a good person and a good son—and even a good brother. His mother and father and sister were good people, and it certainly wasn't their fault that he was different from them—different, in fact, from all the normal people in the world. He was what he was, and apparently there was nothing that could be done about it. He'd heard of abnormals like himself getting operations to make them more acceptable to society, but it was all hearsay and not something that could be depended upon. There were times he felt so frustrated he had to take his anger out on someone—and his folks were the handiest ones around. They'd all be better off if he left and never returned.

He started down the hill toward the road. At the gate he glanced back to discover that he'd inadvertently placed his mother's head on backward, but he was sure the woman would notice this and twist it around. He waved. His mother waved back, but since her body was on wrong, she waved in the opposite direction.

Johnny was hardly a hundred feet down the road when he heard a familiar voice calling his name. Damn. He should've known he couldn't sneak out without Ardeela catching him. She was a pretty blonde girl with yellow fur covering every inch of her body. At least, he thought she was pretty, but then he'd never been able to see her features through all that hair. Only her lovely blue eyes peered out at him.

She caught up and walked along with him. "You're leaving, aren't you," she said wistfully.

"I have to," he said.

She linked her furry arm in his. "You don't have to run away just because you're different from the rest of us. I love you in spite of it, Johnny."

"Do you love me enough to mate with me and have our children, all of whom might be freaks like me?"

"Of course," she said, almost—but not quite—immediately.

Johnny detected the hesitation. "That's what I thought. Goodbye, Ardeela."

Ardeela released him and stopped walking. Her blue eyes were moist. "Goodbye, Johnny. Take care of yourself."

"You, too," he called back.

Johnny continued walking until he got to the dirt road and the bus stop. He hoped he wouldn't see any of their neighbors. They were all polite enough, but the way they looked at him made him squirm uncomfortably. But he saw no one until the bus arrived. The big yellow machine stopped, and the door snapped open. Johnny climbed up the steps and deposited a coin in the receptacle beside the driver.

The bus driver was a man with two heads, both of which appraised Johnny unfavorably. Johnny made his way down the aisle to a vacant seat, trying to appear inconspicuous, which wasn't easy, considering his abnormality. Across the way, a mother was nursing her child from a nipple on her right shoulder and burping the kid at the same time. She also had a nipple on her forehead and one on her neck; she probably had them all over her body, ready at a moment's notice. Johnny also saw that her child had a completely flat head from his eyebrows back. Lucky, normal kid. In the rear of the bus a quartet of male singers sang, changing colors with each note like a human color organ.

Johnny glanced up to see one of the bus driver's heads staring curiously at him in the rearview mirror, while the other head paid attention to the road ahead. Johnny closed his eyes and settled into his seat as the vehicle lurched forward and accelerated down the road. His family was used to him, but he expected he'd be stared at a lot in the Big City, until he found others like himself where he'd fit in, assuming he ever did.

Johnny listened to the hum of the tires on the road and daydreamed of a world where everyone was like him, where people didn't have fur all over, where every man and woman had a skeleton, where skin color didn't change with each note sung, where bodies were always the same shape and size, where there was only one non-detachable head to a customer. Maybe there was no such world, but if there was, he wanted to find it.

It wasn't such a wild idea. He'd known from an early age that his mother wasn't his real mother, his father wasn't his real father, and his sister wasn't his real sister. They'd found him wailing in a field, a baby someone had abandoned or lost, and they took him in and raised him. Little wonder Johnny felt apart from these people no matter how much they all loved each other. He often thought that somewhere out there were his real parents, and perhaps even a real sister, people like himself whose bodies were alike.

As the bus journeyed toward the Big City, it stopped occasionally to take on and let off passengers, but Johnny paid them no notice. He wasn't in the mood to face their stares of shock and revulsion when they saw he was different from them, so he just kept his eyes closed and dozed on and off. Hours later, the bus came to its terminal, and everyone left the vehicle and scattered.

Though he was eager to find others like himself, Johnny couldn't help but gawk at the tall, shiny, metal and glass buildings that towered overhead, blotting out the sun and a lot of the sky. People were everywhere, so many of them that they didn't really notice him—which was a relief. It wasn't until he felt hunger pangs and stopped in a coffee shop that he encountered any trouble. A four-armed waitress, loaded with dishes, took one look at him, shrieked, and dropped her load clattering to the floor. The angry manager, a man with three eyes, rushed him back into the street and told him never to return.

In the street, Johnny stopped a man who immediately burst into flames. Annoyed, the man slapped the flames out with his hands and said, "Sorry, you startled me. I do that when I'm startled." He eyed Johnny carefully. "Oh, you poor fellow," he said, sympathetically, "how can I help you?"

Johnny didn't want sympathy; he wanted help. He asked, "Where can I find others like me?"

The man pondered this. "Well," he said after a moment, "you might try the zoo." And he gave directions, adding, "Good luck."

"Thanks." When Johnny was halfway there, a policeman accosted him. The policeman had his torso on upside down, with legs growing from his shoulders and arms from his thighs. His upside-down policeman's face was angry.

"Here, here, what are you doing out of your cage?" He brandished a nightstick menacingly. "Come on, come on, get back to the zoo where you belong!"

"I was just on my way there," Johnny said, but the policeman, busy poking him in the ribs with the nightstick, wasn't listening, so Johnny shut up and allowed himself to be prodded to the place where he wanted to go anyway.

It wasn't a big zoo, but it had a nice collection of tiglons, cameleopards, seaskunks, tigerbears, elephant-apes, and giraffemonkeys. Johnny had never seen any of these creatures before, but he read their names and habitats off signs in front of their cages as he went past.

The policeman shooed him past signs proclaiming THIS WAY TO THE HUMAN FREAKS until they arrived at a large square room that had a gate in the bars covering its front. Johnny's heart and his pace swiftened as he approached. Inside, there seemed to be a cocktail party in progress. Soft music played from hi-fi stereo speakers, and there was the bubble of laughter and the buzz of conversation as glasses clinked and everybody seemed to be having a good time. As Johnny drew closer, he saw that there were a half dozen people in there—and he knew even at that distance that they were all like him.

The policeman opened the gate and gave him a shove inside. "And stay there!" he growled, turned, and went about his business.

A tall, attractive blonde woman in a cocktail dress, a glass in her hand, spotted Johnny and hurried over.

"Hello," she said, taking his arm. "I haven't seen you around before. My name's Sally, what's yours? Isn't this a delightful party? You must join us. What would you like to drink?"

Johnny's head swam. He couldn't believe how pretty this girl was—and how much like him, with her smooth, satiny skin with hardly a trace of fur or hair, and a long, slim neck that was firmly fastened to her shoulders, and a skeleton that made her lovely body seem just about perfect.

"My name's Johnny," he told her. "This is a wonderful party. Do you do this a lot?"

She seemed surprised by the question. "Constantly. What else is there to do?"

Before Johnny could answer, he heard sounds of embarrassed laughter. Outside, a group of visitors was staring in at them, laughing and pointing and making fun. Johnny felt annoyance rankle him.

"Isn't there someplace we can go to get away from them?"

"Of course not, silly. This is the only place we have. Besides, that's what we're here for, to entertain the normal people."

Johnny shook his head. "That's not what I'm here for." He wrung his hands in desperation. "Isn't there some alternative to living here like this?"

The girl hesitated, then leaned forward confidentially. "Well, there is one possibility. You could go see Dr. Groaner."

"Who's Dr. Groaner?"

"Dr. Groaner is a scientist who sometimes helps people like us, sends them to a world where all the people are just as we are."

Johnny's breath caught. "A world where all the people are like us?" he whispered in awe.

The girl nodded. "A world of freaks," she said, her voice rising to an almost hysterical pitch.

"So why haven't you gone to see him?" Johnny asked suspiciously.

"Not me," the girl said. "I'm among friends, I get fed every day, and it's always party time." She took another swig of her drink, emptying the glass. "Excuse me, I've got to get another one of these. Sure you don't want one?"

Johnny shook his head no. He sure didn't want to stay here is this cage, letting the normals stare at him and ridicule him. No, he'd go to Dr. Groaner. He headed for the cage door, expecting it to be locked, but it opened easily. He closed it behind him and stared back. The girl was with her friends, drinking, chatting, humming to the music, her visitor apparently forgotten.

There was only one Dr. Groaner listed in the telephone book, and his office was right there in the downtown section of the Big City. Johnny walked briskly along, paying no attention to the curious stares of the people around him, his heart alive with joyful anticipation. He found the building with no difficulty and rode the self-service elevator to the fifteenth floor and Dr. Groaner's office. When he entered the reception room, the nurse, a cute blonde with a hand growing out of the top of her head dropped a folder of papers she was busy filing.

"Oh my goodness," she said, staring at him, "you'd better go right in to see the doctor."

"I don't have an appointment."

"It doesn't matter. I can see you're an emergency case. It's that door there." The hand on top of her head pointed the direction.

Johnny went through the door marked DR. GROANER. A middle-aged man with graying hair leaped up from behind his big mahogany desk. For a moment Johnny thought the doctor was like him, but then he noticed the man had hoofs instead of feet and shoes.

"My name's Johnny—" Johnny began.

Dr. Groaner pumped his hand profoundly. "Glad to meet you, Johnny. As you might have guessed, I'm Dr. Groaner. Here, sit down and tell me about yourself."

Johnny sat down and told Dr. Groaner about himself— about his foster parents and about the farm and about his feelings that he felt out of place in this world.

When Johnny was through, Dr. Groaner got up and paced the floor for a few minutes, frowning thoughtfully. After a moment he stopped and perched on the front of his desk, swinging a cloven hoof idly.

"Well, you have good reason to feel out of place, Johnny, because you are out of place. Your body doesn't do anything. It doesn't come apart. It stays the same color all the time. It doesn't have interesting things attached to it. It—But why go on? Let's face it—you're a freak."

Johnny wet his lips. "At first I thought maybe an operation—"

The doctor laughed. "You mean you want me to graft on a tail or give you another eye or surgically remove your skeleton or—well, things like that so you could pass as normal?"

"I'd consider it."

"Well, take it from me, my boy, it won't work. Oh, maybe from a distance you might get away with it, but our biotechnology along those lines hasn't progressed sufficiently to pass a real close scrutiny. Believe me, you'd be worse off than before."

"I have to do something. I can't go back to the farm. I certainly don't want to live in a cage and have people ridicule me. The girl at the zoo said you knew of a world where all the people are like me."

Dr. Groaner nodded gravely. "There is a place where all the inhabitants are just like you, where—" the doctor laughed at the absurdity—"where we normals would be considered freaks!"

"It sounds like heaven. How can I get there?"

"I can send you," the doctor told him. "Oh, not by bus or airplane, but by a machine—a machine that was invented a long, long time ago, capable of transporting a person into an alternate universe, another world, another dimension."

"Have you sent other people like me there?"

Dr. Groaner nodded. "My father and grandfather and great grandfather owned this machine, and they helped misfits just like you. I even remember some of the names from the record: Leonardo da Vinci. Christopher Columbus. Thomas Edison. Sigmund Freud."

"I never heard of them."

"Of course you haven't, and probably no one else has either. Undoubtedly they just got to that other world and lost themselves in the crowd."

"As I'd like to do," Johnny said softly.

"As you can do," Dr. Groaner amended. "The machine is right here in the next room. Say the word, and I'll zip you into that other dimension where you can live happily ever after among your own kind."

"The word," Johnny said, without hesitating, "is yes!"

"Follow me," Dr. Groaner said, prancing across the room toward a closed door.

Johnny followed the doctor into a room filled with tubes and coils and wires and lights and dials and switches and buttons, with only a small area in the center that was open.

"Complex and impressive, isn't it?" Dr. Groaner said proudly. "Well, I don't know how it does what it does, and I don't think my grandfather or his grandfather did either. The important thing is, it works. See that opening there?" He pointed and Johnny nodded. "Just step over there while I warm the thing up."

Johnny stepped past the doctor, dodged a console, and threaded his way into the opening. Around him, thanks to Dr. Groaner's prodding, the machine whirred, buzzed, flashed and crackled into life.

"You can't come back," Dr. Groaner said in final warning.

"I'll take my chances," Johnny said determinedly. "If there are others like me there, I'm sure they'll make me welcome."

Dr. Groaner flipped a switch. "Goodbye then, and good luck."

Johnny waved. "Goodbye, and thanks."

Johnny's world became a nightmare of noises and brightness. He felt his body being stretched, pulled apart, disassembled, put back together. He closed his eyes. When he opened them, it was to the darkness of a cool night with the fragrance of a forest pushed by gentle breezes. There was the smell of rain in the air, and a full moon rode dark clouds overhead. He found himself in a clearing, surrounded by a dozen men dressed in ghost-like robes carrying flaming torches. Johnny knew they weren't ghosts, because he didn't believe in ghosts.

As the nearest man approached him, Johnny impulsively leaped forward and ripped off the man's hood, confirming his suspicions. The man's pale white skin revealed a face just like his. He'd found what he was looking for. Finally, he was home.

"You're just like me," Johnny cried with a laugh.

For a moment the man seemed perplexed by Johnny's action. Then, recovering, the man spat, "You insolent son of a bitch!" and swung his torch so it struck Johnny a hard blow on the head.

Johnny's mind reeled. His skin burned where the torch had struck it. Before he could recover, the others were swarming over him. Too dazed to fight back, he was dragged to the nearest tree and a rope was placed around his neck.

"Wait," Johnny cried, "you don't understand. I'm not different anymore. I'm just like you."

A firm tug on the rope choked off his words, and his body was dragged skyward. He couldn't speak. Worse, he couldn't breathe. His throat turned raw. A few seconds later the darkness of death smothered him with its icy cold embrace.

The white-garbed men-ghosts laughed and joked at Johnny's dead, swinging form, and after a while, tiring of the sport, they filed past him to go home, their torch fires flickering indifferently over Johnny's different, charcoal-colored skin.

THE MAN WHO WAS SLUGGER MALONE

George Clayton Johnson

GEORGE CLAYTON JOHNSON has quickly become one of my favorite people to call late at night. I first encountered George by phone at the direction of Richard Chizmar, who asked me to contact him about coming aboard *Cemetery Dance* magazine as a columnist. One brief conversation led to countless lengthy ones. Not only has George found a home in the pages of *CD*, but my press (Subterranean; www.subterraneanpress.com issued a career-spanning retrospective of his work, *All of Us Are Dying and Other Stories*. Of its contents, George has written:

> My friends Ray Bradbury, Richard Matheson, Charles Beau-
> mont and Theodore Sturgeon all taught me by example—as I
> watched them exercising different sets of mental muscles, switch-
> ing from one form to another as required by the story or the mar-
> ketplace—that if I hoped to earn a living and have a writing career
> like theirs, I would need to learn to write effective film scripts as
> well as stories and articles.

George's list of credits testify that he has done exactly that. He's scripted for *Star Trek*, *The Twilight Zone*, *King Fu*, *The Law and Mr. Jones*, and has had stories in *Metahorror*, *F&SF*, and countless other magazines and books.

George lives, as he has since the 1950s, in a multi-hued house in Pacoima, California, with his lovely wife, Lola.

His contribution to this volume, "The Man Who Was Slugger Malone," is tinted with autobiography, and would have made an exemplary episode of *The Twilight Zone*.

W.K.S.

Slugger Malone peered into the drowned night. Rain gushed down on the crosstown bus turning the passing neons to torch smears.

Up ahead the driver worried the wheel.

There was one other passenger, a young man seated across the aisle reading a paperback, his eyes close to the pages in the dim light.

One could read a history in that face, his capable hands, the determined set of his jaw.

Rain boiled across the glass and Slugger found himself thinking he'd lived his life in storms. The rain sledding on the glass was the same water that tore his tent to soggy rags in Venezuela. The same wetness sent the Orinoco river in mud floods to the sea.

He thought of the time he and little Bristol trucked the guns to Del Brio in the hills and the roads were black glue. And the dark-haired girl with Spanish eyes who bathed his broken hand.

He'd seen Yukon ice in his time and tasted pemican smoked over a fire that put out no heat. He'd smelled the rank scents of native bazaars and felt desert heat suck his tissues dry. He'd heard the drumming of prairie hail and watched the winds pile Northern seas in strange torn forms. Yes, he'd lived in storms and they'd cut and whittled him into an ancient shape.

Slugger shook himself. It was all far away and in another time.

He thought of La Pet, the pockmarked Frenchman who'd betrayed them. The rapids that chewed his raft to matchwood. The piranha that finished La Pet.

He hunched his shoulders in a rueful shrug. He was nothing but memories. When he thought of his life or the meaning of it, he found himself turning to memories of an older time. His running legs had stiffened up. He'd grown suddenly old and come at last to ground.

A man was his memories. Take away those and a man would crumble in upon himself and become nothing.

The bus slewed through the gripping water toward the curb. He raised himself stiffly and pulled the cord. As he stumped back toward the rear door he idly noted the young man rising also. They met at the door. Two hands gripped the polished metal grab pole as the bus shuddered to a halt.

The door gasped and the rain slushed in.

Lightning seared the sky.

There was a stunning jolt and Slugger almost went to his knees clinging to the metal pole. Something stirred and rushed. A wind blew through him. And then it was gone, leaving a hollow where he had been full.

A stunned light flared up in the young man's eyes.

He slid in a heap at Slugger's feet. As Slugger bent over the fellow he sensed the bus driver crouched beside him.

"Jesus," said the driver. "Don't move him. Is he breathing?"

Slugger stared slackly at him.

The driver saw his look and became instantly concerned. "Are *you* all right?" He steadied Slugger to a seat. "I'd better get some help."

Slugger hardly heard him. It was a damn funny feeling he had now. Not pain—not weakness. It was the kind of feeling a guy gets when he loses a tooth. He can't keep his tongue out of the hollow spot in his jaw. Damn it! What had he been thinking about when the lightning struck?

The young fellow was coming out of it. He groaned and sat up. When he saw Slugger he gave a visible jump. He looked down at his hands, fingers, flexed them. "It can't be," he said.

"What happened," said Slugger, slowly, confused. "What happened?"

"Oh, God," said the young man. His face was pale and his jaw was clenched tight. He came carefully to his feet

and peered at Slugger's familiar face in the dim light. Then
he felt his own face and groaned again.

Comprehension.

The young man touched Slugger's shoulder gently. "I
think I'd better get you home," he said.

Slugger blinked. "Home?"

"It's just down the street. Come on. I'll give you a
hand."

Slugger pulled his arm free. "I don't know you. How do
you know where I live?" He stopped. He had that empty
feeling again and it was big. Abruptly, he was frightened.
"Who am I?"

"You're Slugger Malone and I'm taking you home,"
said the young man gently.

He helped Slugger out of the seat.

Stepping out of the bus was like diving into a swimming pool. They were drenched by the time they arrived at
the boardinghouse. "Up the stairs, Slugger, there'll be a
fire waiting."

Inside the warm room he helped Slugger out of his coat
and settled him in a chair by the flames. He went to the hot
plate in the corner and flipped it *on* under the coffeepot. He
looked around at the room. On the walls there were several
framed photographs. One showed a younger Slugger
standing with several husky dogs beside a rude lean-to.
There was snow on the ground and Slugger's face grinned
out of the folds of a fur parka. His brows were frosted with
snow. Another showed Slugger standing with a group of
rough looking men beside what seemed to be a broad slug-
gish river.

Beside the fireplace, hanging on a wall was a pistol in a
well-worn holster. Scattered on tables and dresser tops
were various curios and mementos of an adventurous life:
a tarnished clip of .30 caliber bullets, a strangely carved
musical instrument with three strings, a conch shell, a

black rock smooth as an egg. The young man looked at these bits of trivia affectionately.

The coffeepot began to bubble, sending off a fragrant aroma of coffee steeped in chicory. He went to the cupboard and took down two cups. When he turned he saw Slugger standing in front of the photographs on the wall, looking confused and frightened. "That's me," he said, wonderingly. "But, who are the others?"

The young man came to stand beside him. "La Pet, Bristol, Del Brio. Don't you remember? The Dutchman took the picture."

Slugger was very frightened now. "Who are you?"

"My name . . ." there was a perceptible pause, "doesn't matter. I'm a writer—that is, I try to be. I haven't sold anything yet. Up to now I didn't have anything to write about." There was that in his tone that said now things would be different.

Slugger had a lost look on his face. "What has happened to me?"

The young man looked at him pityingly. "There is a name for it. Amnesia. Funny, you hear all the time about someone losing his memory. You don't hear about someone else finding it." He turned toward the door.

"Where are you going?" cried Slugger.

Surprised, the young man turned. "Why home, of course. I'm going home to my typewriter. I'm going to write about La Pet and Slugger Malone and Del Brio and little Bristol. I'm going to write about a dark-haired girl with Spanish eyes whose name I never knew. When the others left she bathed my broken hand and stayed with me while it healed."

A dim spark blinked in Slugger's eyes. He looked down at his hand and the scar tissue and the etched white lines against the tan. Something was working there.

"It's a book, don't you see?" said the young man. "It's got everything, exotic locale, adventure, romance. Any publisher would take it in a minute. And when I'm finished I'll do one about the Yukon and another about Arabia and the desert that no one knows but me!" He paused. "Now."

"Wait!" said Slugger, harshly.

"Yes?"

"What about me?"

Looking into those wild and staring eyes the young man remembered what that powerful body and those hard fists were capable of. He began to back away.

"Come back!" cried the man who was Slugger Malone before the robbery took place, but the thief, frightened now, fled through the rain.

And later, believing himself safe in his warm home, the young man told his wife of his decision to quit his job and become a full-time writer.

"What do you mean?" His wife, who loved him with all her heart, looked at him worriedly. "How will we live?"

"By writing stories and selling them to publishers," said the young man. "I don't have to write about the Yukon or Venezuela. Now that I know what the world is like I can write about anything. I can make things up!" he said with growing excitement. "I can write about things that touch the heart, about things that give you chills, who we are and why we are here and what it all means. I can write about the far future or the living past. Anything! Don't you see! Now that I *know* there are a million things to write about." Was he truly unaware of the shambling form outside the window, peering in through the rain, holding a heavy wet pistol in his hand?

"Here," said his worried wife who saw the familiar slipping away. "I'd better get you a bathrobe or something. You'll freeze to death."

But the young man hardly heard her, lost in reaches of thought and feeling.

"Do you want me to call a doctor?" she asked. She had needs but she hid them. She had hopes but she saw them broken. Where would it all lead? She looked around at the tiny crowded apartment, and the simple furnishings, and at her husband pacing the floor with his eyes full of blueprints. And then there was the bathroom floor to clean and wax and the diapers to wash and the beds to make. And what would they do without a job to bring in some little money? Hairs grayed on her head as she looked at the very real and fearful possibilities.

"Oh, My God!" he cried, suddenly angry. "We'll survive somehow!" looking at her beautiful face all stricken.

And then the young man was at the typewriter, everything forgotten, in the grip of a seizure as his gaze turned inward and his fingers felt for the keys.

He wrote feverishly, oblivious to his surroundings, and the pages began to fly from the typewriter into a growing pile.

Outside, heavy feet made a quagmire of the flower-beds as hard fingers pried at the window screen.

The young man, hammering the typewriter creating an explosive clatter, suddenly felt vise-like fingers driving into his shoulders, and he whirled about to stare into the clenched face of the man who was Slugger Malone.

"I followed you here. You know who I am and what has happened to me." He brought the gun up into sight. Perhaps Slugger had lost his memory but his hand had not forgotten how to hold the weapon like a deadly tool, fingers strongly gripping in an intimate way so the gun became an extension of the fist.

All this the young man could see, and, knowing the blood history of the man who threatened him, he saw death in that gun barrel. "Wait!" he cried. "Look!" He thrust the handful of pages before Slugger's blazing eyes.

Slugger, at last, understood, and taking the typewritten pieces of paper, relenting a little, the gun ready, bending into the dim light, rainwater dripping from his sodden coat to stain the pages and puddle the floor as he read the title:

THE MAN WHO WAS SLUGGER MALONE
By
George Clayton Johnson

He began to turn the pages. When he finished reading he glared accusingly at the young man. "You have my memories and there is nothing I can do about it?"

The young man nodded.

Slugger became aware of the gun in his hand. "Perhaps if I kill you my memories will return."

"That won't help," said the young man with sudden insight. "It would only destroy you."

"But what have I got to lose," said the victim of the theft. He raised the gun swiftly and fired.

Or, perhaps it was some other noise that wakened the writer's wife. The dark-eyed young woman came from the bedroom, rubbing her eyes sleepily, seeing the wet footprints, or, perhaps, not seeing them.

The young man lay slumped over the typewriter with the neat stack of typewritten pages beside it. She went to him and touched him. "Come to bed," she said shaking him gently. She helped him rise. He leaned against her, followed her. "Come to bed, Slugger," she repeated. "I miss you when you go traveling."

PILGRIMAGE
Ray Bradbury

RAY BRADBURY is a name synonymous with quality fiction, and over the past five decades he has become one of America's best-known writers. Born in Waukegan, Illinois in 1920, Ray moved to Southern California with his parents in 1934, going on to attend Los Angeles High where he graduated in 1938.

He sold his first story in 1941—and has sold 400 more since, along with numerous essays, poems, plays, articles, scripts (he had his own TV series), and novels. He's won a multitude of awards (including an Emmy) and has seen his works featured in some 1500 anthologies and textbooks.

Bradbury was married in 1946, has four daughters, and continues to reside in Los Angeles (a city he loves) with his wife, Marguerite. In the 1950s–60s he functioned as a mentor to the Group, and has written fondly of this period.

A list of his credits is unnecessary. Suffice to say that readers sometimes forget that, in addition to the poetic nostalgia (*Dandelion Wine*), science fiction (*The Martian Chronicles*, *Fahrenheit 451*) and fantasy (*Something Wicked This Way Comes*) for which he is best known, Bradbury is a writer with a lean, hard edge, as you'll see in "Pilgrimage."

W.F.N. & W.K.S.

Paul walked quietly across the green, close-cropped grass, breathing it in all along the way. There was not a part of it he wanted to forget. It must all be remembered. Later, when he was in his room, or driving west again, perhaps in Denver or Salt Lake or San Francisco, he would puff the smoke from a freshly lighted cigarette, squint his eyes, remember, and say, "It was this way," or "It was *that*. The temperature mild, the wind ever so slight. I wore a tweed suit. I drove in at the cemetery entrance at noon. There wasn't a cloud in the sky. A perfect spring day. There were more birds in the trees than leaves, it was that early in the year. The sun made everything glisten. It put my shadow under me as I walked up the gravel path. The gravel made a small sound under my feet."

Paul stopped at the top of a small rise. The gate man had given him directions. Right *here*, left, then right again, just beyond a marble pyramid. He was to look for a pink stone.

He walked on. He glanced back once at his car, sleek and warming under the spring sun. He could have driven in, the gate man had waved for him to do so, but he had taken the keys from the ignition and climbed out. He wanted to see all of this. There was no telling when he would be back this way again. You got into California and once you were there there was no leaving. It had taken him fourteen years to make it east once. Now, he might never return and he wanted to notice everything intensely so he could go over it in his mind once he got home.

Somebody had been mowing the vast green lawns, there was a little path of reaped grass ahead of him. Far away he heard the puttering of the motor-mower climbing some small hill. It might be back this way in ten minutes. But he would be gone by then.

Paul stopped by the pink stone. He looked down silently and read the name:

JOHNATHAN S. MELLIN
BORN 1920 - DIED 1933

The stone looked perfect, new, as if not a rain had touched it. The grass was bright and moist over the grave. There was a rusted tin cup in which someone had put flowers last autumn. They were now shriveled down within the cup.

He thought of Johnathan. If you'd lived, you'd be my age now, he thought. Twenty-seven.

He remembered them running, Johnathan and himself, down through the humming summer ravine, together. Johnathan so proud and blonde, chinning himself on chestnut trees, climbing grapevines, plunging into the creek. How they had wrestled together; Johnathan, stronger, always pinning Paul flat. And the way the schoolgirls slid their eyes when Johnathan walked by. And the way Johnathan ran, like an animal, light heels flicking up dirt behind, coming down rabbit-soft. And the way Johnathan looked at you with his bright grey eyes and closed his eyelids and shook his head back to clear the blonde hair out of his vision. Johnathan never used a comb, he always shook the hair back.

But all that was gone. Paul had traveled west with his parents. Johnathan had died a year later. Paul hadn't come back for the funeral. Not until today.

Paul stood for perhaps three minutes, looking down at the stone, not moving. He bent down to touch and feel how each letter was incised sharply into the gleaming rock. He fumbled his hands over the dates 1920–1933. He smelled the grass, quietly. He saw how thick the grass was. He watched a butterfly go by on the air. He noticed how the wind blew his pants cuffs, gently. There were several birds on one empty oak tree, alone, chattering. In the blue distance, above the horizon, he saw a white cloud. He felt the tweed of his pants against his legs, he felt the way his hat sat on his head, and the way his coat hollowed about his arms. He was sweating from the little walk.

Then, without a word, he turned and walked away, over the green hill and along the gravel path, not making a sound, walking steadily and quietly.

When he reached the gate the watchman said, as Paul was getting into his limousine, "Well, did you *find* it?"

"Yes," said Paul.

"You're from California, I see."

"Yes."

"Come a long way to visit here today. A relative?"

"My cousin. Not so very far. I'm on my way from New York to Chicago. This was only seventy-five miles off the main highway—"

"Still," said the watchman. "It's not many people bother. Seventy-five miles is seventy-five miles."

"I *had* to come," said Paul quietly.

"You must have liked him an awful lot."

"Liked him?" said Paul, reaching down to turn on the ignition. He looked up at the watchman intently. "I hated his god-damned guts."

He started the car and drove quietly off along the highway.

About the Editors

William F. Nolan is a two-time winner of the MWA's Edgar Allan Poe Special Award. His output to date weighs in at 65 books (in 185 world editions, including *Helltracks, Night Shapes,* and *Things Beyond Midnight*), 135 short stories, 600 nonfiction magazine pieces, and 40 scripts for film and television. His current novel, *Sharks Never Sleep,* is the latest in his Black Mask Mystery series. Nolan lives with his wife, Cameron Nolan, five cats, and 10,000 books in Southern California.

William Schafer is the founder of Subterranean Press (www.subterraneanpress.com), which publishes signed books by some of the finest writers of the dark fantastic. He is the co-editor (with Richard Chizmar) of the International Horror Guild award-winning anthology *Subterranean Gallery,* and he is also a World Fantasy Award nominee. He lives in Michigan.

Sharon Shinn